a Woman's Touch

a Woman's Touch

NEW LESBIAN LOVE STORIES

Edited by Valerie Reed

alyson books
los angeles

MANUFACTURED IN THE UNITED STATES OF AMERICA.

THIS TRADE PAPERBACK ORIGINAL IS PUBLISHED ALYSON PUBLICATIONS,
P.O. BOX 4371, LOS ANGELES, CALIFORNIA 90078-4371.
DISTRIBUTION IN THE UNITED KINGDOM BY TURNAROUND PUBLISHER SERVICES LTD.,
UNIT 3, OLYMPIA TRADING ESTATE, COBURG ROAD, WOOD GREEN,
LONDON N22 6TZ ENGLAND.

FIRST EDITION: JULY 2003

03 04 05 06 07 **a** 10 9 8 7 6 5 4 3 2 1

ISBN 1-55583-794-8

LIBRARY OF CONGRESS CATALOGING-IN-PUBLICATION DATA

A WOMAN'S TOUCH : NEW LESBIAN LOVE STORIES / EDITED BY VALERIE REED. — 1ST ED.
 ISBN 1-55583-794-8
 1. LESBIANS—FICTION. 2. LOVE STORIES, AMERICAN. 3. LESBIANS' WRITINGS,
AMERICAN. I. REED, VALERIE.
PS648.L47W645 2003
813'.085089206643—DC21   2003043697

CREDITS
COVER PHOTOGRAPHY BY YVETTE GONZALEZ.
COVER DESIGN BY MATT SAMS.

To Karen C.
with love

"I got the house because I could afford it; she got everything else because she couldn't bear to leave so much history behind. Take it, I'd said, take everything, because I knew she was right. The plaster and concrete walls were too fresh, too new to hold anything of us; the memories had been collecting in our things, and I was glad not to have to face every day the carved heads from New Mexico, the blue throw rug from North Carolina, the rainbow puppies from San Francisco, and all those damn candles everywhere, fat, thin, tall, round, square, honeycombed and pressed and colored and painted and scented and plain. On some nights, she lit them all, and incense too, and I sneezed like mad. But the flickering, uncertain light inspired her, made her romantic, and we always ended up making love, so I swallowed my irritation."

—"THE DANCE FOR LUCY" BY K. BHOJWANI

Contents

Introduction: Call Me a Fool

The other day I read an article suggesting we are "neurologically wired to look for romance," that our crafty enamored brains release chemicals magnifying our date's good points (Wow! Karen is gorgeous, sexy, *and* sweet!) while downplaying her bad points (Karen isn't *really* a pathological liar, she's just a very creative storyteller). These chemicals can keep working for years, but when they wear off, well, that's the bad news. And as I was reading this article, I thought to myself, *Oh, so that's what happened with me and Karen...* But that's another story. (And Karen, if you're reading this now—honey, I forgive you!)

Thinking of love in terms of science—cerebral chemicals, Darwinian impulses, and such—well, frankly, it just gives me the creeps. But then, I don't want to *think* of love at all; I want to feel it and to have faith in it. Because whatever my brain is doing, my heart has got to be doing it better and in more miraculous ways. Call me a fool.

I want to thank all of the contributors to this anthology. It takes guts to write a love story, and these excellent and gutsy writers have managed—using settings and scenarios as diverse and improbable as love and lovers themselves—to give us a satisfying and believable journey into the hearts of lesbians everywhere. Enjoy.

—Valerie Reed

Big Good Dumb Boy

Carol Guess

In the distance is the forest: stern green, as if damped down.
Only the bricks of the high school break the fir line, and
they're worn, greening themselves. Beside me, Jessie untangles
Pete's leash, and he trots around the asphalt track obediently.
"Dumb boy," she says, as he stops to chew the grass on the
margins. "Big good dumb boy."

Jessie is older, the first older lover I've ever had. But 31
doesn't seem impossibly far from 22, and 22 feels old today.
The high school reminds me of my high school: imposing,
penitential; the summer-vacant gape of the windows doesn't
detract from the resemblance. Jessie wipes her glasses on her
sleeve, then zips her half-open fly. "Dumb ears, let's go." She
turns her back on the forest, and we take the gravel path leading up from the track.

The apartment building is perched on the slope overlooking the school. "Pine View," it's called, and there are pines,
and there is a view, even from the ground floor. At night I
push the window open until it cuts the trees into trunks and
tufts: beauty in manageable pieces. Sometimes someone stops

to peer inside, but I don't care. Neither does Jessie. She's unafraid of visitors, of eyes, of drunks and curious peepers. "Nothing will happen," she always says, "except they'll get a free show." She goes back to kissing my hand then, or my stomach, or my armpits. She turns the music louder sometimes. Sometimes she gets up, has to get something to eat.

We met in a Waffle House. I was waiting tables, trying to decide whether to bother asking the drunk at booth five to tone it down some. I barely saw her to take her order. I was taking my time that night, slower even than usual, tired from school, where I'd spent the morning warding off my homeroom teacher's salt-palmed advances. As I pushed my hair back behind my ear and tapped my pen against the order book, I felt that morning's impatience rise up in my throat again, the angry taste of waiting. "What'll it be," I said, pouring coffee into her cup before she'd even had a chance to ask. "Soup's minestrone."

Retelling the story, Jess changes it: an auto shop, where she pieced together my dying Chev, the Kmart off Highway 37, where our hands met by accident as we poked at clothes in the half-price aisle. Sometimes she gets carried away, makes the setting entirely implausible: bank vaults, sea cruises, cathedrals. Her eyes go wide then; she likes her stories tall.

"Years saved," she always finishes. "Five years saved at least." She means I might never have known I liked women without her. She means she brought me out, that I tasted salt between her legs and came back for more.

Her friend Margery lords it over me; playing pool, when she beats me, she jokes it's because I've never had another woman lover. "You can't tell from just one," she says, leaning across green felt, her breath sap-sticky on my cheek. I'd never want to kiss Margery; I could never want her the way that I want Jess. But that's not enough of anything to mean I'm not certain. The way the old butch dykes sit in the back and watch me through smoke wreaths when I dance by myself? I know what I feel for them. I know I could lie beneath any one of them and lose myself under the weight. I have an imagination. But there's only been Jess in the real world, only Jessie's particular heaviness, her slim fingers circling.

This morning Pete's reluctant to finish his walk; Jess has to lower her voice and threaten before he'll take the three steps leading up to the door. I'd just tug on him, but Jessie is patient. "Never use force," she says, meaning Pete but also cooking, politics, sex. Maybe this is why she's out of work. She starts to make pancakes, but I put my hand on her hand as she reaches for the box.

"I think I'll grab an Egg McMuffin." I want to say, "I have a job, Jess," but that would hurt, even if all it means to me is, "I don't have time."

"I can't believe you'd pass up my cooking for trash. We have berries, you know. I could do a blueberry number."

"It's 20 till, Jess."

Her expression changes. "Right." Suddenly she's reaching for the car keys. "At least let me drive you." She tucks her T-shirt into her jeans, pats Pete, and opens the door for me before I can shake my head or nod. So I grab my purse from the back of the chair and follow along. Seated in the Chev beside her, I watch her hands as she steers us out of the cramped lot and onto Wayport Road.

It usually takes 14 minutes to get to the Kiddie Prep Daycare Center, but today Jess makes it in ten, so we can stop at McDonald's across the street.

"Wait here," she says, but I tag along, and she reaches for my hand in the lot and holds it right up until we reach the glass doors. When I get in line, she stands just slightly behind me, letting her hip graze mine.

"Orange juice and an Egg McMuffin," I say, aware that she's humming against the Muzak. She lets her hand brush my back as I reach across the counter for the bag, as she takes the bag from my hands and walks behind me to the door.

When we get to the car, Jess peels the foil top from the orange juice. "Here you go," she says, and I take the juice, and the crumpled foil, and bend my head toward her chest, and let my cheek rest for a second on the freckled skin in the V of her T-shirt: a constellation of stars. I stand that way for a moment, listening to the irregular pulse of cars behind us, as she bends over me and kisses my hair. For a second, we're like stopped traffic: mesmerized by color and sound, ready energy stilled, wanting only to push forward. But I'm late again, so I gulp at my juice, handing her the rest as I grab the paper bag from her hand and book across the street against the light.

It's 11 minutes past, but no one's standing in the coatroom to notice. I tuck my purse inside my locker; nibbling my McMuffin, I slip into the sixes-and-sevens room. Mary Alice Farmer, my supervisor and co-owner of Kiddie Prep, is combing Jillian Norris's hair. As I busy myself picking up the already scattered wooden alphabet blocks, she pushes her frilly cuff back from her right wrist and looks over her watch.

"Hello, Tracy," she says, not smiling at all.

I grin broadly—"Morning, Mare"—and continue picking up the wooden pieces till Jennifer Kendricks grabs me from behind, around the knees, nearly knocking me over. "Jenni-FER!" I say, but she only giggles, and then Jonathan Black arrives, his fur-coated mom trailing perfume and impatience, then Natalie and Neddy Allen, and then Matt Martin, his too-large Ninja Turtles T-shirt worn backwards, and—like me—eating an Egg McMuffin. "Taste good, Matt?" I quiz him, and he stares up at me, crumbs on his cheeks, as if puzzled by the question. "Is that your favorite breakfast?" I try a different tactic, but he just looks shyly into his empty paper bag and shuffles his feet. I turn back toward the blocks, hoping to impress Mary Alice with my exactitude.

"Trace!" Matt tugs on my skirt. "Trace! Guess what?"

"Umm... Why did the chicken cross the road?" I say.

"No! You're supposed to guess! Anyway, we saw you at McDonald's. Me and my dad. We were eating breakfast in the car and we saw you and you went inside like me and my dad only then you didn't get back in the car again."

Jennifer comes up behind Natalie and hits her with a sty-rofoam brick. Natalie begins crying instantly, dense tears like a flooded river. I turn to her, cup her chin in my palm, and wipe her eyes with the hem of her jacket. I'm hoping Matt will take an interest in the blocks, in the bricks, in Jennifer, who's grinning wildly, in Tasha Fiddler, who's kicked off her shoes and is retying them around the leg of a plastic chair. But Matt comes to me and puts a sticky hand on my stomach. "My dad said that it was a lady you were kissing but it looked more like a man to me. Was it a lady, Tracy? Is she your mom? Does your mom work at the same place my mom works? Are your mom and dad divorced? Do you have a hamster? Do you have blocks at home like these? Do you have a VCR or a cordless phone?"

Matt turns contentedly to the blocks, uninterested in answers now that his questions have been aired. I don't look at Mary Alice; instead, I continue wiping Natalie's streaked face with her jacket, till Neddy taps me on the leg and asks if he can take care of her for me. I let him, and move on to untangle Tasha's laces.

By lunchtime I'm exhausted. I slink into the staff room and collapse in a chair, covering my eyes with the backs of my hands. "How's sixes-and-sevens today, Trace?" Sue takes bread, peanut butter, and grape jelly from the fridge. "Want a PBJ?" All the day-care workers at Kiddie Prep eat children's food: peanut butter and jelly, apple juice, graham crackers, chocolate milk. My first day at work, I brought some of Jessie's Irish soda bread and baked beans in a plastic yogurt container; Sue just laughed and told me to give it up. Now she slices my sandwich into quarters, hands it to me on a plate with a neon-colored dinosaur emblazoned on the face. She looks around, pretends to glance under the table and behind the curtains:

"Mary Alice getting to you, huh?"

I once tried to tell Sue about Jessie. We were talking Romance. All the kids were gone but one, and we were smoking on the stoop out back, watching Loni dig happily in the sand while we waited for her juvenile delinquent sister to pick her up. Sue knew I didn't have a boyfriend; she'd asked me that on my first day, even before she asked where I'd gone to high school, or where I'd grown up. All I said, though, was, "I haven't got a man now," which was true enough. So there we were on the stoop, smoking and talking; when the topic of men came up, Sue started prodding a little harder.

Mostly I guess she wanted advice; her fiancé, Kirk, had hit her three nights before, after she'd stayed out late drinking with Betsy Jenkins, her supervisor in the toddler room. Sue got back at 1:30, curled into bed beside him ("in my red nightgown and everything"), and then bam!—he slapped her across the forehead. "Not hard," she said to me, "not hard at all. But you know, I have principles. I told him right off I wouldn't take physical shit from him. I told him that three years back, when we first started dating after graduation. So I don't know, Tracy." She tugged her engagement ring off her finger, and put it against her cheek, diamond to skin. "I want a husband real bad, but no one can hit me and get away with it."

Sue's eyes looked like Jessie's then, so brown they're almost black, and I wanted to say that, to say I had someone too, that I didn't know what it would mean to stay with a woman as beautiful and troublesome and clueless as Jessie. "I've never been hit by a lover," I said, starting slowly. "By my folks, but not by a lover." Sue looked at me and shook her hair from her shoulders. She was obviously waiting for me to go on, but I was stuck: Which way from here? I could say "my lover" without using a name or pronoun. I could say "Jess" and let her assume it was a man's name. I looked down at the scab on my left knuckle. Maybe I should ask her if she'd seen the Oprah show about lesbian mothers.

But Sue took my pause for embarrassment. "Tracy, have you ever even had, like, a boyfriend? You never talk about men, not even Don Martin." Matt's father was divorced, rich, handsome, and ebulliently kind to his son; all the women, even the married ones, swooned over him when he came to pick Matt up. Sue sometimes made kissy noises if she happened to see his BMW pull into the lot out back.

"Don't you think Don is gorgeous, Trace?" She turned her head and exhaled. "I think he's hot. But not, like, to pry or anything, but have you ever even had sex? I mean, you can tell me. I don't think there's anything wrong with being a virgin, you know. You can tell me, Tracy. I was pretty strict with myself till I was 16 and met Jerry. Are you Catholic?" Sue got up as Loni's sister pulled into the lot; as we waved goodbye, she turned and smiled at me, a genuine smile. "I think it's cool that you're not a whore like Betsy. I have a lot of respect for you, Trace."

After that, Sue seemed to feel as if we had crossed some sort of line. She started confiding in me: stuff about Kirk, about her mother's drinking, about how she'd throw up after she ate sometimes. About cheating on her income taxes. I liked it, liked having another woman get close to me. I liked the way she looked at me when she told me intimate things, and I liked how she'd put her arm around me when the kids were all gone and we walked through the center, putting stray toys away, moving the chairs back beneath the tiny tables. So I thought hard about telling her, both because I felt more and more that I wanted to, and less and less like I could risk it.

Now, watching her eat her sandwich, I find myself staring

at her hands. Not tapered and thin like Jessie's; not creased and tobacco-stained like Margery's. For a split second I imagine Sue's palms on my breasts. The ring and the press-on fingernails would have to go.

"So what's pissed off Miss Mary Alice this time?" She's cut the crusts off my sandwich, placed them neatly in a row beneath the dinosaur's stomach. "I'd die if I had to work with her. Thank God I have a degenerate like Betsy for a supervisor."

I shrug my shoulders and lick peanut butter from behind my teeth. What to say? I start to explain, hesitantly, aware in advance of what I'll have to leave out. "Matt Martin came in today with his T-shirt on backwards, eating an Egg McMuffin, and he asked me…"

"Shit, girl! Don't tell me Don made a pass at you. Don't tell me, or I'll die. Was that what set old Mary Alice off? I always said he liked you. I always knew it. Was that it, Trace? You can tell me."

I push my chair back from the table. "I don't want to talk about it now; she might walk in, and we could get blasted. Maybe later, if we have to wait for Loni's sister or the Ericson carpool."

Sue looks at me apologetically. "Hey, Tracy, I didn't mean to pry. Like, it's none of my beeswax about you and Don Martin. I mean, if there is anything between you and Don, anyhow. I just thought you might want to blow off steam is all." She sounds hurt, so I stand behind her and put my hands on her shoulders. Without thinking, I bend down and kiss the top of her hair lightly. She doesn't seem startled, doesn't seem to really notice.

"Sue, I'm sorry. I'm just tired, really tired. I was up all night talking to my roommate and the kids have been crazy all morning. Jennifer must've had a chocolate bar for breakfast, she's so hyper."

Sue gets up and puts both dishes in the sink. "No problem.

Hey, I didn't know you had a roomie. Someone you knew in high school? Do I know her?"

"Her name's Jessie. She's a couple years older, and she went to South for high school. You probably don't know her."

Sue looks at me. "We should all go out sometime. Kick back, have a few beers."

"What if Kirk gets mad?" I say, meaning to be funny.

"Screw him. I could probably do better." She sighs: "Yeah, I could, probably. But I'm tired of looking, you know?"

"Yeah. I know."

"Now, if Don Martin looked at me the way he looks at you!"

I fake a laugh, and Sue giggles, nudging me.

"But really, you should let me meet Jessie. Would we get along?"

I don't answer, because it's hard even to imagine: Jessie and Sue, sharing a booth at the White Lion, ordering a pitcher of Bud Light, nibbling popcorn. What would they talk about? Instead, I wipe the rim of the jelly jar and screw the lid back on the peanut butter. "We're almost out of Skippy. Remind me to write that down on the supply list before we close."

After lunch, Jennifer throws up and has to be sent home, which makes things much easier on me. Neddy continues to follow Natalie around solicitously, a fact I point out to Mary Alice.

"Have you ever seen a sister and brother that close before? And they're not even twins!" I marvel, hoping to elicit one of her lectures on the joys of sibling friendships and maybe indirectly patch up whatever Matt's comments might have fractured this morning.

But instead: "Tracy, I want to speak with you after the children leave." That's it.

So as Sue and I sit on the stoop, waiting for Loni's sister and (unusual for him) Matt's father, I try desperately to think of some way to explain Jessie to Sue. I look at Sue's feet:

pink-and-white aerobic sneakers. Jess owns three pairs of shoes: cowboy boots, hiking boots, and a pair of men's black penny loafers. Don's car pulls up just as Loni's sister slides into the lot, nearly nicking his fender. They emerge almost simultaneously.

"Why, if it isn't Alyssa Portland." Don stops, staring at Loni's sister as she takes Loni's backpack and drops it into the backseat.

"Don Martin! I didn't realize you brought Matt to Kiddie Prep!" All of Alyssa's sentences end in exclamation marks, accompanied by stylized hair tossings.

"Oh, yes." Don seems mesmerized by Alyssa's tank top. Beside me, Sue stiffens noticeably.

"Bye, Sue, bye, Tracy!" Loni makes a last-minute swerve away from Alyssa's car and runs to embrace our shins clumsily. Matt follows behind and waits for her to finish.

"Bye, Sue," he says softly, then comes up beside me and cups his hand around my ear. I smell cherry Kool-Aid and soap. He bends closer till his mouth is almost in my ear: "Tracy, I like you a lot. A whole lot." He stops to take a breath. "I hope your mom and dad aren't divorced." Then his dad claps his hands impatiently.

"Matt. Time to go."

Sue nudges me; I know instantly what she means. Don Martin is watching me, not the way he watches Alyssa, but more carefully, as if I were a newspaper, or a road map to some distant city. I shiver. "Let's go inside." We wave goodbye to the kids and leave the two of them leaning casually against Don's sleek black car, Alyssa with her arms akimbo, Don with one hand atop Matt's head.

Sue practically drags me inside the center. As she locks the door behind her, and before I can warn her that Mary Alice is still lurking somewhere within, she blurts out, "Goddamn! Just goddamn him! Talking to that whore as if she were worth one of my little toenails! Or," she adds, turning to look at my expression, "one of yours. Goddamn!" Sue sniffs, and for a moment I think she might begin crying. Then she laughs, oddly but infectiously.

"As if she were worth a used diaper!"

I start to laugh too. "Or the beans in a beanbag."

"Or the crust on the finger paint!"

"As if he were worth a stepped-on potato chip!"

"Aw, hell, Trace, he's worth a lot more than that. It's that stupid Alyssa who's the worthless one. Just because she's got boobs like a Barbie doll and spindly old legs."

The light in the room to the left goes off and Mary Alice's voice rings out from the darkness: "Tracy? I wanted to speak with you."

Sue's eyes widen, and she whispers, "Darn, I didn't realize…" but I pat her shoulder.

"It's OK, Sue. I should've warned you, but I forgot. You gonna be OK taking the bus home? You probably shouldn't wait; this might take a while."

Sue raises her eyebrows sympathetically. "I oughta get home and start cooking dinner. Don't want Kirk to have any reason to whomp me again."

I just nod and hold her coat open for her. "Bye, Sue. See you tomorrow."

"Bye, Trace. Don't forget to ask your roommate when she wants to party."

As the door closes, Mary Alice flicks the lights off in the hall and beckons me into the staff room. "Do you want some coffee, Trace?" I've never heard her use my nickname before, and it sounds all wrong, like Jessie's mom calling her "Jessica Lynn."

"No, thanks." I feel sick for a minute, but then just as suddenly the feeling vanishes. The lines around Mary Alice's mouth and eyes make her look tired, more tired even than I feel.

"Tracy. Perhaps you know why I asked you in here?" Despite my "no, thanks" and despite the fact that she never drinks coffee, Mary Alice is carefully smoothing the fluted edges of a brilliantly white filter. She measures a little plastic cupful of grounds into the coffeemaker and pours in a quarter pot's worth of water. Her hands shake steadily the whole time.

"Actually, Mary Alice, I'm not sure I do know. Is there a problem with one of the kids? I felt like things went especially well today, although I know Jennifer Kendricks got a little out of hand in the morning session."

"That's quite an understatement, Tracy. Jennifer was entirely out of control, and I hold you responsible for that."

I sigh inwardly.

"But that's not why I asked to talk to you today. I think our business is a little more serious than your inadequate reaction to a child's misbehavior."

I watch as the first drops of coffee sputter into the glass pot.

"Tracy, I overheard Matt Martin's comments about your... about your behavior in the parking lot this morning. Because I feel that this sort of...issue concerns the Kiddie Prep Center, I called Don Martin at work. He and I talked for quite some time, and he confirmed..."

From the long low window above the sofa, I can see the jungle gym, the tetherball pole, and half of one of the hopscotch courts. A bird is perched on the orange ladder leading up to the slide. I watch as the bird hops up two steps, then stops and begins preening its feathers. I try hard to think of how I'll describe its markings to Jessie when I get home. Is it a sparrow? I'm not good with animals, not even Pete. Jessie always says you can be good with kids or animals, but not both. It's growing dark outside, and the AC is still on in the center. I pull my skirt closer around my legs.

"... effective immediately. I'm sorry, Tracy. It's difficult to let you go, and I understand that it will be hard for you to accept."

Outside, another bird, darker and larger, perches on the

rubbery seat of one of the swings. I try to imagine what Sue would say if she were here. Would she remember my kiss? I try to imagine her in a tiny trailer kitchenette, cutting the crusts off a sandwich for Kirk, setting the placemats exactly six inches apart. I try to imagine the expression on Kirk's face as she says, "Remember that girl Tracy I told you about? Well, turns out she's a homosexual person, Kirk." Nothing seems real but the birds and the goose bumps on my arms.

I don't say a word to Mary Alice, just push my chair away from the table, go into the coatroom, and undo my locker in the dark. Halfway through the combination, I remember the peanut butter. I stop and grope for the supply list on the bulletin board. I find a pen in my pocket, scrawl "Skippy" in mammoth letters across the list.

Then the light goes on. Mary Alice steps into the room, not too close to me. "Tracy, I want you to know it's nothing personal. It's for the sake..." I finish the combination on my locker and pull out my purse.

"Sure," I say, walking through the door and past Mary Alice, careful not to touch her. "Sure, Mare."

I stop at Target on the way home. I buy a pack of Lucky Strikes, two boxes of Tampax, and a nylon dog toy shaped like a steak.

Even before I open the door I can hear Pete growling; inside, he stands on two feet, nearly knocking me over. Jessie's nowhere, but there's a note on the table: a white square, with "Tracy" in her up-slanted print. The clock reads 6:49. I put the note in my left skirt pocket, wash a glass, gulp some Coke, and slip the choke chain around Pete's ears. "Out," I say, as he tugs me to the door. "Big good dumb boy." It's cooler than it's been for some time, and the breeze is pleasant; the trees rustle almost musically. I walk Pete around the track till we get to the baseball diamond. I let him off his leash and toss a stick into the outfield. "Go get it." His legs slide till he reaches grass.

I break open the Lucky Strikes, light one up, and squat by home plate. Pete brings the stick back and I toss it out again, and again, and again till he gets bored and starts sniffing the metal fence by the dugout. I pull Jessie's note from my pocket. The bottom edge is sealed with tape. Taking the cigarette out of my mouth, I try the right corner. It won't take, so I pull out my lighter and watch as the paper goes gray, as my name turns to ash that I grind into the soft red dirt of the diamond. "Pete!" I call and call, but he's loping, more like a deer than a collie, headed for the green line of firs, which bend as the unexpected breeze tears in from the east.

To the Core

Lori Horvitz

After I sent a photo attachment of myself to Lisette, a woman who answered my Internet personal ad, she responded: *Nice photo. You look familiar. Where might I have seen you?*

In the small Southern town where we both live, I often see the same faces in the local bookstore, café, supermarket. After a flurry of E-mail exchanges with Lisette, I figured out where she could have seen me. We both frequented the local Y—she worked out in the weight room; I used the swimming pool.

I E-mailed her: *Perhaps we've been sweaty and naked in the sauna at the same time. Could that be it?*

And she replied: *I've never been in the sauna, but I'll make sure to go there now.*

So I suggested we meet face to face, so to speak, in the sauna. Why not let it all hang out to begin with? But when I swung open the door, there sat an enormous woman reading *Family Circle,* wheezing like a circular saw as she chomped on an apple. Although I knew this woman couldn't be

Lisette, her presence wouldn't exactly serve as a romantic backdrop. I spread my towel upon the upper bench and sat down, feeling nervous and exposed. I breathed deeply. The apple-chomping didn't help the situation.

Lisette had sent me a blurry photo of herself. I deciphered a long-haired brunette with a square jaw and piercing brown eyes. *I'm a mixed breed,* she wrote, *part Cherokee Indian, part Irish, part Japanese.* Exotic and sexy, from what I could unearth. But maybe that's what I wanted to see. From this blurred photo, did I create a fantasy woman in my mind? This woman who says she works as a gourmet chef, loves to dance, paint, and laugh?

Before Lisette, I'd met two other women through the Internet, so I knew how this medium worked, how disappointing the end result could be. The first woman brought me a bouquet of daisies, asked me the exact date and time of my birth to see if we were astrologically compatible, and within the first 15 minutes brought up the idea of traveling the world together. Besides that, she looked nothing like the sexy photo she had sent. The other woman claimed to be a highly spiritual person who meditated often and practiced Kundalini yoga. We exchanged personal E-mails about our past relationships, families, and dreams. Only after I'd gone out with her three times did she admit she had a girlfriend. And her girlfriend was out of town tending to her dying father.

The apple-chomping seemed to grow louder and more frenzied. From the sound of it, this woman felt incredibly passionate about her apple. But I felt panicky. Sweat beads slid down my breasts. Part of me wanted to throw on a pair of pants, a coat, and run for the hills. Then the door swung open and, as if she were a flash of lightning illuminating a darkened sky, Lisette appeared. She electrified the scorching, cramped room. Even the chomper had to cease her chomping and look up. More beautiful than I'd ever imagined,

Lisette was dark and muscular and voluptuous, with a three-colored tattoo of a seahorse on her upper arm.

On the other side of the chomper, she spread out her towel, sat down, smirked at me. I smiled back. The apple-chewing proceeded. Must've been one hell of a big apple, but it couldn't go on forever, could it? Lisette and I made a silent agreement to not speak until the chewer left the sauna. And so we played catch with our furtive glances, throwing them back and forth across our sauna-monkey-in-the-middle. I couldn't help but notice Lisette's full, velvety breasts, the muscle definition in her legs, her pierced navel. I caught her eyes drifting from my breasts down to my crotch, up to my eyes. Her tongue, moving ever so slowly across her lips, came to a halt when the chomper took her final bite and exited, making sure to take her flimsy, mangled core—but she left her magazine. Perhaps she thought one of us would be interested in the cover story— "Elizabeth Dole: mother, wife, political force."

"Next time we meet here, I'll make sure to pack a picnic," Lisette said.

"What'll you bring?" I asked in my most sultry voice.

"What do you want?" Lisette got up, turned the light out, moved her towel next to mine. Now our naked flesh almost touched.

My skin was sizzling. I could almost hear my body hairs scream out in unison. "I want to kiss you," I said, surprised at myself. Usually it takes months for me to work up this amount of courage.

Lisette brushed strands of hair from her face, leaned toward me, and planted her lips on mine. We embarked on the sweatiest, sexiest kiss imaginable. Moving her body closer with each tongue swirl, she ended up sitting in my lap. Nothing could stop us. Not the sauna heat. Not the sweat. Not even the chomper, who re-entered the sauna to retrieve her magazine.

She flicked on the light and gasped. "Jesus Christ! Pardon me!"

Before flicking the light off, she grabbed Elizabeth Dole's face, leaving us to our kiss.

Just as that woman had eaten her apple, we weren't going to stop till we got to the core. And even after that, we'd keep going. Not even stems and seeds could get in the way.

THE DANCE FOR LUCY

K. Bhojwani

Death had been bellying up to my fence in tightening circles of disrespect for a year by the time Lucy died, though I hadn't seen it coming. Four years old, my neighbor Tammy's daughter. She used to waddle across her mother's cropped lawn—a dazzling South Florida green—and squeeze through the weak part of the gate dividing us to carouse with Buster, my beagle, in my weed-eaten backyard. Lucy couldn't speak (a neurological disorder), but Buster made her smile. He dropped the ball at her feet a thousand times, and each time she furrowed her brow when she tossed it, as if unsure that he would fetch it. Every time he brought the ball back, she cupped her hands to her face in joy, amazed at this unexpected devotion, thrilled with the gift of a dirty ball wet with dog spit.

I was making love to Marge when it happened, Lucy's passing, and Marge was the first one I called when I heard about it.

"Were you close to her?" Marge asked.

"Not really. I think Buster'll miss her more than I will."

Through my patio doors I saw Tammy take the garbage out.

From this distance, you couldn't tell that she'd just lost her little girl. It seemed heroic, her continuing to keep the house clean; I ought to help. But I brushed away the thought. I felt selfish just then, tired and unwilling to face her grief. "Can you come over?" I said to Marge.

"Not tonight, hon."

I knew from the way she said it, tightly, through her teeth, but I asked anyway, to punish myself: "Why not?"

She hesitated. "Pete's on his way home…we're going out…"

My gut clenched. On any other night I would have stopped there, but maybe I needed a little grief of my own to feel better about not sharing Tammy's. "Can't you make something up?"

"It's our anniversary. I just can't tonight. I'll make it up to you tomorrow. I promise."

Fuck tomorrow, I thought. And fuck Pete. Actually, don't fuck Pete. But just to complete the torture, I asked, "How many years?"

"Eighteen," she said, and I detected her pride.

"Congratulations." My sarcasm filled me with disgust. I tossed in a "Happy Anniversary" before hanging up. I wanted to break something, but the house was so damn empty there was hardly anything worth the trouble.

When Sarah left, she'd emptied the place of our short lifetime of accumulated objects. I got the house because I could afford it; she got everything else because she couldn't bear to leave so much history behind. Take it, I'd said, take everything, because I knew she was right. The plaster and concrete walls were too fresh, too new, to hold anything of us; the memories had been collecting in our things, and I was glad not to have to face every day the carved heads from New Mexico, the blue throw rug from North Carolina, the rainbow puppies from San Francisco, and all those damn candles everywhere, fat, thin, tall, round, square, honeycombed and pressed and colored and painted and scented and plain. On some nights, she lit them all, and incense too, and I sneezed like mad. But the flickering, uncertain light inspired her, made her romantic, and we always ended up making love, so I swallowed my irritation.

Even in daylight, the candles held more for her than they ever did for me. The melted wax was art, she said. She would study them and point out shapes to me. Sometimes I could see them. Other times I had no patience for her generosity. I liked my art intentional, distinct and framed, not to be stumbled upon in the random and messy remnants of last night's perfection while waiting for the morning coffee to brew.

Not long before we separated, she stopped trying to show me. Without her vision as a guide, the candles looked ugly and worn, and I was glad she tossed them all before she left. I kept thinking I would buy new things, build new memories, but the place remained spare and simple, big enough to hold a grief of my own.

Tonight, my empty house stared back at me, as bereft of comfort as Marge had been. It had started to rain, a soft slow drizzle that couldn't soak you if you kept moving, so I laced up and took Buster for a run. My new sneakers snuggled my feet and I flew over the asphalt, sweating out the dirty anger crowding my insides. After 30 minutes, I could feel the motion of the muscles in my upper back with each stride. I loved that. It made me feel useful and alive. The soreness the next day, the stiffness in discrete muscles, made me feel tangible, and I liked knowing that I could be broken down into parts, that my body was held together by more than just fragile threads of tissue and feeling.

As I let myself in the back gate, Tammy took another load of garbage out. I waited, blocked by the big frangipani tree so she wouldn't see me. Just thinking of what to say to her tired me. What does one say to a mother who loses a child?

Inside, I boiled spaghetti and curled up with Buster in the blue armchair and Miles on the stereo. The chair was the one post-Sarah piece of furniture I'd managed. It embraced me perfectly, and I had splurged on it, hoping to find comfort in its folds. In the year she'd been gone, I'd worn a groove in its middle, right in the heart of it.

The trumpet wailed and the notes settled on me, seeped into my pores. I could enjoy Miles now because I had stopped trying to make sense of him. My ears, tuned to pop and classical, kept waiting for resolution; only when I gave up expectation could I let jazz in.

This too was Sarah's doing. She divided me: pre-Sarah and post-Sarah. B.S. for the bullshit I was into before she swept me off my feet our last year in college and P.S. for the incidental nature of the last several months, the body of the letter (the letters of my body) having already been consumed.

She left because she fell out of love, she said, and five years dissipated in a haze of forgetting and a few simple words. I didn't have the strength to let anyone else do that, didn't want to have to gather the fragments and reassemble the shell all over if it broke again. But nights like this made me wonder how long I could last. Marge started as a stop-gap measure, a P.S., a fuck buddy, a way to kill time. Now it looked like time was killing me.

I could always count on the binary code, but it offered me no comfort the next day at work. If I followed the steps, unlocked the code, understood the truth of the program, I could always get from one step to the next, forward movement in increments. But the jumble of numbers today was just that, a meaningless jumble I hadn't the strength or inclination to pursue. The image of Lucy with Buster's ball at her feet crept along the edges of my mind. It was hard for me to absorb that she would no longer be there, that she was gone. It was harder still for me to think about her lying in her coffin, her flesh disintegrating into a mess of soiled silk.

I packed my briefcase, closed up the office, and went home. Ashes did go to ashes and dust to dust, but in between were babies and puppies, people and dogs. Buster had made it, but Lucy hadn't. Why?

"I need to know there's more than this, Marge," I said at dinner. "I need to know we're not just going to be snatched away, that at the end of the day everything we've built isn't going to be worth a damn."

"Oh, but honey, we can't know, don't you see? We just have to keep on living."

I stared at her, refusing to accept that. Then she said, "Have you ever read *To the Lighthouse*?"

"No."

"There's a character, Mrs. Ramsay, and her purpose in life is to create moments of beauty for the people around her, for her family. I'm like that," she said, smiling. "I'm Mrs. Ramsay. I create moments of beauty."

I looked at her. "That can't be all there is, Marge. Life has to add up to something more."

Marge smiled at me in her let-me-envelop-you-in-love-and-goodness-and-make-it-all-right way. "I once tried to go where you want to go. And then I realized that the search for meaning is meaningless. Unconditional love, honey. That's what it's all about."

I pushed my plate forward and walked away from the table. "What are you doing here if that's what it's all about? What about Pete and the kids?"

"I haven't left them, have I?"

I turned to look at her. She sat placidly, still smiling. I'd never expected her to leave Pete. In fact, I'd never even thought much about it. We were way stations for each other, each enjoying what the other offered without hollow promises of the future weighing upon our moods. I'd cleared my head of expectations after the first time we slept together. She looked much the same tonight as she did that night almost a year ago, a little tipsy, aroused, and apparently unconcerned with consequences. I had felt the same way that night, which was how we ended up in the bedroom.

That night, Marge had sat on the edge of the bed, holding the middle of me with her thighs, her feet on the floor. I kissed her forehead and placed my finger at the bridge of her nose, tracing a path down her face and letting her skin reveal the inside of her to me. She closed her eyes, leaned back, and stretched herself across the bed. I crawled up her body, supported by one hand, the other gliding across her torso, under her blouse, still searching for her essence, looking to feel who she was through her skin. I moved up, closed her eyes to kiss them, ran my lips across the side of her face, over her ear, down to her lips. She parted them for me, and I ran my tongue across her teeth. Her tongue met mine, and I swallowed the fear that had kept me from this intimacy for the last year, I swallowed the remnants of Sarah I had been carrying.

My hand roamed down her belly, under her panties, into her wetness. I stroked the tip of her with my thumb, slid a finger into her, casting for the part of her she kept hidden, the deepest reach, wanting in. When she arched her back and groaned, I remembered what it felt like to provide for another, take care of a woman, hold her pleasure in my hands. The feeling filtered into the familiar places in my body, filling the empty spaces. The vein pulled tight across Marge's neck. Her outstretched fingers, the thrust of her ribs, thrilled me, topped my spaces with a froth I would sip in my alone moments to remind myself that women gave themselves in ways they couldn't imagine.

"Fuck me," she said, grabbing my arm.

My fingers went limp. I had forgotten. This was only sex, not a gentle plea for entrance into another's heart. I complied with her request, even when she said *harder,* even when it seemed that the roughness she demanded couldn't possibly be enjoyable, even as I tried to remember why I had decided to sleep with her. Her final howling gave me no joy. I pulled out after a grace period of two minutes and lay on my side next to her spent body, knowing I had no one but myself to blame for expecting anything different.

Sarah's thighs flashed before me then, the sensation of resting my head in the groove of her hip, falling asleep in the radiant aftermath of her satisfaction with her hand stroking my hair. Marge lifted herself up, ran her hands along my arm, groping downward. I let her loveless fingers smooth me out, hoping to plunge into the pool of forgetfulness, to leave my sticky past on her.

Afterward, she flopped down so her face was under the air conditioning vent, her feet inches away from my head. As if remembering something, she placed a hand on my knee. She said, "Did you know that when you have sex with someone their aura stays with you for weeks?"

I shuddered.

After she left, I scrubbed my insides, my skin, my scalp, with steaming water, trying to wash out her smell, trying to recover Sarah's. After an hour or so, I caught a whiff of Marge, a stray scent lingering in my kitchen. I took another shower, scrubbing the space around me to wash away her aura. I felt as if I had betrayed Sarah, or at least my memory of her. I carried my cache of recollections with me like a talisman, a reminder of how things could be, of how miraculous and devastating love was. It scared me to see how ready I was to fall into the same trap again.

When Marge seduced me the second time, I was prepared. Sex was all it was, and sex was all it had been for the last year.

Marge looked at me now from across the table. "When's the funeral?"

"Tomorrow."

"Maybe you should go."

I'd never been to a funeral, and I wasn't sure I was ready for one. "We'll see."

I flew to New York the next day to visit the old neighborhood in Brooklyn. Tammy's grief for Lucy was still too fresh for me to handle, and I wanted out of the dead air that hung around my house. Marge's platitudes were not much comfort. In fact, I felt almost ready to break it off with her. But I had started to slip back into the murk of memories I'd built with Sarah, and I didn't want to go back there either. There I was, sandwiched between the pain of the past and a future filled with false hope. Why was it so hard to stay present?

I met Esperanza at the drugstore on the corner of the block where I once lived. I stood in the colorful presence of cold medications, dazed by the selection. I glanced over my shoulder and saw her staring at me from the checkout line, a half-dozen eggs and a pint of Ben & Jerry's pistachio ice cream in her hands. She wore a black ribbed tank top and jeans, and the silver of her belt buckle glinted in the store's fluorescence. I returned to the medications, and when I turned around again her eyes bore into me in a curious way, not sexual but searching.

She paid for her things and approached me. "You look like you could use some help," she said with a shy smile.

Long after Esperanza downed her espresso, I was still blowing on my coffee to cool it. She had a way of listening that made me want to tell her everything. She didn't have answers for all life's problems the way Marge did, didn't offer philosophical responses to every weighty question. I told Esperanza about the funeral, about how I didn't understand why Lucy's death troubled me this much. By the time we went to dinner, she knew all about Sarah.

"I had my own Sarah," she said. "Ten years we built together. And then she left. We had grown apart, she said."

I exhaled a slow whistle. "Ten years. Wow. That's a long time."

"Yeah, but you know what? She was right. We did grow apart. But I couldn't see it. I was holding on to the past. Too afraid to let go of time invested. But that's a shitty reason to stay in a relationship. Time invested."

"So what did you do?"

"I rediscovered myself, recovered myself, actually. It's scary how much of ourselves we lose in relationships without realizing it. How much we sacrifice to keep our partners happy for fear of losing them."

I mulled the thought over a bite of penne. "So why be in a relationship then? We lose ourselves to the other person, and then they leave. What's the point?"

She studied my face. "Are you serious?"

Was I? I thought about Lucy. Yes, I was serious. How must her mother feel now? What did the weight of that loss feel like? I couldn't imagine.

"Can you really live without love?" she asked.

I thought about Marge. Did we have love? A variation of it, I supposed. We'd been sharing thoughts, feelings, and body fluids for a year. It wasn't love like the kind I had for Sarah, but it was something, a diversion, a collection of beautiful moments strung together like Christmas lights. "I guess I can't live without love. But a part of me would like to be able to."

"That's just fear of loss. But love weighs a lot less than fear, so love always floats to the top. Love always wins."

"If love always wins, why did our lovers leave?"

"I'm not saying the person you love will stay with you forever. I'm saying your desire to love, to give and receive love, will always surface. You can fight it, which only makes it harder to enjoy the feeling, but it'll find its way out."

I chewed on mushrooms and Esperanza's ideas. "How can you be so sure?"

She laughed. "Who says I'm sure? I just know what works for me. My life is unbearable if I don't love. Lack of love is the only true death."

I flew back the next day and went to pay my respects to Lucy's parents. I had an idea of what a house of grief should look like, so when I walked into Tammy and Rich's I expected an unnatural quiet. Instead, chattering people draped themselves over two voluptuous black leather couches. Three young kids sat below them, alternately staring at the television and tugging on a large plastic truck, red and green and yellow and blue. I said hello. The adults glanced up, and one or two nodded; someone smiled, another said hi. Then their faces returned to each other and their conversation.

I wandered gingerly into the house, half-looking for Tammy. I didn't know Rich that well, and I thought it would be awkward to see him first. I stopped at the kitchen entrance. Three women waltzed between the sink, stove, and countertop, hovering and stirring, the smell of burning cheese lingering. Tammy was not among them. I moved on.

Something in the dining room caught my eye. A collage balanced on a flimsy wooden easel. A collection of photographs of Lucy laid in varying geometric patterns, all non-Lucy parts clipped, myriad Lucys crowding one another. Her expression in almost all of them was bewildered, strangely vacant; if I studied the pictures, tried to place them in chronology, I might have found a progression of the essence missing from her eyes growing more absent, a steadily reclusive gaze withdrawing into itself each month.

"Julia!" I stood up and turned. Tammy grabbed me in a hug. I placed my hands lightly on her back and tapped a rhythm meant to console. I held myself buoyant, weightless against her warmth, uncomfortable with her readiness to include me in this...celebration, it felt like.

"I'm sorry," I said.

"We appreciate your prayers. I'm glad you came over. Lucy loved Buster."

"He'll miss her." I peered into Tammy's eyes, surprised at

their clarity, at the pitch and speed of her voice. "How are you doing?"

"I cleaned up today, disinfected the whole place, moved all the flowers outside. They were making me crazy. Allergies. I only kept this one." She pointed to a bouquet by our feet, next to the collage. "It was on her coffin."

I swallowed and looked at the arrangement of white roses. I imagined a shrunken pearl-white box cradling in silk a once-pink, now pearl-white child. Eternal Resting Place of a Pretty Little Pink Girl. "You look like you're handling this well," I said.

"I have my moments, but today's a good day. Rich and I have a strong faith. We know she's in a better place. She's an angel in heaven with God now." Tammy's eyes lit with the intensity of forgetting.

I took a step back, amazed at her forthrightness. This was not how I imagined grief. I thought it traveled like death, cloaked in stealth. Tammy's grief was full of good cheer, open and welcoming.

I stared at her, not knowing what to say. I wanted to ask her how she knew, how she could be so sure Lucy was in a better place, but I knew better than to question faith. I envied her grief then, the kind of grief that rested comfortably in the body's grooves, in the certainty that all was as it should be.

She turned suddenly to ask a man reaching for chips on the table, "Where's Rich?"

"I thought I saw him go into the bedroom earlier," the man replied.

"Excuse me," she said to me and hurried away.

I watched the man scoop dip onto his chips, his body rigid with intent, his eyes focused on the dip. He looked up, and our eyes locked. I turned my head and wandered in Tammy's direction to tell her goodbye. I glanced into the bedroom, its door ajar. Rich lay on the bed, face-down. Tammy stroked his hair, her face close to his ear. He shuddered in soft intervals, each trembling motion more relaxed, farther apart, each whispering breath of Tammy's bringing him back to his life. She got him to rise, helped him off the bed, and held him close to her. They stood motionless for only a moment before having to sway to keep their balance, before the momentum of holding on to each other took hold of them.

From the kitchen came the sound of a pot crashing to the floor. Someone called for paper towels and Tammy looked toward the door. She took Rich by the hand and pulled him out of the room. I headed for the front door, retreating from the soft, slow hum of mourning punctuated by Tammy's commands in the kitchen, her voice individual and distinct in its authority, its determination to restore order.

When I got home I called Esperanza, hoping I could keep death at bay a while longer.

ELUSIVE LOVE

Ronna Magy

Cherries
You came back to me last night, or was it in a dream? The moon outside a milky white. You came at first through touch, then sight. My hands around your shoulders, that white shirt slipping off to one side. At first, I do not remember your feel and wonder if I want you close. So many times together and apart. You stroll smiling inside my house. Hair pulled straight back behind your ears.

I remember your look as you lay down. Rose of your skin blending in with the couch. Fingers combing back my hair. I remember your smell, the scent of your skin, like food not tasted but recalled. There are your breasts beneath the shirt, your legs so long and deeply tanned. There is your body one more time.

I feed you Bing cherries as we stand stroking all the curves, naked. I bite into each blood-black fruit, and pass the flesh into your mouth. Cherries stain my hands, your face, your lips, a purple.

There is no time when we are there. Or when we lie so

close in bed. I remember it all, the curve of your back, the sound you make before you come, the way you turn cat when you are stroked.

The words "My dear" and "I still love you" remain in the air, as if waiting for this moment to happen anew, waiting for this love to begin again. I have not forgotten, nor have you. You came last night, or was it in a dream? And when you left we walked outside. There is the memory that you were there. And a half-filled bowl of cherries beside the sink.

Beach

In the hours before winter sunset I think of you. High waves lash our curve of beach, tall palms and night blue agave silhouetting the bluffs. In bed, I remember the feeling just breaths ago. You slid your hands along my skin and I could feel what before wasn't there. I was alive then, as were you. This beach trip scene returns days later when you have gone up north. I play the waves back, we are still there, all touch and kiss as long, long as we can until I feel it between my legs, then you, yours. My hand goes down into that place where your fur-lined thighs open to me, wide. I play it back and you, my love, are alive, and in this space we live together. When you are gone on that trip, day upon day, when you are gone, there is no more we than ever there was. As if we are broken and never have been. As if one could erase our years of love.

What did we do on that trip to the ocean? Nothing, you say, but that wasn't all. We let the moments pass by, still. Felt them later, each on its own. The crunch of apples, sips of lemonade, sand in our shoes, sun on water on waves on sand on beach on feet on deck chairs under umbrellas. What did we do there? Nothing. Drank strong coffee and watched winter mornings arrive not yet yellow. Sat in the window and took in the waves. Talked to the birds and made pictures in the sand. The things one does on an adventure at the beach. With your traveling to Sequoia, the beach trip ends. What sweetness lingered in the air gets lost. Calls from your cell phone scratch over the lines. Your voice cloaked in heavy fog. "Hi, honey," you say. It is your voice. I try to feel our love, but no longer am sure. Your body is no longer holding mine. Your real voice no longer in my ear. This is what happens when you are gone. I traipse through days as if in the dark. Close myself up in unlit rooms. Only slivers of sunlight slip in through the slats. Sleep in daytime, awake at 3, eat cans of soup, and climb back in bed. A flickering light lives across my wall. Black, white, and color glow off its screen. TV characters parade into my mind. In a world where there was an I and you and you are gone, parts of both of us die. In a world where the I and you die, what remains? The words we spoke no longer float in the air. Our touches exist only as memories in dreams. What then do the ethers hold of us? My writings, your writings, thoughts on paper, yours and mine. Your sculptures and the images of women that they hold.

You Sculpt Women

You sculpt large women with lots of breasts and lots of hips, full bodied. You sculpt women and when you do, you talk to them and enter their bones. As you lay the clay across their forms and press each piece so tightly on, as if you know the way inside.

You show me your latest figure in clay. The woman's breasts large, a lot like mine. Her stomach and shoulders amazingly similar to the way my reflection looks up close. She is gray and solid in form. And I am flesh and I am alive. Is the sameness between us just in my mind? Or do you really want to have me again and again? In flesh, in clay, throughout your world.

If I sculpted women as well as you, I'd sculpt, oh, yes, a group of them. Old and young, I'd sculpt them all. Large and small. I'd breathe my breath into the clay and invite my women to come out for tea. And give them each a set of clothes, a hat, some gloves, and shoes to match. Each would have a place to sit. At a table, round, covered by white cloth. Their glasses filled with iced lemonade. Little tea sandwiches on each plate. They would talk and talk to their hearts' content and hold their daughters upon their laps, and children would play around their feet.

I'd give them all a summer's day. Out in the yard where roses would perfume the air. And with my words, for I like to write, I'd give each one a story or two. To tell when it was her turn to talk.

If I could sculpt women with life inside, I would have my women sit down with yours. Yours would dance and sway in the breeze. Mine would clap, and then they'd sing. Yours would be solid and full of life. And mine would love, and so would yours.

If I could sculpt you as you have me and I could put life's breath inside, perhaps I would not feel such pain when you are gone away on a trip, even for a few days. That pain of loss I try not to feel when you have gone away.

The Door

Click, behind us you close the white door. Across the bed stretches a comforter in white. At its head four pillows encased in lace. I wonder where on your bed we will lie. Take off our clothes and begin to touch. Will you remember my taste, my smell? I wonder if you'll remember the way we were.

Inside this bedroom there has been our love. Clothing removed with abandon and desire. Jeans and black sweaters strewn at the foot of the bed. Silk stockings and lace bras that covered our curves. And once again, now, we enter this space.

Elizabeth Sims

She didn't want to suffer, this time around. But how do you die slowly, and too young, and not suffer? How can you not suffer a hell of a lot? I knew what she meant, and I saw to it that she suffered as little as possible. I was willing to do anything, short of finishing her off myself.

Faye knew suffering. She'd gone through hell the first time—hell and back again—and she beat the goddamned thing. Then, four years later, the other shoe dropped. She turned to me that afternoon in the doctor's office, the nice office with indirect lighting and something Persian underfoot. The doctor waited for her to react to the news that it was inoperable. She'd known it all along, though. And she said simply, "I don't want to suffer."

Was she a coward? No, not Faye. She could have withstood murder by inches at the hands of a team of gold-medal sadists—and done it gracefully too—if she'd felt it necessary.

We could have forestalled death for perhaps a year. That's what they said, when I asked. A year is a long time. Enough time for her to have written another book. Enough time for her to have advanced theoretical mathematics by one more fraction. Enough time to have won one more prize, or half a dozen.

The point for Faye wasn't that she couldn't handle another go-round; it was that she didn't want *me* to have to handle another go-round. She didn't want me to have to witness it again: the wasting, the vomiting, the peeling skin, the friends coming by bearing soup and ghastly smiles.

She didn't have to explain any of this to me. Do you see what I'm telling you? *She chose a shorter life for my sake.* Oh, I could have handled it, you know: You do what you have to. And I would have. She just wasn't sure what would be left of me afterward.

So I ordered a hospital bed and put it on the second floor so she could see the bare treetops. With the doctor's help I laid in a supply of morphine and learned how to give it to her. And I sent to California for cases of the peppery Cabernet she liked and was able to drink and keep down.

Unless you're a math geek yourself, you surely don't know anything of Faye. What was Faye? She was brilliant, of course, a crackerjack mathematician, a world-beater, but more than that, she was a theorist, an artist of the gray matter. She wasn't merely inventive. She was nimble in those mysterious regions of imagination the rest of us only poke into, then hastily retreat from, suffering badly from brain-hurt. She came up with new theorems and she didn't leave the proofs to future generations. She proved them herself, by God.

People—odd, nearsighted people—came from all over the world to see her, to listen to her talk and draw numbers on a board. They came to shake her hand and begin conversations I couldn't follow.

Fortunately for me, she could make other talk too, and do more things with her hands than draw numbers.

We were Faye and Dede, Dede and Faye, the painter and the mathematician, and we lived in a pleasant house all our own, with a big garage for our cars, which we loved to distraction, the both of us happy to tinker and send away for parts and exchange greasy kisses while we worked.

One afternoon about two weeks from the end she came out with something new. There was a fireplace in her room; I'd used some good seasoned apple wood to build a pretty fire in it. I'd just added a chunk and stood watching the flames curl around the gray bark when she said in a clear voice, "You break my heart, you know."

She wasn't asleep, as I'd thought. I turned.

When horror unfolds before your eyes, you begin to manage your emotions as though they were unruly children. *Fear, come here and settle down now—and you, Despair, I'd like to know why you're not on your mat with the rest of us. Anguish! Please stop that stomping around.*

We looked at each other for a long moment.

I said, "Would you like some custard?"

She licked her lips. "Seeing you standing there. Your face."

"I made some of the maple kind this morning."

"I can't imagine going away from you."

"You like the maple kind."

"Don't cry. Come here."

I climbed onto the bed, careful not to bounce her. Her body was like a pile of pick-up sticks under the blanket.

"There are things I haven't done," she said, "things left to do."

"Tell me." I stroked her sharp shins through the blanket.

"You should be painting, you know."

"I—I'll—I'm sketching a little now."

"Between loads of laundry and running to the store and bathing me." In spite of the morphine, she was pretty lucid.

"I'll paint."

"I know you will. And you'll make a lot of people happy."

"Maybe. That isn't the point, though."

"Why do you paint?"

She'd never asked me that question before. I said, "For the sake of painting."

"For its own sake?"

"Yes."

"Has it always been that way for you?"

"For a long time." There was a frayed spot on the blanket. I circled it with my finger. "I don't think I've ever really had a choice."

"Dede, why don't you want my money?"

I shook my head. "It's hard to explain."

"You'd never have to worry."

"That's what worries me."

"So the university will build a new library and put my name on it. Endow another chair." She turned her eyes to the window. "Yippee skippee."

I said nothing.

With effort, she said, "I took care of everything, I thought. But now that I've been lying here, I realize... You know how when you go on vacation and you're halfway there and you start to wonder whether you've left the stove on? I don't want to leave the stove on."

"Yes."

"My book."

"Yes?" She meant the most recent one. The math people were going wild for it.

"It's...big. You know."

"It'll immortalize you, as they say."

She coughed out a little laugh. "I want to sign those five hundred copies. I want to autograph each one, and I want you to send them out. I know they're still sitting there."

"I'll help you. We can do that. You want them to go to the people on your mailing list, right?"

"And I want Uncle Wendell to have that Cadillac."

"Good. He should have it."

"You'll have to drive it down to him."

"Well... Couldn't I use the shipping company?"

"Dede. Listen to me. First of all, no truck driver could

possibly get close to Wendell's place, let alone get a car carrier in there. And I don't want some stranger to drive it down."

"Well, how am I supposed to find him? I've never even—"

"You'll find him. You can drive right in. I'll write everything down for you."

"All right. Yes."

"And I want you to redo the floor in the garage. We should have put that sealer on it the first time."

"Uh-huh."

"The oil is just eating right through."

"I'll take care of it."

She was tiring. "And..."

"Yes, baby?"

She murmured, "I want you to take my ashes to the most beautiful place on earth."

I closed my eyes. "Oh, Faye."

"That's where I want to be."

The summer after she recovered from the first tumor, we mounted an ambitious expedition: We wanted to retrace the routes of the voyageurs, up the waterways from Lake Superior into the Canadian shield, into the wilds as far as we could get, eventually to Hudson Bay.

As girls we'd both been mesmerized by stories of the French fur trappers and the missionaries, the tales of independent adventure, the privations and the solitude. The lonely beauty of the rivers and lakes. We'd read all the history, and since there had been no girl voyageurs as far as we could tell, we decided to redress that in our own way. We used Faye's period of suffering and recovery to plan the trip.

When she was well, we did it. We acquired a large canoe and the proper gear and we trained our bodies, lifting weights and running and taking vitamins.

We paddled and portaged north from Thunder Bay. When September arrived we found ourselves in a magical campsite at the head of a tributary of the Albany River, not far from Hudson Bay. It was a creek, and it invited us to paddle it. The creek narrowed until we encountered a sudden wet meadow and the biggest beaver lodge we'd ever seen.

The bite in the air and the stillness of the marsh and the dark woods surrounding it made a magic world, even compared to the fairylands we'd already passed through. We grew breathless and reverent.

We were out of stove fuel, so we gathered sticks and made a conservative fire for cooking. We camped there three days. Finally the air grew colder and forced us to turn our canoe downstream.

There is no explaining the mechanics of magic. We watched the V's the beavers' noses made in the water, heard the abrupt slap of their tails at night: *ker-ploot!* The moon was blinding. We exchanged perhaps ten words in that camp. In fact, from then on, we required fewer words to communicate. That place, of all the places we'd ever been, changed us most. It deepened us.

When we left there, I said a silent farewell, knowing I'd never see it again.

Faye spoke again. "Dede, I mean it."

"I hear."

"I know you can do it."

"Um. Ah."

"You're thinking we didn't use a map that last week before we reached the bay."

"That's exactly what I'm thinking."

"Well." She sank into her pillow. "It'll be a matter of feeling your way."

"But Jesus Christ, Faye."

"I know you can do it. Promise me."

"I promise. I promise. Yes."

She squeezed my hand. I lifted hers to my lips.

The next day she was noticeably weaker, but she insisted we set to work. I brought the books upstairs a stack at a time.

"You had to get a great big hardcover deal," I said, grunting. "Couldn't you have condensed some of this? Skipped a few formulas? Saved a few trees?"

I picked a book off the stack at her bedside, opened it to the flyleaf, set it on the pillow I'd placed over her stomach, and positioned the pen in her fingers.

It took her about a minute to sign each autograph. She managed five or six, fighting sleep, fighting that final sleep we both dreaded so, before she drifted away for a while. I capped the pen and waited, glad at least to have a goal, for the both of us.

Seven days later, I said, "That was the last one. You've done it, honey-cake."

"Oh," she whispered slowly. "Do your arms ache? That neck of yours?"

"Not at all."

"Liar, I've worn you out."

"No, darling."

"Promise me you'll get your sleep. I've asked too much of you."

"No. No."

I spent two days writing out mailing labels, getting nowhere near done. I left them on the dining room table.

At the end, she didn't want me to leave her for a minute. I got a few of her former students to look after the house, shovel the snow, and fetch groceries, while I stayed with her and fed the fire. I heard their voices, low and solemn, as they tiptoed around downstairs, searching for the ice-melt crystals and the toilet cleaner.

I was lying on the floor beside her bed when I became aware of her breathing. It was midnight. The sound grew louder, and I realized she was laboring. I got up and held her, lightly, and listened. Splinters of moonlight came through the window. I held her and I believe she heard me murmur, for the last time, the things only lovers can murmur.

The funeral was a blur, naturally. Everybody came: almost all of those mailing-list people, and the relatives and the students and the colleagues, all of them in acute distress, as much from being nerds in forced fellowship as from the fact that Faye was gone.

I got back to the book project as soon as I'd finished cleaning her room. I thought about Faye as I pasted labels, stapled envelopes, and hauled the lot to the post office.

I wandered through the house, my heart shredding with every memory. I wanted to drive off a cliff. I wanted to burn every canvas I'd ever touched. I wanted to cut myself in half. The utter futility of life hit me in the face like a baseball bat.

The Cadillac was a 1996 Fleetwood, the final model year. Faye had bought two of them, one to drive and one to put in storage, with the intention of cannibalizing its parts in order to keep the first one running forever. The stored car hadn't yet been touched, and this was the one Faye intended for Uncle Wendell.

Faye was a Cadillac girl from the get-go. Her parents both worked for GM from cradle to grave: her father on the line at Fisher Body, her mother ladling sauerkraut and peas in the plant cafeteria. They sent their brainy daughter to the General Motors Institute, which became her springboard to MIT and theoretical mathematics.

I think they were always a little disappointed that she didn't use her genius for the advancement of General Motors. But the fact that she liked Cadillacs and always drove one—as they did—appeased them somewhat.

Uncle Wendell had worked at Cadillac too. Now he lived in East Bejesus, Florida, or someplace. Without electricity.

I pulled the canvas off the Fleetwood and folded it away. The car was heavy and sleek, in a pearly gray finish. It was a shame they hadn't sold better. I put the wheels back on, with fresh new tires, jacked it down, added all the fluids, put in a new battery, poured in three gallons of gas, and cranked her. She sprang to life as if she'd just rolled off the line. I felt my face do something strange, and realized I was smiling faintly.

I got on I-75 and headed south. The Fleetwood drove nicely. A squashy sort of ride, but I like squashy all right in a big car. Me, I'm a Ford woman. I stuck with the Thunderbird through thick and thin, all those horrendous model years, keeping my faith alive in the shrine of my powder-blue 1964 convertible. In winter I drove a stripped-down Taurus.

I'd done all the crap in the pamphlets the doctor hands you. I'd had plenty of time to prepare and to say goodbye to my girl. But I still couldn't believe she was gone. My heart felt cold and tightly sealed, like a cut of meat in a freezer case.

I drove deeper into the South, over the bridge in Cincinnati into Kentucky. It was two weeks since the funeral, three months since the diagnosis. We'd made love just twice after that day.

The velvet hills of bluegrass country rolled beneath the expressway, and I remembered Faye's hands on my body, her fingers, her toes, her mouth. We were sublimely sensitive to each other. She was such an accomplished lover—something that should have merited mention in her biographical notes.

Her breasts were delightful. Two cheerful drumlins always ready to be caressed, always warm with the scent of Faye: a cross between carrot cake and a summer forest.

Yes, I'd hoped at least one interviewer would say, "Well! So much for $E=mc^2$, professor. Now, please tell us something about your sexual technique, which must be awesome, judging by the demeanor of your friend here."

It was warm in Tennessee. I stopped in Chattanooga for the night and found a place to get something to eat. Even though I wanted very much to drive that car over a cliff, I knew I wasn't going to do it.

The woman who served me my barbecue sandwich was a girl, really, no more than 19. She wore a horrendous amount of foundation and blush, and she needed a manicure. But the way she met my eye and the delicate manner she employed when she placed the extra sauce and a premoistened towelette at my elbow made me remember that I'd experienced sexual pleasure before knowing Faye. Was it terrible to think sex might bring me out of this?

The next day I left the expressway south of Ocala, followed a two-lane route for a while, then left that for a narrower crowned road. The pines grew tall here, and I inhaled their resinous perfume before I rolled up the window and turned on the air conditioning.

Uncle Wendell could have retired to one of those old-timer complexes in Florida—the ones with shuffleboard courts and van service to the doctor—but somebody sold him a vast chunk of property in the central part of the state for next to nothing. I guess he'd never heard that saying, You get what you pay for.

I turned onto a dirt road. Here the pines began to fight for turf with live oaks. A strip of cloudless blue sky hovered overhead. I found the crossroad Faye had written down, then drove slowly along until I saw what looked like the right two-track.

It was a dense landscape. Spanish moss dripped from the oaks, and gigantic black flies threw themselves at the Fleetwood's windows, smelling me right through the gaskets and the clear-coat. I put the car in low; the two-track was soft and sandy. My watch said 1 o'clock, but I had to turn on the headlights. As I steered the car carefully around a bend, a buck deer sprang right over the hood, nicking the ornament with a rear hoof.

Eventually I came to a clearing where an old man was cutting up a felled pine trunk with a chain saw. His back was to me. I waited until he lowered the saw after making a cut, then gunned the Fleetwood's V-8 to let him know I was there. Without turning, he dropped the saw, clawed at his chest, tottered sideways, and fell to the ground.

Uncle Wendell's funeral was a small affair, attended by a man named Septus, Septus's wife, Jo, the minister, five chickens, and me. Improbably, Uncle Wendell's wife, Aunt Flory, had died herself just ten days before, of natural causes.

"Coulda dug em both at once if I'd'a knowed," the tight-muscled gravedigger muttered as he held the cemetery gate open for us.

If Faye's funeral was a blur, everything about Uncle Wendell's stood out like razor blades: the hot flat Florida sky, the pine needles scattered over the hardpan of the cemetery, my own bewildered eyes in the Fleetwood's mirror. I remembered to give $50 to the minister.

That night Septus and Jo hosted a little dinner for the minister and me at their home, miles deeper into the woods than Wendell's place.

"Ever et possum?" asked Jo, handing me a quart bottle of Budweiser. I couldn't tell whether she listed to one side because of a defect or because she'd started on Bud much earlier.

"No," I said, "but I've had muskrat."

She looked at me closely, then said, "Nowheres near the same experience."

"I feel terrible about Wendell."

She took hold of my sleeve. "Looky here, Missy. Wendell didn't amount to much."

"He worked at Cadillac."

"And that's a fine thing, a fine thing."

"I thought he was a good guy."

"You didn't know him at all, then?"

"No."

"Jes' as well."

"He was kin to my lover. Who just died too."

"Oh." She said it kindly. We sat together for a while. She patted my arm, and I felt better.

The opossum stew was good. Septus and Jo were a helluva couple, I decided. The minister, Reverend St. John, wasn't bad either. The four of us got roaring drunk on Budweiser, and then Jo got out her autoharp and we sang gospel songs till almost morning. That is, they sang while I hummed along, making quick sketches of them with a soft pencil on brown grocery bags.

"It's magic!" Septus shouted, looking over my shoulder delightedly. I'd reduced his overbite considerably.

At one point we rested from singing. I weaved over to Reverend St. John and said, "You know, Jesus isn't somebody I've ever hunted very hard for."

He took a long pull from his Bud, wiped his mouth and said, "He ain't been hidin' from you."

I said, "How do you reconcile yourself to a terrible loss?"

He winked. "Plenty of beer!" he yelled, and together we laughed maniacally.

Around noon the next day Septus drove me in the Fleetwood to the crossroad, where I could catch a bus to Ocala. I gave him the keys and told him the title was in the glove compartment.

"You're a good person, Dede," he said.

Back home I tackled the job of the garage floor, the next thing on Faye's list. I did it in two halves, moving our equipment from one side to the other. We'd kept the place pretty orderly, but it had its mysteries. Behind an empty waste carboy I found a hair ribbon I'd been missing since it flipped off my head during a close call with a fan belt.

And when I moved a metal case of nuts and bolts from a back corner, I found an envelope wedged beneath it. It was a note in Faye's handwriting that said: *Dear Dede, see how strong you are? I love you. Don't miss me very much. Faye.*

I went to the store and bought a quart bottle of Budweiser, and drank it while I worked into the night.

The warm weather crept up north. It was time to escort my lover to her final rest. The heavy work in the garage had gotten me in shape for it. But I didn't want to do it. I really didn't want to do this one. Why? I felt tired, not so much physically as emotionally. The Uncle Wendell thing had really shook me up.

I wouldn't do the whole trip, I decided. She hadn't asked me to do the whole trip; she'd asked me to take her ashes to the most beautiful place on earth.

I paced the house. Faye eyed me from the library table. Well, it was the box Faye was in that eyed me, a sturdy little cardboard box that you might want for mailing a batch of brownies to someone. Only Faye's eyes were now just little bits of cinder. Oh, it was unbearable.

Looking at a half-finished canvas in my studio, I could see exactly how I wanted the picture to end up, but I could no more paint than prove one of Faye's theorems. I forced my hand to pick up a tube of viridian green. I held it for a moment, then dropped it back into the tray.

A little voice that lives in my head sometimes says shameful things. At this moment it said, *Why not just, like, flush her?* Sometimes, of all the people in the world, I hate myself the most.

The next day I made plans to drive to Canada and hire a plane to fly me and a small kayak into the Albany River, a hundred miles upstream from its mouth.

"Get it done, get it done," I muttered as I dug through our stuff searching for topographic maps and my lucky tin cup. I gathered equipment and a small pack of supplies, and bound the cardboard box of Faye tightly in plastic wrap and duct tape.

I waved to the pilot, and he rocked his wings and was gone. Just a hundred miles between me and Fort Albany, on the mighty Bay of Hudson.

The sky was bright; I'd checked the forecast and the high pressure was supposed to hold for a day or two at least, though an arctic storm was mixing it up in the western provinces. I'd packed a small tarp and plenty of waterproof matches in case I had to hole up for a bad spell.

Faye was lashed on top of the kayak's nose. I imagined she felt secure there.

"You and me again, baby," I said as I shoved off. "God, it's beautiful. The spruces, baby, remember the spruces? Smell them!" I talked to her as if she were blind. "There's a mama moose and her calf! I'm paddling, I'm paddling. I'm not getting close."

I'd forgotten how important it is to go to the woods. I studied the ribbon of sky above the river. Compared to the hot flat light of Florida, this Canadian light was somehow more golden, despite being colder and harder. I liked it.

"It's more gorgeous than I remembered," I told Faye. "How am I supposed to go home without you?"

We had both remembered that our tributary had led off to the east, so I headed up every right-hand turn I saw. Some were easier than others. Topography changes. Rivers switch courses, floods sweep away beaver dams, and beavers build new ones. Trees blow down.

I paddled my ass off. I hoisted the kayak around snags, I squeezed it through chutes, I muscled it over rocks. I felt savagely calm.

The chatter of a small party of canoeists reached my ears as I was slipping back to the big river from a tributary. Not wanting to make voyageur small talk, I eddied out and waited until they were well downstream.

As I paddled up a creek on the second morning, a feeling developed in my pelvis, a sort of downward pull. I recognized where I was.

When I arrived at the meadow, there was the beaver lodge.

I made camp a comfortable ways into the forest. I wanted a little shelter from the wind, which was picking up. The air tasted so good and clean, I wished I could drink it. Then, finding dry kindling beneath the deadfalls the beavers had left, I built a small fire, as Faye and I had done together. I heated water and brewed black tea.

Sitting on my haunches holding my cup, watching the meadow and the pond, I couldn't believe how familiar everything looked and smelled. A beaver glided by, and I thought I'd seen him before too.

The wind kept up strong, but not cold. I unrolled my sleeping bag beneath a tamarack and looked up at the stars swirling through its tossing top. The crowns of all the trees were getting mightily slapped around, but I felt only a light breeze on the ground. I wanted never to leave.

In the morning heavy clouds were drawing themselves across the sky, like torn cotton shrouding. I felt my face do that strange thing again: I was smiling up at those clouds. The rain began just as I'd eaten some cereal and tidied my camp.

The rain could go on for days, and my food wouldn't last more than another two.

"This is it, honey-cake," I said, unlashing Faye's box from the kayak.

The meadow beckoned me. My plastic poncho whipped about annoyingly, so I set down Faye and took it off. Then I squirmed out of my pullover. The rain was almost warm. I carried everything to the kayak and stowed my poncho and pullover. Then I undid my shoes and stripped off my T-shirt and my shorts and my underwear. I picked up the box and smiled, to be naked with Faye in the rain. The meadow grass was pleasant beneath my feet. I carried the box along the edge of the meadow until we came to the beaver dam. I waded into the pond and swam, pushing the box ahead of me. It floated.

The water was clear to the bottom and amber-colored near the shore. Grasses swayed on the bottom, in response to the wavelets kicked up by the weather. I hoped a beaver would come along and swim with us, but none did. Leaving the box floating, I dived down around the lodge, searching for an opening, just to see it, but it was too dark there. Bobbing up, I floated on my back and opened my mouth to drink down rain. The raindrops splashed on the pond's surface like millions of tiny meteors. They drummed on the floating box.

Returning to shore, I tore the duct tape and plastic away with my teeth, and lifted off the lid. The rain instantly mixed with the ashes inside, pattering in and disappearing. I stuck a finger in and drew it out coated with ash. I held it out and the rain washed off the ash. I poured some ash into the lid of the box and made mud with it. The ash was gray and gritty. I picked out a fragment of bone and used it to scoop up some ash-mud. I painted a streak of it across my belly. Another between my breasts. Using the mud like raw pigment, I drew it over my legs and buttocks in swirls and bars. When it thinned it felt very slick, like clay. I made more mud, and painted my face with it, tracing my jawbone with my thumbs. I decorated my arms and watched it trickle away in rivulets.

Licking my lips, I tasted the ash, the ash mixed with rainwater. It tasted like earth, like wine, like iron. I slipped back into the water with the box and submerged it, cleaning it in the clear amber water. Clumps of ash floated to the surface, where the steady rain battered them down. I wadded up the box and tossed it ashore. The rain shimmied across the meadow. I laughed, and my throat opened to the wetness of the world. I was alone and all right.

I kicked out into the pond and swam a while longer, thinking of nothing. I swam, and the reeds and underwater grasses caressed me like a lover.

Fighting Fire

Yvonne D. Jennings

It took K.C. 45 minutes to get up the nerve to enter Goldie's. The outside of the old dive looked the same as it did the last time she had been there, about two decades before. It had probably looked the same since the Prohibition era. But when she finally did get inside, she felt like a fool. Men crowded the place—all types of men, but certainly gay men. Some danced closely to the *thump thump thump* of the too-loud music. A few near the door stared curiously at her, letting their eyes linger on her firefighter's uniform, on her blunt face framed by dark-red hair.

"Oh, jeez," she grumbled.

The letdown of seeing Goldie's like this struck her a little harder than it should have. It wasn't just the 45 minutes outside, though that alone could have been enough. She had sat on a bench at the corner, watching the late-night traffic rush by. Just sat there—hunched over with her hands clenched. How was it that day in, day out she could run into burning buildings and pull mangled people from the wrecks of cars, yet she could not muster enough nerve to enter a dumpy little women's bar?

It finally came down to the liquor coursing through her

veins, saturating her mind in a bath of false courage, pro-
pelling her off the cold bench and down the block to the bar.
She was drunk, sure was, for the first time in countless
years. And she was single. This was the biggest motivator.
She was single again, after 23 years. Maybe, then, it wasn't
so much the liquid courage that got her off that bench after
all. It was the loneliness of her other option: She could go
into Goldie's or go back home to the emptiness.

Janet had taken half the furniture, their two dogs, even the
plants. The hollow house still seemed to ring with the sound
of the door slamming behind her. The noise of it threatened
to deafen K.C. Sometimes she woke up in the night, her ears
stinging and her chest burning, the air seeming to vibrate with
the displaced molecules of a thousand slamming doors. K.C.
did her best not to cry on these long nights.

But tonight the drinks were beginning to numb her. She reasoned she had come all this way, so why not get another high-
ball. She dodged and shouldered her way across the crowded
bar until she managed to find a stool at the far end, wedged next
to a video poker machine. The worn vinyl felt slick and yielding
under the thin navy cotton of her uniform pants. She settled in,
then tugged out the baseball cap she had stuffed in her back
pocket. She put it on backward over her soot-dusted hair before
tapping the muscle queen next to her on the shoulder.

"Since when did this turn into a gay bar?" she hollered
over the music.

He shrugged. He had a handsome face and bright blue
eyes. K.C. guessed him to be no more than a couple of days
over 21. "Hasn't it always been?"

"No, it used to be a *lesbian* bar," she snapped. Her sense
of foolishness upon entering the bar had evaporated into
bitter entitlement.

The young guy smiled cattily. "Honey, I wouldn't know
a thing about it." He turned back to his friends.

"No shit," she said under her breath.

The bartender—a woman as thick and solid as a linebacker—ambled up to her. "What can I getcha?"

She looked at the woman, searching her padded face for someone she might recognize from 20 years ago. "Tall scotch and soda."

The bartender gave K.C. a kind smile and said gently, "Sure, sweetheart, whatever you need to cure those blues."

K.C. quickly averted her eyes, ashamed it was showing through. When the woman came back with the drink, K.C. leaned across the old, chipped bar and asked her, "Whatever happened to this being a lesbian joint?"

The bartender again flashed her kind, dimpled smile, this time in apology. "You know how it is—as soon as a coupla boys start coming, the floodgates open and they all start coming. But a few women still show up, younger ones. Not many old-timers, though."

K.C. nodded, then reached into her pocket to retrieve her wallet. The bartender gave a quick wave of her hand. "The first one's on me." Then she sauntered away.

Old-timer, huh? She took a sip of the drink. Janet would have been offended by that. She was fond of saying, "You're only as old as you feel." Last year, at 41, Janet had quit her job and enrolled in college for the first time. It was like a reawakening. Unfortunately, K.C. didn't fit into her new outlook.

The scotch and soda was going down easy. K.C. wasn't usually much of a drinker, not since a drunk-driving accident in her mid 20s. But tonight seemed to be taking her down a different path. It started after work. The captain had announced his retirement and all the guys decided to take him out and celebrate. They wouldn't let K.C. weasel out this time. After the 24-hour shift, the whole group of them, still wearing their navy blues, went straight from the firehouse to O'Sullivan's Tap, the tavern down the street. K.C. had hoped she could sneak out after a beer, but then the captain specifically requested to share a round with her.

It was then that he told her how proud he was of her, the first female on the force.

"These kids today, coming out of the academy thinking they're hotshots, they don't have a fucking clue." He slurred a little, his white mustache slack on his upper lip and his arm tight on her shoulders. "'Specially the gals. You paved the way for them, and now they just sail on in. They don't know the shit, the sacrifices it took. But I know, I know."

K.C. looked down at her beer and her face burned. Everyone knew she became the first woman in the department because her father, a captain himself at the time, had pulled every string. In the beginning, each day was a new struggle. There was a general resentment directed at her by everyone. Certain guys took it further. Their intimidation bordered on violence. But she outlasted that. She made herself just another face, quiet and private. Even now, the walls she'd built around herself those first few years remained.

The Captain continued, his voice low and sentimental. "I know that your mother, bless her soul, died when you was young. And your father—damn near a legend in this department—gave his life in the line a' duty." He tipped his beer in a quick salute. "And you, as good as any man on this force. I wanna tell you, for your folks' sake, that I'm proud of you." He jerked a thumb at the soot-smudged faces in the room. "And that you've got a family right here. You can't beat a family like this."

She nodded, but knew better than to believe it. Sure, they'd carried her father's casket 15 years ago, and over the years had come to treat her with respect; but they weren't her family. Janet was her family—or had been until she left.

And her leaving had come like a wrecking ball dropping out of the sky. After 23 years, Janet had left her because, in the fury of a midlife crisis, she decided that K.C. should quit the force or come out of the closet and break down another barrier.

"You just can't live two lives forever," Janet had yelled at her one seemingly unremarkable Sunday morning. "It's not fair to you or to them. You could teach those meatheads something; you could help make this world a better place."

K.C. had just come home from the 8 A.M. to 8 A.M. shift and was exhausted. Janet sat at the kitchen table, an untouched plate of fried eggs in front of her. She pointed her fork at K.C. "You've been introducing me as your 'friend' for way too long. You don't have to hide this. Our relationship is as important as any marriage."

And then K.C. noticed the wedding invitation—it must have come in the mail the day before—resting on the table next to her coffee mug. It was addressed to K.C. alone. A rookie from her district had mentioned he was tying the knot.

"I'm never included." Janet's anger set in her jaw, clipping her words. "I'm sick of being invisible."

But what Janet didn't understand, couldn't understand, was that invisibility had come to be K.C.'s manner of survival. She did not forget her early years on the force, when being a woman was crime enough, or later, when her own father stopped talking to her. She had just moved in with Janet and he had been forced to accept what he didn't want to acknowledge. His last words to her were, "Don't you ever embarrass me. I would never have gotten you this job if I had known." And then there was what happened to that openly gay rookie. He was a pariah, the butt of all jokes. When the word FAGGOT was etched on his locker, he cleaned out his locker and left that very day, after only three weeks on the force.

She had told Janet about it, and Janet, fresh from her first semester back as a college student, questioned why K.C. hadn't rallied to the poor guy's side. "How could you let that happen? Leaving him to stand there alone." Her eyes narrowed and her voice cracked. "Don't you know that silence condones hatred like this? Don't you know?"

As if it was K.C.'s fault, as if she could have done anything about it.

When Janet had left her, packed her bags to move to her own place in another part of the city, she had mentioned the gay firefighter. She brought it up like heaving the weight of a heavy yoke off her shoulders. "I knew then," she had said through clenched teeth, "that you would never change, that you weren't proud enough to love me. I waited for you, but you just kept your head in the damn sand. You just don't have the guts, and I can't love a coward anymore."

K.C. had tried to control herself, but the words flew out of her hot, like aerosol sprayed at a lighter. "What, did you learn that in your damn women's courses at the fucking community college? I live in the real world, honey, and you're too old to start actin' naive as a teenager."

Then Janet stormed out and slammed the door after her.

As the Captain talked to her in O'Sullivan's Tap, K.C. wondered if maybe it wasn't true: She had sacrificed too much for the job. It wasn't the kind of realization she wanted. When the Captain ordered the next round, she switched to scotch.

The video poker machine next to her started to buzz. She came out of her thoughts and turned to look at the thin old man who had put in his money and was now pressing the buttons. The machine made all sorts of beeping noises, annoying her. She leaned away from it and nearly fell off her stool. The scotch glass in front of her was empty, and she knew it was time to go. She stood up slowly.

"Hey." Someone behind her tapped her shoulder.

K.C. laughed to herself. *Like clockwork. How could I forget the typical routine at a bar? No one shows any interest until you are about to leave.*

She looked over her shoulder at the girl who had spoken and was surprised to see a clear, young face. She was a little shorter than K.C., her shiny brown hair pulled back in a ponytail.

"Are you leaving?"

K.C. shrugged, giving herself time to think of something smooth to say.

The girl didn't wait for an answer. "Because if you are, I'd like to take your seat."

"Go ahead." K.C. felt a blush rise in her face. For the second time that night she felt like an utter fool.

But the girl wouldn't let her pass. "Is that a fireman's uniform?" She looked down at the initials stitched above the left breast pocket. "K.C.?"

K.C. nodded and took off her baseball cap. She ran a hand through her red hair, then put the cap back on. She caught a glimpse of her hands and they were dirty, especially around the nails, so she stuffed them quickly in her pant pockets.

The girl was smiling. "Can I buy you a drink? You know, for giving up your seat."

K.C. was about to shake her head 'no,' but the girl was already leaning across the bar, talking to the bartender. She noticed the wink the bartender gave her, over the girl's head.

"What's your name?" K.C. asked as the girl handed her a shot glass.

"Jessica." She seemed small and boyish. Her shoulders were broad but thin, like they were made to hold a considerable weight but hadn't yet had to. K.C. felt like a giant next to her.

Jessica toasted, "To finding another pair of tits in this sea of testosterone."

K.C. laughed, startling herself. It had been so long since she had heard her own laugh. The liquid was sweet in her mouth, like lemonade.

They both stood around the empty stool, leaning on the bar. "So what's K.C. stand for?"

It had been a long time since anyone had asked her. She never used her full name. She was named after her mother, and when her mother died, just after K.C.'s tenth birthday, her father started calling her by her initials. He couldn't stand to use his dead wife's name. K.C. saw no harm in telling the girl—she seemed nice enough—but she couldn't get her own mouth to say the words. She said, "It's just K.C."

Jessica laughed. "Trying to be mysterious, aren't ya?"

K.C. shook her head. She couldn't stop staring at the girl's face, the perfect arch of her eyebrows. "There's nothing mysterious about me."

They talked for the next half-hour, meandering from the history of the bar to the heyday of the neighborhood. Then their conversation, buoyed by another drink and a growing sense of hope, wandered over to K.C.'s job. Jessica asked a lot of questions and K.C. told her that some days it was crazy, and others it was downright boring—she passed her time reading science fiction books. Jessica said that she too liked to read but had never given science fiction a try. Their words volleyed smoothly back and forth. Jessica laughed easily and K.C. joked in her old way, the way that had been so natural just four months before and now felt like putting on an old pair of gloves. They stood close together, close enough to hear each other speak in normal voices over the thump of the music. When they both leaned in to say something at the same time, it brought them even closer. K.C. didn't hear—or just didn't pay attention to— what Jessica now said, but she watched her lips move and didn't back away. Their faces were only inches apart. She wasn't sure who initiated it, maybe neither, maybe both. But soon the inches shortened until there was nothing but soft, smooth skin and wet, explorable warmth.

As they kissed, there by the video poker machine at the far corner of the bar, K.C. felt like there was no one else in the room. In the past two decades, the only other mouth hers had touched had been Janet's. This was an entirely brand-new sensation, like eating cotton candy for the first time. As they separated for a breath, K.C. stared hard at Jessica's face, hoping to obliterate all thoughts of Janet. She reached for Jessica once again, slipping her arms around the girl's back and pulling her in. Jessica's hands came up onto her face and gently inched back until they tugged at the hair under her baseball cap. She tasted sweet, like the lemonade shot, and smelled of fresh soap and shampoo. K.C. felt muscles tightening like a ripple in her lower stomach, a sensation she had nearly forgotten, with its peculiar mix of pleasure and queasiness.

"Shoot," she moaned when they separated for the second time. It was too easy, too perfect. She wanted to give the girl a way out. "You're a lot younger than me. We shouldn't be rushing into this."

Jessica laughed. "I'm old enough."

"It just seems kind of weird here." K.C. glanced over at the bartender and was glad to see she wasn't watching. If by odd chance the bartender recognized her from 20 years ago, she might also know Janet. K.C. didn't like taking chances with gossip.

Jessica looked at her closely, then nodded. "Wait here a minute. I'll get my coat."

She slipped away into the crowd.

K.C. took hold of an empty beer bottle and started picking at the label. *What if she never comes back?* She strummed the bar. *What if she changed her mind?* The thought brought an awkward sense of relief.

A hand came down over her own, surprising her.

"Well, let's get out of here then." Jessica smiled. She tugged K.C. by the hand and pulled her through the crowd.

The cab hurried into the night.

"Why me?" K.C. asked, buckled up in the backseat.

Jessica thought for a second then shrugged. "Because you seem to be exactly who you are. Like you said, no mystery. I don't know if you noticed, but most people at that bar are, like, as different as night and day depending on whether it is night or day. Like split personality disorders or something."

K.C. at first didn't know what to make of it, but the

earnest way the girl had said it convinced her that it was a compliment. She allowed herself a slight smile.

They sat in silence for a while. K.C. closed her eyes and tried to simply enjoy holding the girl's hand. But she was drunk—drunk as she'd ever been. Drunk like she used to get right after her father's death. With her eyes closed, it seemed like the world outside of her lids was spinning on a top. She became worried that she might get sick, so she opened her eyes and pressed the girl's cool fingertips to her burning cheeks.

The cab pulled to the side of the road after a short time. K.C. handed the driver a few bills before getting out. She wasn't sure where they were, which was something that hardly ever happened. She prided herself on knowing the city inside and out.

"My place is over here," Jessica called, quickly heading up the steps of a brick, cathedral-like building. K.C. paused when she realized it was a college dorm. BISHOP MCCLURG HALL—ST. MARK'S UNIVERSITY read a sign on the lawn.

She was relieved to place herself. *Oh, yeah, that Catholic school. This place is in my district.* Then the realization settled in, and she came to a halt. Jessica waited for her on the stairs, but K.C. didn't move. She pointed at the sign.

"You live in a dorm?" And in her mind sang out the unasked question, *You're this young?*

"I have to," she sounded annoyed. "I'm on a scholarship for track and field, and part of it is that I have to live in university housing. It's not so bad."

K.C. laughed. It was ridiculous. The girl was half her age and lived in what looked like an old convent. But the issue now wasn't just about her age. No, it was fast becoming more about sleeping with someone besides Janet. It made her nervous, and her laughter subsided into silence. As she stood there on the street with the seconds passing, she remembered Janet calling her a coward.

K.C. looked up at the girl at the top of the steps, her baggy jeans and tight shirt. She wasn't smiling, and it made her even more desirable. A new fear surged in K.C.'s chest. It was thick and sloppy and mean, like a smoky oil blaze, and K.C. recognized it as regret. What if she went home right now and the next fire were to be her last? Worse, what if she went home now and fate left her with never the chance to love a woman again? She would grow old prematurely, with only her pictures—the ones Janet had left—to keep her company. Soaked with booze, she couldn't shake the gloomy thought.

"Well?" Jessica said.

K.C. didn't leave her waiting any longer.

They went in through a side entrance. The hallway was narrow and brightly lit. Pictures from magazines decorated the doors. A noteboard on the wall by the communal bathroom read: THIS IS A SUBSTANCE-FREE SPACE! SMOKING STINKS! Tacked up next to it was the cafeteria menu for that week. The air smelled musty, like dirty laundry, with an underlying presence of industrial-strength cleaners. The halls were quiet, but near certain doors K.C. could hear voices and music. A sign over the water fountain proclaimed QUIET HOURS: 10 P.M. TO 7 A.M. SHUT UP! (THAT MEANS YOU!) Jessica led her to a stairwell.

"I live on the top floor," she explained as they climbed four flights. "They call it the 'penthouse' because the rooms are more like apartments than dorms. Only athletes on scholarship can live up there."

"Isn't there an elevator?" K.C. muttered. Her knees had been worn out over the years, an occupational hazard from running up and down countless stairwells.

"Yeah, but this is a better way to go. I didn't want to run into an R.A. and have to explain what you're doing here."

K.C. nodded, curious herself what the answer to that would be.

On the top floor, the hallway looked much the same as it did on the first floor, if not more narrow. The only thing missing was the communal bathroom. Jessica unlocked the first door on the left. Before letting K.C. pass, she put her finger over her lips. "Shhhh."

Roommates, K.C. realized with a frown. She hesitated, picturing a closet-size room with a bunk bed. A scenario played in her mind of a hellishly long night, complete with a snoring roommate and a ban on all talking. She grabbed Jessica by the shoulder.

"Why didn't you warn me about the roommate?"

"Don't worry," she whispered. "It's not what you think."

She continued inside and turned on the light. They stood in a hallway. On the right was a small kitchen, complete with a fridge and stove. On the left were two doors.

Jessica pointed at the first one and mouthed, "Roommate's bedroom," then the second one, "Her bathroom." She led her down the hallway to a huge living room with a mismatched pair of sofas and a wooden dining table surrounded by an assortment of chairs. Two-story windows stretched up the far wall. A spiral staircase in the corner led up to a loft. Jessica pointed up there. "My room."

K.C. gave a low whistle. "They sure take care of you athletes." She remembered the outside of the building. This apartment was in one of the turrets. "When did they make this place into a dorm?"

Jessica shrugged. "Uh, like a real long time ago. Maybe in the '70s or '80s."

K.C. smiled and decided to stop asking questions. She took Jessica's hand and kissed the palm, then pulled her close. They kissed in the middle of the living room under the high ceiling and the black night of the skylights.

After a bit, they began to inch toward the spiral staircase. For the first few steps they kept kissing, but it was awkward and K.C. turned and hurried up. The loft was narrow, but still bigger than a typical dorm room. There was a walk-in closet at one end and next to it the open door of another bathroom. K.C. peeked over the ledge of the loft at the living room below.

"Not so bad." She grinned. She turned back to Jessica and gently, expertly began to kiss her neck. With eyes closed, K.C. removed the girl's clothing. This was so different, so very different than it had been with Janet. Nakedness had become a matter of course between them, necessary and neutral. But this, now, the girl's smooth, firm skin, filled her with an electric excitement. She clenched her eyes shut, letting her anticipation build, holding the moment, afraid to expose her desperate longing. When Jessica didn't reach for K.C.'s belt, K.C. undid it herself, undressing quickly, self-conscious for the first time in years. At last she opened her eyes. Her breathing paused. The girl was beautiful.

She asked K.C. something.

"Huh?" K.C. managed. The timing seemed a little off for a conversation.

"Oh, I was just wondering where you usually pick up women." Jessica repeated the words flatly, eyeing the bed behind them.

K.C. held her close and walked with her slowly toward the bed. "It's been a long, long time."

"Then where did you used to?"

"Oh, you know. Around."

She sat down on the edge of the bed. Jessica remained standing, directly in front of her. K.C. pressed her lips to Jessica's stomach, right below her navel. She kissed the soft skin there, then began to inch her lips downward.

"Come on!" Jessica abruptly sat down next to her. "Tell me."

K.C. sighed and thought for a second. She had met Janet when they both worked at the factory, assembling the innards of television sets. Janet had been next to her on the line. Day in and day out they did the same thing over and over. Flirting over the hiss of the soldering gun was the only thing that made the job bearable.

"At work," she finally answered, ready to get back to the business at hand.

"In the firehouse?" Jessica gaped, excited by it.

"Oh, hell, no. I'm talking before I was in the department. I used to jump around on the factory circuit. You'd be surprised at how many of the same women you'd see out at the bar the night before coming on down with their punch cards to the factories the next morning."

Jessica seemed to mull it over. "So, how many women do you think you've slept with?"

K.C. was caught off guard. Whatever the girl was trying to get at, all of these questions were threatening to change the mood.

She leaned over and cupped the girl's breast in her hand as she kissed her earlobe. She whispered, "None that I'd care to think about right now. You're the only thing on my mind."

Jessica wormed away and stood up. "Excuse me... It's just I...well, I have to go pee."

She rushed to the bathroom and shut the door.

"Huh?" K.C. asked the empty room around her. She sat on the bed for a while, thinking. *She's sure acting weird.* She began to get curious. Pictures lined the shelves above the bed, while books and papers lay scattered on the desk across the way. She stood up and nearly sat right back down on account of her swimming head. But the wooziness settled and she made her way to the head of the bed for a better look at the photos. Most showed Jessica with her arms draped around the shoulders of a grinning friend or two. However, one framed photo on the far left caught K.C.'s eye. Jessica smiled proudly in it, a graduation cap sitting squarely on her head. K.C. figured it was her high school graduation, but what struck her as odd was that Jessica now looked not a day older.

"Oh, lord," she said. She went over by the desk to investigate further. Jessica had tossed her wallet on top of the messy pile of papers and books. K.C. now took it and opened it up. The picture on the license inside resembled Jessica and the birthdate made her 22, but the name read "Tanya Loftis."

K.C. pulled out the license to see what lay beneath. Sure enough, there was another license there. The photo on it was undeniably her and the name was Jessica Kallen. The birth-date, however, made her 18.

K.C. sighed and slipped both IDs back the way she'd found them. As she put the wallet down, she noticed a school-book: "Women's Studies: Challenging, Succeeding, and Coming Into Our Own."

"Oh, for fuck's sake," K.C. groaned. She went to the bed and sat down weakly.

When the bathroom door finally opened, Jessica emerged with a determined look on her face. Her body, naked except for socks and underwear, rubbed fully onto K.C.'s as she sat down, straddling her and locking her legs behind K.C.'s back.

Jessica caught the look on K.C.'s face before kissing her. "What? What's the matter?"

"Have you ever been to that bar before?" K.C. asked quietly.

"No, this was my first time."

"Who'd you go with?"

"Uh, friends."

K.C. winced. She sounded like a lying teenager.

"Does your roommate know you'd bring another woman up here?"

Jessica's eyebrow jerked up. "She's not all that open-minded."

"So she's never caught you before?"

Jessica looked at her closely, then let her face go blank. Apparently, she had figured out what K.C. was getting at. "There is no 'before.' This is the first time." She put her hands on K.C.'s breasts and kept them there.

"Why?" K.C. asked. "Why me?"

Jessica leaned in and kissed her full on the mouth. "I'm curious," she whispered, pushing K.C. down onto the bed. "I wanna learn from someone who knows what they're doing."

It took only a second lying there like that, with her eyes closed and Jessica's tongue in her mouth, before the spinning world and the weight on her stomach sent her sprinting willy-nilly to the bathroom, her hand clasped over her mouth.

Just when she thought she was done emptying her stomach, another wave of nausea crashed over her. Her fingers gripping the toilet bowl were as white as the porcelain. Her mind reeled, trying to remember if she had ever felt this awful. She could think only of the time after her father's death. It had seemed then that drinking was the sole way to escape the guilt. She would go to the bar straight after work at the firehouse and not leave until Janet came and dragged her home. In fact, she had almost killed both herself and Janet one night, insisting on driving even though she was blind drunk. There had been no other cars on the road, thankfully, as she swerved and hit the median. When the police came, K.C. had been at the side of the road, puking her guts out. Janet told them it had been her at the wheel, that she had swerved to miss a raccoon.

Such a mess. K.C. shuddered, half from the memory and half from the bile dripping like a long string into the murky water of the toilet bowl. All because he had died while still not speaking to her. She hated him for that, hated him even before that. After her mother died, she was left alone to raise herself. He couldn't deal with a child. His only act of love, in her whole life, was getting her a chance at the firehouse. And then, by dying, he forever robbed her of the opportunity of standing up for herself, of proving to him that she was worth more than he thought.

She spit over and over into the water. *And look at me now.*

After a while, her grip on the bowl loosened. Her body was limp, and she could do nothing to stop her throbbing head from lowering to the floor. The cool linoleum felt like a balm on her sweaty forehead. Her body, naked as a baby's, curled around the base of the toilet as she surrendered to the simple call of exhaustion.

"Come on! Get up! Come on! Get up! *Come on! GET UP!*"
The voice—urgent, scared—seemed far away. The words, repeating like a skip in a record, rang out like a bell. Somewhere, somehow, her body began to connect with her mind and she realized someone was shaking her. The bell—or was it words?—kept ringing louder and louder. A sixth sense told her that this was serious, that she must get up, but her eyelids were so heavy, too heavy. She could not budge them. Then sleep, gentle as a feather falling to earth, coaxed her back under.

Her face was freezing and wet. She shot up, hitting her head on the toilet. Water was around her and on her, dripping from her hair and down her nose. Her eyes squinted in the glaring light. She could still hear the frantically ringing bell.

"About fucking time! Now get up!"

She looked up at the girl. She held an empty glass in her hand and wore K.C.'s own uniform shirt.

"Hey!" K.C. croaked. "What the hell is…"

The girl—*Jessica*, it finally triggered in her mind—cut her off. "Get up! The fire alarm is going off! Even if it is a prank, my R.A. is probably gonna come in here and *you've* gotta move!"

"Fire alarm!" K.C. grabbed on to the girl, forcing her to help her up. "How long has it been going off?"

"Who cares! Let's just get out of here before my R.A. comes! You know, I could be kicked off the team for this! I could be expelled!"

Jessica was pushing pulling K.C. out of the bathroom and down the spiral staircase. The ringing bell became louder as they hurried across the living room. K.C. then realized it wasn't the dorm room's smoke detector, but rather the alarm out in the hall. That meant the whole building should be evacuating. More importantly, it meant the fire department—her house—was on its way.

K.C. broke into a run, then skidded to a stop. She was naked!

"Give me my uniform!" she hollered to Jessica, but the girl was already out the door. She felt like a cornered little bird, frozen by shock and rage.

The roommate's door was open. K.C. rushed in and grabbed the first thing she saw—a fluffy lavender robe. She flung it on and jammed her feet into a pair of running shoes. They were small, but K.C. didn't have time to care. She needed to get out of the building before the fire department arrived.

The hall was vacant. The noise from the alarm threatened to crack K.C.'s skull in two. She covered her ears and glanced up as she ran, looking for smoke. Sprinkler heads sat idle along the length of the hall and K.C. knew the problem wasn't on this floor. Perhaps it was a prank after all.

She made it to the stairwell and checked the handle for heat before opening the door. All was clear. She hustled down the stairs, the shoes pinching each time they hit a step.

At the second floor she heard them and slowed down. The sirens from her company's trucks. They were here.

"Shit! Shit! Shit!" She smacked the brick walls of the stairwell with her open hands. How could she explain this? What could she do? The damn girl was in her uniform, and she was stuck in a frickin' purple robe and someone's stolen sneakers. If they didn't see her, they'd for sure see the girl. Her damn name was printed right above the breast pocket. K.C. smacked the wall again and spit on the floor.

"Hey!" It was someone running up the steps. Jessica rounded the corner and cried, "What the fuck is taking you so long?" Her brown eyes were wide with worry.

Now was K.C.'s chance. She'd take her shirt and run back up for the rest of her clothes, then jump in line with the guys as they entered the building, tell them she had been driving by when she heard the alarm. Her hands reached out to grab Jessica—to grab her shirt.

"Listen," Jessica said quickly, looking down at the purple robe. "I'm sorry if you get in trouble for this."

K.C.'s hands paused, then fell limply onto the girl's broad, thin shoulders. They felt solid and able under her hands. "I'm a grown woman, sweetheart. I'm not gonna get in any trouble." She pulled Jessica to her, spontaneously hugging her tightly. "What about you? The team? Your roommate?"

Inside K.C.'s embrace, Jessica shrugged. "Oh, well. I guess they were just gonna have to deal with it sooner or later."

K.C. could tell that she was anxious to head down the stairs and out of the building.

"I don't see or smell smoke," she told her. "It's in another part of the building or it's a prank. We're OK."

She let her go, then put her arm around the girl's shoulders. "It's Karen Christine, my name."

Jessica nodded. "That's pretty," she said. Then, "I'm 18."

K.C. nodded. "Well, let's get it over with. There's gonna be a long line of big guys rushing up those stairs any moment."

They went down each step quickly, purposefully.

When the door on the first floor banged open, K.C. stood up to her fullest height, adjusted the robe, and cleared her face of any emotion.

The Blessing of the Animals

Lynne Herr

I went to a psychic once (gift from my New Age West Coast aunt) who told me that I had "the Blessing of the Animals." *Good thing*, I remember thinking, *since those are the only creatures I hang out with*. Fortunately, the psychic didn't tune in to that thought—she had already moved on to my future, one destined to be spent in a lovely Lower Manhattan office drowning under bags of money.

Later that night I gave my aunt the good news. "Great!" she said. "And what about love? Any good prospects coming your way?"

"Yes, but she was very vague. She told me that I'll meet someone with similar shadows…"

"Huh," she sniffed.

Later that night I stopped by Hamburger Mary's for a quick bite, then walked to the SPCA for my volunteer cat-petting shift. And honestly, that was what my entire shift involved: no litter boxes to clean, no nails to trim, no cages to hose down, just cat-petting, to ensure their continued socialization.

My favorite cage housed the two largest felines in the

facility—Snowpuff and Glug. These sisters weighed 37 pounds between them and were rated a "2," which meant they were friendly without being needy. But despite the "2" the sisters had been in the SPCA for three months (usual turnover being under a month). There were two reasons for this: 1) uhum, they weighed 37 pounds between them; and 2) they were "affection eaters," which means "animals that will only eat after they feel loved."

"Looks like they get a lot of affection then," a girl behind me spoke up. I'd seen her before, smoking cigarettes with some other hip San Francisco dykes out front.

"I guess so," I muttered with a blush—the blush that happened every time I spoke to someone new. The blush that made me blush that made me blush...you get the idea.

"Oh, I shouldn't laugh—I'll be a Glug before long."

"Oh?"

"Quit smoking." She smiled glumly, then pulled up her long john shirt to reveal a tattered patch with a frazzled face drawn on it. "That's me."

"Self-portrait?"

"Oh, yeah, I'm a closeted art genius."

"I can see that..."

A lanky chick with stringy black hair and thick boots came up and tapped her on the shoulder. "Hey, how's the patch going?"

"I think these things have been known to make mice explode."

Lanky laughed, then walked off toward the locker area to get rid of her book bag. The smell of old cigarette butts trailed behind her.

"That's the reason I decided to quit: the smell. It wasn't the lung cancer or the heart disease, it was the smell. Especially here, since it rains so much. Rain and smoking don't go together."

"Yeah." I nodded dumbly, wanting to talk more now that

my redness had faded, though it could decide to rear up again at a moment's notice. "Uhum, you from here?" I hate that question. Everyone on the West Coast asks that question.

"No..." she trailed off, undoubtedly wondering why I chose to ask a standard question when there were so many other things to talk about. "All right, I'm going to head down to Ratso's cage, he's my favorite. See ya."

"Oh—Lynn."

"All right, see ya, Lynn." And she walked off without telling me her name, scratching at her patch.

Snowpuff was sympathetic to my pain, but Glug only cared whether I scratched her left cheek in just the right way. Snowpuff batted her sister on the head and explained that I needed a bit of sympathy here. It had been, after all, two years since I'd had a date and two years and three months since I'd been kissed. Glug hopped off my lap and lumbered to the food bowl, unconcerned.

For the next week I wondered when I would see her again. She hadn't returned at the same time she did the day we met, and I couldn't remember what time she usually volunteered. I used to rely on the sunset to know when she would be there. I would always see her orange cigarette tips before I saw her face. But maybe she'd changed her schedule since she quit smoking.

I saw her lanky friend about a week later and kind of nodded. "Hi..." My face firing up again.

"Hey," she nodded, then continued walking.

A few years ago I'd tried smoking. Art school—you had to at least *try*. And every now and again I'd smoke when I drank, just to ensure that every inch of my body would be toxified. All or nothing, you know. So I decided to bum a smoke from the lanky chick and maybe bring conversation somehow back to her friend.

"Uhum," I called after her. "Are you going to smoke?"

"I could," she answered, sounding much nicer than I had expected. "Need one?"

"Yeah…"

"OK, let's go."

I made a conscious decision not to ask her where she was from, instead sticking to more interesting topics: Have you seen the latest David Lynch movie? When is Sister Spit going on tour? Where'd you get your tattoo? Eventually I managed to ask how her friend was doing with her attempt to quit smoking.

"Oh, Shalene? Oh, I guess all right. I dunno. I haven't seen her in a while. She usually comes in tonight."

And then three things happened simultaneously: 1) my face blazed hot and red; 2) I made a move to drop the cigarette, which tasted like cooked dung—or how I imagined cooked dung tasted; and 3) Shalene walked up, saw my cigarette, sidestepped us, waved, and ducked inside.

Shit!

I didn't want to be obvious, so I finished my cigarette then told Lanky I needed to get back to my shift. She stubbed hers out and came in with me.

"Hey, Shalene—" she yelled as we entered the door.

Shalene turned around. She'd bleached her hair white and changed her glasses to a pair of thick, black—starker than last week's subtle olive—frames. She looked extreme and both more beautiful and more frightening. I stood there—smelling like smoke and wondering if I'd ever have the courage to bleach my hair—while Lanky walked over to her.

I'd never wanted to be noticed (at least not consciously), and somehow that made me noticeable. That and my proclivity for men's pants and four or five layers of shirts. But when Shalene noticed me, she gave me this look—just a quick flash of the eyes—and it changed my whole outlook on being noticed. More than anything—even more than I wanted Glug and Snowpuff to be adopted—I wanted Shalene's eyes on me like that again, only for a much, much longer stretch of time.

Lanky nodded my way before she and Shalene disappeared

upstairs to the behavior modification cages. No wonder I hadn't seen her inside before, she was actually on staff, working with animals who scored less than "3" so they'd get up to socialization speed and earn a presentation cage in my area.

I knew I'd never see her again.

But then I did. Two weeks later she was walking toward Snowpuff and Glug again while I sat on the floor trying to balance each one on a knee. I was explaining to them that if they only climbed their huge scratching tree ten times every morning and night, they could easily trim to 15 pounds each by Christmas and maybe fit into two generous stockings.

"I think people don't want cats that are larger than their kids," Shalene said with a smile.

"Oh, hi," I bumbled.

"Do you know what Glug is?" she asked suddenly.

"Other than herself...no."

"It's a holiday drink from Switzerland. You make it with six bottles of port, a pint of brandy, a pint of Everclear, a pint of rum, some cinnamon sticks and some raisins, I think."

"Shit—"

"Yeah, but I think you only use the brandy to light it on fire while it's cooking. A friend of mine made it for us last night. He torched his knuckle hairs lighting the brandy, but otherwise no one was harmed."

There was a pause while Shalene read over their charts.

"Still not smoking?"

"What?" she asked, letting the chart drop.

"The glug must've been hard to drink without a cigarette."

"No, I'm OK. One month down. It's all good. What about you?"

"Oh, no... I don't... I only smoke maybe four times a year, and I really don't enjoy it."

"Oh, I used to love it. Ah, well. I'm glad you don't smoke. It smells bad."

"Yeah, I know..."

"And it's not so great kissing a smoker."

I think my face turned so red that it looked like I'd fallen asleep on a tropical beach...for 13 days straight. Shalene laughed.

"That's your tell," she said, not making the situation any better. "So does that mean if I asked you out, you'd say yes?"

I just sat there, smiling dumbly up at her as Snowpuff wiggled herself into a comfortable position on my thigh and eyed the food bowl.

"I guess that's a yes? OK, how about we go out for dinner after I get off at 7 o'clock? Meet me at Ratso's cage. I need to say goodbye to him anyway. He's been adopted by a lovely Jamaican man who will teach him how to be suave."

"OK, that sounds great—" I managed.

Two hours later Shalene stopped by Ratso's. He and I were playing fetch with a stuffed mouse. "You really love animals," she said. "And they really love you."

"Yeah... I used to have this recurring dream when I was little that a bomb exploded and the only creatures to survive were me and all the animals."

"Nice dream..."

She took me to a Middle Eastern place about a mile away, fielding my questions most of the way: How did you get this job? Do you ever think of opening your own shelter? Do you have any pets? What was your degree in?

When we arrived at the restaurant, she waited until our food arrived then said, "I think you are probably as interesting—if not more interesting—than me, so you don't have to keep asking me questions."

"Sorry, I'm just so curious about you."

"OK, but let's tag team."

So tag team we did, all night. Three hours, four glasses of wine, and two cups of tea later, we left. By then my blushing had all but ceased. I even looped my arm casually through hers on the walk to BART.

Turned out she lived about ten blocks from me, so she offered to get off two stops early and walk me home. The temperature had dropped to a ridiculous 20 degrees, so I invited her in to warm up. At that time, San Francisco had given up posting exact times for their bus schedules. Our line ran "every 20 minutes," and since we'd seen one driving off as we got out, I knew it would be at least 20 minutes before the next one.

"Twenty minutes or five," she laughed.

"So you don't want to come in?"

"Oh, no, I want to come in."

The real test was my, uhum, fickle cat Leonard, who had a nasty habit of hiding under the couch and growling at new guests, sometimes reaching out to slash their ankles or ruin a new pair of tights. It was part of his charm, I explained between apologies. Leonard loved my grandmother, me, and my landlord, who fed him bacon. He hated everyone else.

Including Shalene.

So the *real* real test (that one was just a warm-up) was whether she moved Knots from his place on the couch, sat on the floor, or plopped him on her lap when she sat down. She chose the floor—a mixed sign.

While I was concocting schemes, Shalene was wondering (as she later told me) how to get me to sit down on the floor with her so we could kiss. Finally she said, "Sit down. I want to kiss you." Subtle.

So then we had the *real real* real test. And she passed. Kissing her made me feel strong and secure and wanted, even from the first night. And it only grew stronger as time went on. I knew I loved her right then, but it took three months of practice to tell her (and only after she told me first).

Six months later, I'd dyed my hair a nearly-bold red and moved in with Shalene, her two cats, and the six mice she'd rescued from her psych lab (they'd successfully completed the maze and were on their way to the snake tank). She took me out to our Middle Eastern place a few weeks ago to celebrate our half-a-year anniversary and asked me if I ever had that dream anymore—the one where everyone dies except the animals and me.

"Yeah," I smiled. "I had it last week."

"Did *everyone* still die?" she fished.

"Well…yes. But I missed you a lot—"

Then she threw a piece of falafel at me.

JUDGING DISTANCE

Dawn Paul

Miss Johanson was hired in the middle of the school year after a flap about our high school's noncompliance with Title IX, the new federal law concerning girls and sports. It's hard to imagine now, when women jocks are selling everything from Wheaties to sports bras, that Miss Johanson started with six boxes of cheerleading pom-poms and three soggy volleyballs. Eighteen of the 30 girls in her first gym class asked to be excused because they were having their periods. No girl had ever run the entire length of the school's basketball court.

Miss Johanson was short and wiry, with Swedish-blue eyes and a kid's grin. She had a scrapbook of clippings from her hometown newspaper with photos of an Anna Johanson— not much younger than we were—holding an assortment of bats, racquets, balls, and trophies. When she had study hall duty, she roamed around the tables in a powder-blue sweatsuit. She ruffled our hair and thwacked goof-offs on the head with a wiffle bat. Smart-mouth kids? She'd pitch it right back at them. Not quite a teacher. Not a kid. We called her Miss J.

Miss J flushed the rust out of the pipes in the girls' locker room. She cleared the pom-poms out of the small room off to the side and made it her office. She went after the boys' athletic director with arm-punching persistence to get equipment and a new gym schedule. We saw her walking the principal down the hall with her arm thrown around his shoulders like he was a second-string quarterback. In one week she landed six new basketballs and practice time on a full court. In two weeks we had our first girls' basketball team.

The gym was overheated all winter. Sweat evaporated off our bodies and condensed on the cold skylights. The new basketballs, full of compressed energy, boomed off the hardwood floor. Miss J drilled her new recruits, running us through lay-ups, dribbling, passing, rebounding. We were not much of a team. Only five girls had shown up for tryouts, and none of us had ever played before.

Fran Mulcahy, with her pugnacious nose and man-size hands, was the only player that earned respectful stares when we walked out onto a court. But she had grown the last four of her 5-foot-11 inches in one year and could not keep track of her body. She fell against other players, incurring penalties and sometimes provoking them to poke her in the face. Skinny Denise LeBlanc had a way of standing knock-kneed, curled in on herself, that telegraphed easy pickings. If her boyfriend showed up at a game she played even worse, and I was never sure if she did this out of nervousness or on purpose. Pam Sherrill was smoking too much pot before school and seemed to have trouble paying attention for an entire game. She had problems at home.

I looked like a player. I was tall, but had come into my height slowly, and I was neatly muscled. I knew how to stop short, slap a sneaker down like a pistol shot, and stand my ground under the basket. It was all bluff, though. I am blind in one eye and have no depth perception. The eye looks perfectly normal. But I cannot judge the distance between myself and other objects. Every time the ball left my hands, the game was as good as lost. I would have warmed the bench on any other team. But good Miss J, out of necessity and maybe a weary admiration for my tenacity, played me every game.

The only one who could really play was Rebecca Golden. She was small and well-proportioned, with tightly-bunched muscles in her calves and shoulders. Her movements had a strength and completeness that was beautiful to watch. No holding back. She had dark-blond hair that she wove into a thick braid down her back before each game. Golden played clean, with none of Mulcahy's bluster or my own theatrics. Her quiet, pensive way made her seem more like a scholar than an athlete. She played an intellectual game—tactical, gauging angles and timing. She could fire a perfect swisher from the corner. I watched her in hopeless admiration.

Miss Johanson held practice every afternoon that winter. Once a week she hauled us off to play games at big city schools where the girls took their basketball seriously. Even their parents came to watch. Miss J didn't have a budget for a team bus, so she'd drive us in her own station wagon. We lost game after game to teams of tall, whippet-bodied white girls with brutal elbows or black girls who whispered taunts under the basket.

At the last game of the season, Miss J gathered us together before we went out on the court. I waited for instructions on defense or passing. Instead, Miss J handed out red satin hair ribbons. She told us a photographer might be there and she wanted us to look feminine.

"Why?" I asked. I knew the reason. But if we had to wear the silly ribbons, I wanted the satisfaction of hearing someone say the word we were trying to avoid. The word we whispered about the tall, serious city girls.

Miss J just said, "Don't give me any grief about this, Collins. Wear it or don't play."

Rebecca Golden took my ribbon and reached up to tie it.

I bent my head so she could wind it through my hair. Her face was inches from mine, her serious eyes fixed on the knot she was tying. I knew exactly why we were wearing satin ribbons.

We lost that game, as we had lost the others, but we begged Miss J to take us out to celebrate. Henri's Ice Cream was the high school hangout, but Miss J drove us across town to a place called Mayo's Lounge. She said she was thirsty.

She led us through a back door marked LADIES' ENTRANCE and we crowded into a dark wooden booth. Miss J seemed to know the slick-haired guy who took the order. She asked for five Shirley Temples and a "CC 'n' 7." The Shirley Temples were disappointing—just ginger ale with a cherry. Miss J's drink had a sweet, smoky smell that was somehow familiar, although my parents did not drink liquor.

"To the team!" Miss J said, and we all clinked glasses. Then she said something about this being better than Henri's, more grown-up. But I was remembering where I had smelled the CC 'n' 7 smell before. Miss J's little office. I wished we had gone to Henri's. I didn't feel grown-up at all.

After basketball season, Miss J unpacked new archery equipment and led us out to the stubbly brown hayfield behind the school. It was April, and it was good to be outside the stuffy gym. She lined us up and stood in front of us, arms and legs bare and sunburned already, a scar curved around her knee like a white scimitar. She held up a bow. It was a slim, no-nonsense bow, without pulleys or any other kind of action. She snapped a brown leather guard over her left arm.

"If you are right-handed, and all of you are except Sherrill, you hold the bow in your left hand. Sherrill, you will hold it in your right. Your arm should be fully extended, like this. The other hand draws back the string until you can rest your fingers against your jawbone."

She stood stock-still, holding the bowstring taut, sighting down an imaginary arrow. The sun glinted off the golden down along her jawbone as she rapped it twice with two fingers.

"You have to pull it back this far. Your body should be perpendicular to the target." LeBlanc snickered at the mention of *body* or maybe the word *perpendicular.*

"OK, girls, select a bow and I want to see you pull that string all the way back."

"Hey, what about arrows?" Mulcahy asked.

"You're not ready yet. You'd kill someone." But she was smiling one of those lopsided grins she doled out to us once in a while.

Drawing back the bow was not as easy as Miss J had made it look. My arm quivered as I tried to lay my fingers along my jawbone. Even big beefy Mulcahy was struggling. Sherrill let her string fly from her fingers and it snapped against the thin skin on the inside of her arm, leaving a red welt.

I held steady and started to sight along my imaginary arrow, as Miss J had done, then realized that my blind eye was in line with the arrow. I was disappointed. I had looked forward to archery, thinking that if I only had to aim and shoot, seeing the distance to the target might not matter as much. I gently let the string relax and watched Rebecca Golden draw back her string, sight, and relax, over and over. Her arm muscles were taut.

Miss J stepped up beside me. "Collins, you're going to have to shoot left-handed. No big deal. Lots of people with vision problems have to switch hands." She rearranged my bow and my hands and arms, and everywhere she touched she left a track of warmth. I stood perpendicular to the target and sighted down the imaginary arrow to the red center of the target.

"Thanks, Miss J. This is better." I pulled the string back to the place just below my ear, liking the feel of the tension, the gathered strength in the bow. I had never told Miss J about my blind eye. I was not ashamed of it, but I didn't want to hold it out as an excuse for bad playing. But Miss J must have known all along. I wondered if each of us had a file somewhere with things besides conduct and grades. Was there a note in Pam Sherrill's file that her father once whipped her legs bloody? That Denise LeBlanc could hardly read? That Fran Mulcahy had a retarded brother who was put away when she was born?

I felt cold wetness on my feet and realized that I'd been standing in one place too long. The field was still sodden with snowmelt and it had oozed up around my sneakers. I replanted my feet on new ground and sighted down my imaginary arrow to the heart of the target.

Miss J drilled us as relentlessly in archery as she had in basketball. My arms and shoulders had a pleasant soreness every day after practice. She mandated push-ups—boy-style, with backs and legs straight—to build up our arm muscles. Mulcahy couldn't raise her chest high enough for her big breasts to clear the ground. Sherrill and LeBlanc complained bitterly and lay still on the ground every time Miss J took her eyes off them. Rebecca Golden and I were tied at nine each. We were working toward a dozen.

Miss J paced back and forth behind us while we shot our arrows. Sometimes she came up behind me and lifted my elbow saying, "I swear, Collins, if I have to tell you to keep your arm up one more time…" She would yank LeBlanc's rounded shoulders back and nudge Sherrill's right foot into place with her own.

But she worked the most with Rebecca Golden, deftly adjusting Rebecca's stance as she stood poised to shoot, eyes straight ahead, never leaving the target. Miss J would place her hand on the small of Golden's back to straighten her spine, place a finger under her chin to lift her head, and once she even placed her two hands on Golden's hips to turn them slightly toward the target. Whenever she finished arranging Golden, she would step back to look at her for a long moment. She'd take in the tensed shoulders and perfectly placed hips, then give the signal to shoot. Golden's eyes would never leave the target.

Sherrill, for all her whining about the push-ups, was a decent archer. "She's just so blasé about it," LeBlanc said, and it was true. Sherrill would take the bow, shift her body into position, nock the arrow, and draw the string. Then she would gaze dreamily at the target for a while before she let the arrow fly. She never hit the bull's-eye, but unlike the rest of us, most of her arrows hit the target.

I was discouraged to find that although I was strong enough to hold the arrows steady, they still went wide of the target. Usually they soared over it into the woods and I wasted most of my practice time looking for them. Rebecca Golden started the same way, launching her arrows powerfully in the general direction of the target. Then she was tracking Sherrill's arrows from the yellow circle to the middle blue one. Then came the day when Mulcahy ran to retrieve the arrows and announced that Golden had just made it inside the bull's-eye.

"It's right on the line, though. Not really in," she amended, and yanked the arrow before Golden could dispute it. Not that Golden would ever dispute it. She would just keep firing arrows at the target until one of them hit so on-center even Mulcahy would have to give it to her.

Fran Mulcahy seemed to resent the extra coaching Miss J gave Golden every day. She started whispering "teacher's pet" when Golden was shooting, and deliberately coughed or laughed just as Golden released her arrows. One day Mulcahy dropped her bow at the moment Golden let an arrow fly. Miss J placed her hand on Mulcahy's shoulder and steered her away from the line to the edge of the field, calling back to the rest of us to keep shooting. The two of them stood there a long time, and we kept glancing over at them in between shots. Even Golden was distracted.

Mulcahy stood with her head down but was still taller than Miss J, who kept her hand on Mulcahy's shoulder even though she had to reach up to do it. Miss J's jaw was moving, but I could not see the expression on her face. Mulcahy would nod her head once in a while and I could see, even at that distance, that her ears were red.

That afternoon, as Mulcahy, LeBlanc, and I waited in front of the school after practice, LeBlanc asked Mulcahy what Miss J had told her.

Mulcahy's ears turned red again. "She told me to quit fooling around so much during practice."

"Come on, Mulcahy," I said. "I shot a whole bag of arrows while she was talking to you, and that's all she said?"

"Yeah, but you shoot real fast because you know you're gonna need all afternoon to look for them."

"That's true. I really stink."

"We all do," LeBlanc said generously.

"Sherrill's getting better. And Golden is good." It was the truth, even if Mulcahy didn't like it.

"Miss J drives her home," Mulcahy said.

"So what?" I didn't want to hear any more. "She drove Sherrill home that night when her parents never came to pick her up."

"She drives her to her own house. My aunt lives across the street. She's on the school committee. She says it's moral tur-pit-tude."

I noticed for the first time the red blotches on Mulcahy's pale skin. And that her teeth were too short and her lips too big and red for them.

"What's that?"

"Do I have to paint you a picture, Collins? You know what they are."

LeBlanc looked away and tittered. Mulcahy had said it. Sort of. Finally. What I had been hoping to hear. I wanted to belt

Mulcahy in her too-short teeth. Then, like those few times when I released an arrow and knew it would fly true, words came to me: "You're jealous that Miss J chose Golden."

I was remembering Golden's hands in my hair, tying the red satin ribbon, when Mulcahy hit me. For a few seconds it didn't hurt, though the force of the punch made me stagger backwards. I hoped she wouldn't hit my good eye. A burn started at my lower lip and radiated out until my whole face was on fire. I bent my head down, feeling my teeth with my fingers. I squeezed my eyes shut so tears wouldn't leak out.

"Stop it, Mulcahy. I'm telling. I'm going to tell that you punched Darcy Collins. I will." LeBlanc's voice was high and squeaky as though she was afraid she was next. I heard Mulcahy's footsteps pounding away down the sidewalk.

"Are you OK?"

"Yeah, I'm fine." My teeth were in solid and I could finally open my eyes. LeBlanc's narrow face was up close. She had the nervous look of a greyhound.

"Your face is OK, I guess." LeBlanc's boyfriend pulled up then in his truck. By the time my ride came, my lower lip was a little swollen, and the thin skin around my eyes was stiff with dried tears. But it was fine. No one asked about anything.

The next practice was the last one before the first tournament of the season. The tournament would be held not at one of the big city schools but at a place called the Marita T. Wheeler Country Day School. Not tough city girls. Rich girls. The practice field was dried hard by then, and tasseled grasses had grown up tall around the edges. Our running back and forth for arrows had worn the middle down to strips of bare dirt. It was a hot afternoon. I was wearing a nylon belt and could feel a ring of itchy sweat around my waist.

I stepped onto the field and watched Golden walking across the grass with Miss J. They were carrying the targets. Miss J stood in the sun with her hands on her hips and pointed out to Golden where to set up two of the targets. Golden had trouble getting one of them to stand upright and Miss J hurried over to help. As they walked back toward me, they clapped their hands and slapped their thighs in unison like they were making up some sort of cheer. They were laughing.

Mulcahy had to be wrong. But the picture of Miss J's sunburned hands on Golden's hips kept floating across my mind. If Mulcahy was right about Miss J and Rebecca Golden, then anything was possible for anyone.

Mulcahy shuffled up the dirt path from the school. She walked up to me, absentmindedly running her knuckles across her lower lip.

"I was acting stupid. Are you OK?"

"I'm fine. Really. And don't worry about LeBlanc. I already told her that if she mentions any of it, I'll punch her just like you did me."

LeBlanc and Golden walked up and threw themselves down on the sparse grass.

"It's too hot for practice," LeBlanc said into the ground. Golden lay on her back with her arms crossed on her chest, staring into the sky. Miss J rummaged in her duffel bag until she found a plastic bottle and took a long swig out of it.

"Can I have a sip, Miss J?" LeBlanc asked. "I'm dying of thirst."

"Sorry, LeBlanc. This is for the grown-ups." Miss J grinned, showing the little creases on the side of her mouth that were almost dimples. "Where's Sherrill?"

"She can't make practice today," Mulcahy said. "I think they searched her locker. I think she's in some kind of trouble. Because of some stuff they found."

"Well, that's just wonderful. We have a tournament on Monday and one of my few hopes that we'll even score is on her way to juvenile court. Why do I bother?" She took another gulp from the plastic bottle. We were sitting on the ground, heads back, looking up at her. Golden's lips were parted as though she wanted to say something.

"This is just wonderful," Miss J continued. "And I've got two other so-called teammates beating up on each other after school." I shot a look at LeBlanc, but she shrugged and mouthed "not me." Mulcahy rested her arms across her knees and hung her head between them.

"So, you two think you're tough? Want to fight it out here?"

"Anna..." Golden finally spoke. None of us had ever heard anyone call Miss J by her first name before. Mulcahy's head snapped up. LeBlanc gave a nervous giggle. But Miss J stared over our heads, talking out to the field.

"You all think you're so tough. None of you know anything yet about how to be tough. Not even you, Collins." I wondered why she singled me out. "You want to learn how to really fight? The way I had to learn?" She was smiling at me, the side of her mouth twitched up, her eyes bright. Mulcahy let her breath out in one big chuff, like a horse, and I realized I'd been holding my breath too.

LeBlanc stood to brush off the seat of her shorts. "If we're not going to practice archery, I need to get home. My sister's getting married this weekend, and I have to help with things." She gave a tight smile but did not look at Miss J, who took another long drink and watched her hurry down the path.

"How about it, Collins? Want to learn?" Miss J was looking at me like she knew I wouldn't do it. I looked around. There was no one in the field. Trees shielded us from the school. Everyone had instructions to stay away from the field during practice because of all the errant arrows. I stood and faced Miss J—Anna. I crouched a little with my arms stretched out, the way I'd seen men stand in the movies when they were getting ready to fight. I rocked on the balls of my feet to find my balance and bent my knees to drop my center of gravity. A blue jay shrieked an alarm and I could feel, rather than see, the four of us jump.

Miss J stood up straight in front of me, feet slightly apart in clean tennis shoes, jersey tucked neatly into her shorts. Her arms hung loosely at her sides and her palms were open, as if in proof that they were empty. She did not look like she knew how to wrestle. Or like she was going to go through with this.

I saw a flicker of motion and I was on the ground. Miss J was on top of me, her weight crushing. My cheek was pressed into the grass and I could smell dry dirt and Miss J's smell that was baby powder and the CC 'n' 7. I tried to get up, but she had pinned my arms behind me. My shoulders hurt, and I couldn't move my legs.

"Enough?"

"Enough," I said. I would have said anything to free myself. I stood up, peeling a blade of grass off my cheek. It was embarrassing how quickly it was over. I looked over at Golden, but she was looking at Miss J, not me.

"How did you do that?" I asked.

"I came at you from the left. From your blind side. Learn to guard that. Come on, Golden, you're next."

"No."

"Come on, I won't hurt you. Right, Collins?"

"Yeah. I'm fine."

"You're going to get in trouble doing this." Golden put her chin in her hand and regarded Miss J the way an adult would wait out a child. I wanted to see Golden and Miss J wrestle. I wanted to watch them roll all over the field through the grass and the dust.

"Go ahead, Golden," I said. "Do it. What are you afraid of? That you'll lose too?" For all that Golden was a winner, she always encouraged the rest of us to try, to never be afraid of not succeeding. I liked her for it and felt bad using it against her. But I knew it would make Golden stand up and fight.

She did. She jumped up and leapt on Miss J so quickly that Miss J was taken off balance, and they both keeled over. Golden was on top, but Miss J pushed her off easily. I thought it was over then, but they both jumped up and circled each other, staring intently into each other's eyes. Miss J's neck had a thin layer of sweat, and one drop made its way slowly out of the hair at her temple. Golden's braid was coming undone, and bits of dead oak leaves were stuck in it. Mulcahy let out another chuff, but I didn't dare breathe. I wanted them to forget we were there.

Miss J feinted left then grabbed Golden's shoulder with her right hand, stepping forward and placing her right leg behind Golden. Golden toppled backward. Probably what happened to me. She bent down to grab Golden's arms and turn her over, but Golden was quick. She twisted out of Miss J's hold with a snap of her arm, and Miss J, surprised that this wasn't working a second time, lost her balance and fell on top of her. They lay there, legs tangled together, Miss J's breasts pressing into Golden's chest, the two of them breathing hard. Miss J was smiling down at Golden, but Golden was red-faced and looked like she might cry.

"Anna, get off me." Golden almost whispered this. Miss J smiled and blew a stream of air at a sticky wisp of hair on her forehead.

"Don't play with me, Anna. Not here." Miss J looked bewildered for a minute and then looked over at Mulcahy and me. She lifted herself up heavily, as though she was suddenly very tired. Golden jumped up and started to loosen her braid. She combed it through with her fingers. She had her back to us. Miss J leaned down to pick up a bag of arrows.

"What about me? Don't I get a turn?" Mulcahy stood up and put her hand on Miss J's shoulder to turn her around. The sun was behind them and I could see them in silhouette, Mulcahy big and hulking over Miss J.

"I told you before, Mulcahy. Leave me alone."

"No. It's my turn now." Mulcahy still had her hand on Miss J's shoulder and was shaking her a little.

"Fran, I'm sorry. I really am." It was hard to tell, with the sun in my eyes, whether Miss J stumbled then or if Mulcahy pushed her. In any event, Miss J regained her footing and gave Mulcahy a powerful shove that toppled her as though she were a little girl. Mulcahy fell on her side and was trying to push herself up when Miss J deliberately stepped over her and then sat down, straddling Mulcahy's hips. She grabbed Mulcahy's wiry hair in both fists and started banging her head on the grass in rhythm to a chant of *Why-can't-you-leave-me-alone?*

"Stop it, Anna!" I heard Golden behind me but could not take my eyes off Miss J. She was crying now, and the chant was slurred. Her face and neck were blotched with red.

"Anna. I'm not kidding, Anna." I turned to look. Rebecca Golden stood with bow in hand, arrow notched—not drawn and aimed, but ready. Her hair rippled over her shoulders and glinted in the low sun.

Miss J untangled her hands from Mulcahy's hair and stood up. The skin at her open collar was bright red. Mulcahy stayed huddled on the ground, but she didn't look hurt. Miss J dusted off her hands.

"Mulcahy, get up and go break down those targets. Collins, get the bags and the bows. Put them in my office and lock the door behind you. Golden—" Miss J looked at her, apologetic. "You need to go home." Miss J picked up her bag and shambled down the path, cutting to the right to head straight for the teachers' parking lot. Mulcahy sat up and rubbed the side of her head.

"Do what Miss J said, Fran," Golden said gently. "Go pick up the targets." Mulcahy heaved herself up without a word and lumbered across the field. I picked up the bag of arrows and the bows. I reached out to Golden for her bow and arrow. She handed them over with an embarrassed smile.

"Do you need a ride?" I offered.

"Thanks. Yeah. I guess I will need a ride." She rebraided her hair, yanking the strands so tightly into place that I winced. "Why don't you leave this stuff here, let Mulcahy take it. I don't want to go back to Anna's office."

"No, that wouldn't be fair. To leave it for poor old Mulcahy. I'll just take it in and meet you out front."

I walked down the path and through the side door, which was propped open with a cinder block, then down the cool dark hall to Miss J's office. It was odd to be in the building by myself. Miss J's door was open and a reading lamp was on over her desk. I looked around the office at things I never noticed when the whole team was crowded around the desk with Miss J. Her college degree on the wall in a gold frame. The red stuffed moose we had given her at the end of the basketball season. A bunch of dried flowers in a jar that looked like they could have been picked in the practice field. I breathed in Miss J's scent—sweat, sweet powder, and whiskey. What would the new gym teacher be like? Would she be willing to drive the team in her own car? Would she have to worry about red satin ribbons?

The picture of Miss J lying on top of Rebecca Golden, smiling, kept running through my mind, and I kept trying to push it away. I dropped the archery bag and sat down in Miss J's chair. I closed my eyes and made myself look:

At Miss J's hands on Golden's hips.

At Rebecca Golden, standing in the sun holding her bow and arrow.

At me, watching and waiting. Wanting.

There was a file cabinet next to the desk with a drawer marked "Student Files." I thought of opening the drawer and taking out three files—Collins, Darcy; Mulcahy, Frances; Golden, Rebecca—to read what was written there. Blindness? Jealousy? Courage? A need to prove herself in areas that are unimportant for girls? A tendency to like the look of strong muscles in a woman's arm? I reached down to turn the handle of the drawer.

Cousins

Lisa E. Davis

For victims of September 11, 2001,
from the villages of Puebla—Acatlán
de Osorio, Tlachichuca, Teziutlán

Dolores and Alicia came in to work on the subway together, early in the morning when light was just breaking over the river. In the winter it was dark as night, with a wind that chilled to the bone. But on that morning poised between summer and autumn, the sky stretched out bright as a flag.

They had seats because they got on near the beginning of the run from the bottom of Brooklyn to Manhattan, pressed closer together at each stop along the line by hundreds of passengers up before dawn. They didn't mind; in fact, they liked the comforting warmth that passed between them from knees to shoulders, made sweeter because nobody noticed. Not like home—a dry, empty place east of Mexico City—where everybody knew everything, and suspected the worst.

"Estás dormida." Alicia put her hand on Dolores's knee.

"You're sleeping. You didn't have to get up so early. I could've come in by myself."

Dolores laughed and sat up taller, her back muscles taut, arms hard from years of farmwork and packing produce for $1 a day in a drafty shed. Her coffee-colored eyes were warm and caring. "I'd rather be with you," she said. *"Prefiero estar contigo."*

She had always stuck close to her cousin Alicia, to whom she was related—people said—by the complex bloodlines that encompassed most of the villagers. They had sat next to each other in the tattered village school and afterward had played beside streams that swept down the steep hillsides. They had made up adventures and told each other secrets, holding hands in the shelter of a friendly cave.

"But you could've slept another hour," replied Alicia, who was never late, never sick, never took a day off.

The boss at the restaurant where she worked in food preparation—a good job if you had no papers—had asked her shift to come in early. "We've got a big breakfast meeting," he'd told them the day before, "and I need everybody here on time and ready to go."

Alicia was small, even dainty, with coal-black hair to her shoulders. She had been giddy and terrified when she went for the job interview, sent by a friend who lived in the Bronx. She thought she was going to faint in an express elevator that lifted her 100 stories into the air in seconds and deposited her at the door of a wonderland of glistening chrome, glass, and marble that outshone anything she had ever seen or imagined. She was hired on the spot, just like that, no questions asked. Good help was hard to keep, especially in boom times, the Dominican cook Ysidro said. He was a dark-skinned giant who showed her the ropes, then started her in chopping peppers, onions, and carrots. She shed many tears, at first, over the onions.

By the end of the week Alicia had earned a paycheck and

lost her fear of heights. If she had questions, she asked Ysidro, and she spent any spare moment staring enraptured out the great windows that encircled the restaurant—at the city, the river, and the countryside that stretched for miles beyond. Like a miracle, she sensed what power meant and that some of it was hers. She didn't care what it had cost her, what it had cost them both in family, danger, and hardships. She knew how it felt to be free.

Back in the village, the last straw had been a proposal of marriage from an uncle whose wife had died of breast cancer. "It's a good match," Alicia's mother had insisted, "and you need a home of your own." While her father negotiated with the uncle, Alicia buried her heart in heavy housework, which had fallen more and more on her shoulders. She was kept close to home, cooking for hungry men and washing their dusty work clothes. At the same time, Dolores was sent north to pick crops. Silently and implacably, the life they had shared drained away.

"*Y usted, adónde va?* Where are *you* going?" Alicia's mother had asked her one evening, after dinner was over, the dishes washed and put away. The old woman's face was thin and narrow like a fox's.

"Just for a walk around the plaza," she lied. She was meeting Dolores for the first time in weeks.

"Take your brother with you," her mother said with a bitter smile. "You think you can go wherever you please? You'll soon be a married woman. *Una mujer casada.*"

Alicia stared. Her parents were serious about the marriage proposal, and even worse, a suspicion crept over her like the shadow of death that they'd been watching her, perhaps for a long time. She remembered other nights she'd met Dolores, and a trip they'd taken all the way to Puebla, the state capital, to visit a widowed aunt—where she and Dolores had slept together in the same bed. Far from home and prying eyes, they'd waited until no more sounds came from the aunt's bedroom then turned to slide softly into each other's arms. The passion awakened would never be denied again. But her mother and father couldn't have known about that night, or those that followed, or that Dolores was the only home she would ever want.

On the evening Alicia had arranged to meet Dolores in the town plaza, she backed down, hoping to allay her mother's suspicions. But the next day they met in secret, beneath a favorite image of the infant Jesus in the village church. *"Díles que no, que no quieres,"* Dolores pleaded. "Tell them you won't do it."

"Shh," Alicia cautioned, "you think I haven't told them that?"

"And what do they say?"

"That it's time I was married, *y ya*. That's all…"

"They didn't mention," Dolores hesitated, "me, or anything?"

"Las amistades, friendships, they said, aren't the same as marriage." Alicia hung her head. *"Cosas de muchachas,* things for little girls."

Dolores got up and looked around the little church, inspecting shadowy corners. Satisfied they were alone, she took Alicia's hands in hers. *"No nos queda más remedio,"* she reasoned. "All we can do is try to get away from here." For her part, she didn't fear hardship or anybody's outrage. "Are you ready for that?'

A door opened up front, and the villager who served as sexton walked past the altar railing. Dolores and Alicia knelt on the stone floor facing that way. He nodded and kept going out the other side.

"I'll be ready tonight if you say so," Alicia answered.

Dolores kissed Alicia on the forehead. "You're very brave," she said, then paused, "but remember, if we go, you may not see them for a long time."

"I've seen enough."

Dolores knew the way north. "We'll need bus tickets, at least as far as Mexico City." They would slip away long before dawn and walk miles to the next village before they boarded. It was safer that way. "And I have to find out what time."

Dolores had a younger brother, Arturo, in Mexico City, a handsome, soft-spoken young man who had left before them, looking for a place to be himself. She knew where to find him and that he would shelter them.

In the capital, the women slept all night in a long queue that encircled the American Embassy, with the thousands waiting for a visa—one month, six months—whatever they could get. Most had no plans to return anyway, among them Alicia and Dolores. They would bypass California. "Not far enough," Dolores said. *"Hay que ir lejos."*

In New York, there was work. Everybody said so. It was a place for dreaming.

That morning, Dolores and Alicia got off at the same subway stop, on Broadway right behind the twin towers—*las torres gemelas,* people called them—almost in front of a large discount store where they went sometimes on payday. "Look how pretty this is!" Alicia would exclaim over a rayon blouse with bold flowers. *"Rebajada.* It's on sale."

Whatever they could afford, they reveled in—like jeans with labels you never saw back home, scented candles, and gadgets that whipped and chopped. Alicia bought flowers every Friday—carnations, *claveles,* so they would last—for the small apartment they'd settled in. Their neighbors were also recent arrivals. The women had at first rented a room from a family, but as soon as they could afford it they'd moved on. Their new building clung to a sloping street that, a block further down, dove beneath the Gowanus Expressway, but the heat was good and the subway nearby. The money they earned paid the rent.

On weekends, they bought dark, heavy squares of sugary chocolate and melted them with milk and cinnamon. They drank steaming cups for breakfast or when they snuggled on the secondhand couch in front of the new television set—their biggest purchase, on time, *a plazo,* from a neighborhood dealer. *Las novelas*—the soap operas from Mexico, Puerto Rico, and South America—spun tales of amorous intrigue, marital infidelities, and illegitimate children. *"Fantasías,"* scoffed Dolores, who changed to the English-speaking channel when Alicia wasn't watching, even though she understood very little of what was going on.

"We have to learn English," Dolores decided one day, "so we'll know what people here think." She gave Alicia an encouraging nudge. "Once we have English, we can apply for other jobs."

"Classes cost money," Alicia reminded her, and that perhaps it was better to keep to themselves. Without papers and because they loved each other, going unnoticed was, in fact, essential. At the neighborhood market, they always introduced themselves as cousins to the other women with toddlers and infants clinging to them. To avoid suspicion, Alicia fussed over the children, but she envied the women nothing. She was one of ten, and Dolores the oldest of eight.

For months there was no news from the village, and neither of the women initiated any contact, except to send money to Dolores's brother Arturo in Mexico City, to thank him for his help. Dollars were worth a small fortune in pesos. Because he was the only one who had an address for them in New York, it was Arturo who wrote in the summer to Dolores to say that he was well, but that Alicia's mother wasn't. "She never speaks Alicia's name," the letter said, "and forbids anyone else to. People say she's wasting away from the anger inside." Dolores put the letter down on the kitchen counter.

"What does Arturo say?" Alicia asked.

"It's not all good news."

"What's wrong?"

Dolores handed over the letter and sat down at the table,

at a respectful distance. "I don't know how much of this you want to hear," she said, "but I can't keep anything from you either. *Mejor no guardar secretos.*"

Alicia read and wept, then lay across the bed in Dolores's arms. "She has banished me."

"Just for now," Dolores comforted her.

"How do you know?"

Dolores didn't answer. "Do you want to go back and see her?"

"That's not possible. It would mean the end of everything." Alicia tried calling instead, at the home of a neighbor in the village who had a telephone. Her mother refused to come to the phone. The receiver went dead in Alicia's hand.

"*Corazón de piedra.* Your mother's heart has turned to stone," said Dolores.

"I cannot be what she wants," Alicia murmured. "Better not to think too much about it." There was a desperate edge to their lovemaking that night, and there were no more letters from Arturo.

Dolores didn't forget about the English classes. "There's a woman at work," she reminded Alicia, "who goes to a class for free, *gratis.*" The next week Dolores enrolled in the elementary class at a Manhattan settlement house. A young American with a bristling beard wrote his name on the blackboard—Joseph Carson. He said they could call him Joe in class. That seemed to Dolores too familiar, but maybe Americans were like that. He listened cheerfully to Dolores's answers to the simple exercises— What is your name? Where are you from? How old are you? Where do you live?—and Dolores imagined a bond forming between them.

At home Dolores practiced reading the lessons given out in class and shared what she learned with Alicia. They watched more TV in English, and Dolores thought she was getting the hang of it. She spoke to Mr. Carson before and after class, not hiding her admiration. On the night that ended the ten-week session, she hung back as the other students were leaving.

"Thank you," she said.

"Will you take the next English class?" he asked, pulling on his jacket.

"Oh, yes," said Dolores eagerly.

"Good, I'll see you then," Mr. Carson offered her his hand to shake, and she took it. "Goodbye."

She kept studying and wished for American friends for herself and Alicia. She longed for the world she glimpsed beyond their neighborhood in Brooklyn, beyond the sweatshop in Queens where she folded sweaters into plastic bags all day alongside a few hundred other illegal women. Nothing would keep her from a chance at that world.

When Alicia went to work at the restaurant, Dolores quit the sweatshop in Queens. A neighbor from Brooklyn had a job in a hotel that sat in the shadow of the twin towers. She agreed to introduce Dolores. They were always looking for good workers.

"She's my cousin," the neighbor lied. "She needs the job." One look at Dolores told the boss that she could handle vacuuming, scrubbing, and making beds. Most of the hotel staff was just off the boat, relatives of somebody or the other who worked downtown.

The move brought more happiness. "We can ride in to work together every day," Alicia mused, and she kissed Dolores on the cheek.

That morning, hundreds of people exited the subway station with Dolores and Alicia, then spread out across the immense plaza. The women walked arm in arm around the great bronze sphere at its center, chrysanthemums blooming in a semicircle, to Alicia's building. The tower rose almost out of sight into the clear, sparkling morning.

"*Te veo luego*. Till this afternoon," Alicia said as they

embraced. Early arrivals hurried past them, under the slender, silver arches, to a thousand different jobs—a vast community dedicated to keeping the world's economy from faltering.

"I'll wait for you," Dolores said. "And what are you serving this morning?"

"*Cantidad de huevos*. About a million and one eggs I'll have to break." Alicia laughed. "Do you think you'll be late picking me up?"

"No." Their eyes mirrored each other for a long moment. "I'll be right here." Dolores nodded toward the entrance, and Alicia was swept along by the crowd.

At the hotel, Dolores drank coffee and gossiped with some of the other women before they began their rounds. She was on the 11th floor overlooking the plaza, sprinkling cleanser into the sink of an executive suite, when she heard a thunderous blast. Right after, the earth shook the way it did in Mexico during an earthquake, *un temblor*. She reeled against the bathroom wall, then raced to the window. Fire and smoke engulfed the top floors of the building where she had left Alicia hours ago.

Dolores dropped her cleaning rag and ran into the hall. The elevator was crammed with people, but she pushed her way in. Men in dark suits spoke together in hushed tones, in an English she couldn't understand. By the time they reached the hotel lobby, a hailstorm had struck the plaza, like a great winter snowfall, Dolores thought foolishly. *Las grandes nevadas de Nueva York* that halted traffic and silenced the streets. But instead of snowflakes, shards of glass shattered on the ground, and a maelstrom of papers fluttered down.

The tower blazed. Dolores saw the first firemen arriving and knew they would save Alicia. They would bring them all down. Then another blast, like demons from hell screaming, split the sky, and the second tower burst into flames. People stared skyward helplessly.

Dolores fell to her knees.

The restaurant 107 floors up swayed sideways, then popped back like a car antenna. Smoke rose in monstrous clouds up the elevator and ventilation shafts from the wounded tower beneath. Alicia careened against the counter. Beyond the kitchen, she heard muffled screams, then Ysidro took her by the hand. "If we can make it to the roof, the police have helicopters. They came last time."

She didn't move, so he carried her out toward the stairwell. She weighed nothing.

The hostess was on the phone at the entrance to the main dining room, but she hung up as they passed. "Everyone should stay put," she said to the customers who had begun to gather around her. A few huddled near the elevator doors. "We'll be getting instructions."

Ysidro kicked at the door that would take them up to the roof. It didn't budge. The floor groaned under them, and a crack opened in the ceiling while Alicia watched him crash his shoulder against the door. He shook his head and took her hand again. Through the dense smoke, they saw the hostess shepherding the customers down to the restaurant's lower level and followed. From there they could hear the beating wings of the helicopters as they circled above then pulled back.

The smoke pursued them along the walls. Ysidro drew a handkerchief over his nose and a cell phone out of his pocket. "*Voy a llamar a casa,*" he mumbled. Alicia saw others cradling tiny phones, bending over computers. People would know what was happening. Dolores too must see the smoke and flames. Alicia longed for her gentle hands, for the way they held each other at night in the silence.

Ysidro touched her shoulder. "You can call out if you want to."

"Nobody's home," she cried. Not even an answering machine in the apartment.

Ysidro and Alicia felt the panic quicken around them. They drew closer together. Someone threw a computer through a window, and a breath of air rushed in.

"Do you have family here? *Tienes familia?*" Ysidro whispered.

Alicia remembered her mother's hard face, the sweet faces of her younger brothers and sisters. "I have only my cousin," she sobbed, and she let herself slip to the floor that heaved and shook beneath them. *"Mi prima."*

Paula Neves

Christine had been a Goth chick in college—black hair, black clothes, pale makeup—very different from the way she looked now; she still wore basic black, only now it was tagged Talbot's, The Limited, or Eddie Bauer, depending on her mood. Otherwise, about the only thing she seemed to have in common with the girl she was then was an enduring love of the "alternative" music she introduced on her conservative campus during a stint as the college DJ, white noise she now played for us in the evenings while we did our "bond troll" work—as she called it—for Blumenthal Securities. The six of us sat in pairs for several hours every evening after our inadequate day jobs and proofread aloud the minutiae of bond offerings and other financial page-turners, each page looking exactly like the one before it.

When Christine's golden protopunk oldies were no longer enough to liven things up, she suggested after-work drinks at a favored dive in nearby Rocky Hill—"a little social lubrication." We all liked one another well enough and made it a Friday night ritual.

But then Christine started wanting to get lubed on other nights of the week as well. James, the aspiring grad student, wouldn't go for it—too much studying for the GRE's. Ben, the lawyer, had a wife and kids to go home to. Donna, my partner, had daytime unemployment woes to go home and nurse. Lisa still lived with her parents and tried not to push it. And I usually managed to step out of there before Christine got to me.

But one night James couldn't come up with an excuse about balancing studying with his girlfriend's needs fast enough, and I—having neither of those prospects—couldn't either. Christine swooped by my desk, squeezed my shoulders, and, mouth lowered to my ear, said, "Paula, you'll come out with me, won't you?" It wasn't really a question.

"Christine, I'm really tired," I protested, thinking of the hour's ride back to Newark and the early-morning job interview I had the next day.

"Aw, come on. Just one, my treat."

I hesitated, and it did me in. "Great," she said, and gave my shoulders another squeeze before gliding back to her work station; all I could manage to do was look at her slim retreating form encased in black leggings and an oversize sweater.

At the bar, James acted the perfect academic wanna-be, soberly considering what kind of job a graduate degree in English lit could buy him, since the undergraduate degree hadn't done diddly, and how hard he had to study for the subject test of the GRE. Christine and I looked at each other once or twice, her eyebrow slightly raised in what I hoped was regret at having dragged us out. I studied her profile as James droned on. She and I shared a common Mediterranean background, but maintained a pleasing contrast within it: her long, straight, dark, soft-looking hair vs. my short, wavy, dark, coarse-looking hair; her large, almond-shaped hazel eyes vs. my almost black eyes; the same cheekbones and nose—though hers was slightly larger, a fact I'm sure she wasn't too fond of. But I wondered most about her skin. When I was nine or ten—old enough for my mother to leave me alone when she went to work—my best friend, Irene, who was Azorean, and I liked to play a game where we stripped down in front of the bathroom mirror and stood precariously together on a chair comparing our bodies and our skins, mine a brownish olive, Irene's paler, almost luminous against mine. It was the same contrast between Christine and me. She caught me looking and smiled.

She had pressed us both for this one drink, tried to draw it out beyond half an hour, but James soon enough said, "No, my girlfriend's waiting. I have to go." When he got up to use the bathroom, Christine turned to me and said, "P.W.'d. That boy is big-time P.W.'d."

"Christine," I said in mock shock, "P.W. is not P.C."

"Oh, fuck P.C. Hey, those aren't your initials, are they?" she laughed.

She said it just as the waitress I'd checked out when we first walked in came up to ask about a second round. While Christine considered another chardonnay, I enjoyed a closer look at the woman's slim waist, long hands, and firm body, reminding me with a pang of long-gone Michele. So, I reacted accordingly: had smiled inordinately when ordering my Bass Ale, smiled again too much now when declining a second, and let my eyes follow her as she walked away.

"Paula, why are you flirting with that waitress?" asked Christine.

"Because she's there," I replied.

"I see, " she said. "And do you always flirt with anything that takes orders?"

"Sure. Or gives them," I tossed back just as James emerged.

"What's so funny?" he asked, checking his fly as we laughed. He *would* think that.

I was surprised to feel slightly looped after just one beer

and dismissed the sudden careless joviality as the result of my fatigue and her two chardonnays.

"I'll get this, you guys," she said, reaching for her purse when the check came, and when I protested she added, "I'm giving the orders now. You can get me the next time."

James was clueless.

As we filed out of the bar, her foot caught the back of my shoe. Earlier, when we were leaving Blumenthal, I had stepped on her brand-new black leather boots. "Now we're even," I said lightly, not sure whether or not she had done it on purpose.

"Not quite," she answered.

As we waved James off and walked to our cars, she said my name, drawing out the middle so that it sounded Italian and at the same time funny. "Paoo-la! One of my professors in college was named that."

"Christine, are you OK to drive?" I asked.

"Oh, sure, honey."

Our cars were parked next to each other. Hers was a white Bronco, and I couldn't resist. "Is that the car you use for your slow-speed chases?"

"Of course, those are the best." She winked as she climbed in.

I got in my car, expecting her to tear out, but she didn't. She waited, pulled out after me, and followed until the turnoff on 206. I hoped the cops weren't out doing road checks.

The next afternoon, my partner, Donna, didn't show, and I wasn't surprised. Depressed, like we all were, she had mentioned possibly bagging out. Ben, Christine's partner, usually appeared around 6, but as the clock ticked on 6:15, then 6:30, it became apparent that he was either going to be very late or not show up either.

"Want to work together?" Christine asked as I brought up a document.

"Sure, let me get something to eat first."

She followed me into the kitchen, sure to remark—like she always did—on my voracious eating habits. She always had just a salad and some coffee. "I'm not pregnant anymore, but my butt still is," she'd say, and look on enviously as I piled my plate high. It wasn't that I was a pig, I was just poor, and I did the majority of my eating there. I hadn't grocery shopped the whole two months I'd been at Blumenthal, thanks to its generous pantry.

As I was stuffing my face with some tortellini, Christine asked, "How are you today, Miss Paula?"

"Not too bad," I answered, my mouth full of food. *How attractive,* I thought.

"So, I guess it's just you and me tonight, huh, toots?" Tonight she had on chocolate-brown slacks and a puffy cream silk blouse. The effect was attractive, though not the kind of look I usually went for. "How about after work too?" she continued as I reached for the salad bowl. "Let's go out."

"Again?" I asked. "How about the husband and kid?"

"Why do you think I go out so much?" she said.

I smiled as if to say *whatever,* but said instead, "Actually, tonight I'm kind of tired," like that was my stock answer for everything. She probably had more reason to be tired than I did. But I could never seem to come right out with what I felt. Besides, what the hell kind of smart retort was I going to shoot back? I grabbed a juice. "Meet you at the desk," I said.

At the workstation, she knocked my leg as she moved it to cross her knee. "I enjoyed our conversation the other night," she announced in the middle of a sentence about coupon maturities. She was wearing some kind of fragrance, and it hung in the air between us.

"Huh? When?" I asked.

"Last night, at the bar."

"Oh, I don't recall the conversation being that substantive. Something about James's relationship troubles, right?" I smiled.

"Would that we all had those kinds of relationship troubles," she said loudly, rolling her eyes heavenward and raising her hands in mock supplication.

James looked up and over at us. I felt myself shrink in my seat. *What the hell was this woman getting at, anyway?* "Well," I said, clearing my throat and lowering my voice, "beers and bar d'oeuvres"—I used her term for stale popcorn and other such bar snacks—"aren't usually conducive to meaningful insights."

"They aren't if you're trying too hard. So, are you coming out for more insights tonight or what?"

"Maybe," I answered.

"Good," she said—taking it as a yes. Her large brown eyes settled on me, then shifted quickly back down to the document. "OK, let's get back to this," she said. "But first, some music." She got up to put on the white noise. I wondered what the music reminded her of. As she walked over to the boom box, bantering with the other proofreaders along the way, her new shoes clicking smartly on the floor, I realized with a familiar feeling that I was definitely becoming interested in her—though I would never appreciate her taste in tunes.

"These people must think we're the Blumenthal faithful the way we make a pilgrimage here every night," I said as we entered the bar and made our way toward our usual corner table. "We're beginning to get a reputation."

"That's OK, I already have one the way I show up with different people," she said, unbuttoning her expensive-looking raincoat. *What other people besides the bond trolls? I* wondered.

"That's a nice coat," I said as she took it off. Underneath she was neat and dry while I, as usual, had forgotten weather essentials and shivered slightly in my damp T-shirt. "Is it a London Fog?"

"No, it's made in Korea. It's a Seoul Fog," she joked. But it did look expensive, whatever it was.

I noticed our waitress wasn't around, but then the place was pretty empty. When the bartender came over for our orders, he looked relieved for something to do.

Christine got her usual wine, but I wavered, not really wanting to drink two nights in a row. As the bartender waited, Christine reached over and pushed the damp hair out of my eyes. Her hand felt warm and cool at the same time. "A Virgin Mary, please," I stammered. When he left, I asked, "Do you always do that to people in public?"

"Sorry. Instinctive mother reaction. Sara always has her hair in her eyes. She won't let me take her to get it cut."

"Smart kid. My mother's a beautician. You wouldn't believe the atrocities she practiced on my poor little head. She gave me a perm when I was in 7th grade—in the class picture half the picture is the class, the other half is my hair. Kids called me Killer Bee 'cause my head looked like *The Swarm*."

She laughed. "Well, I can see how that might have hurt."

"It stung," I deadpanned.

"Ohh," she groaned.

"Tell me about it. When I tried to play football with the neighborhood kids, they were envious that I had a helmet and they didn't. Ruined my tomboy status." I traced circles from the wet rings on the tabletop while she watched me. She started to ask something but I said abruptly, "It must be hard raising a kid," cutting off any questions my personal anecdotes might bring up. "Does your husband watch her while you're at work?"

"No, he's too busy lawyering and cross-training. Running is his latest extracurricular obsession," she explained. "Whatever interests him, he's got to conquer it. My mother watches her. And you're right, it is hard. I'm glad for the chance to get away from the brat for a few hours every night," she said, glancing at the bar.

"The brat? Your daughter, your mother, or your husband?"

"Yes," she laughed. "Don't get me wrong, I love Sara, but

it is hard. She takes up an unbelievable amount of energy and patience. And waiting isn't my strong suit," she added as the drinks arrived.

"Well, I didn't think I took that long," the bartender said as he set down the drinks.

"Oh, too long, honey, too long." Christine picked up her drink and smiled at him.

"Now who's flirting with the help?" I said once he'd left.

"Doubtful, I think he's gay."

"Oh, really? Well, sometimes what looks one way isn't."

"That's what I always think too," she answered, meeting my eyes for a second.

I rolled my glass around in my hands, hating that my face felt the color of its contents; after all, I had nothing to hide.

"Sara sounds very bright," I said, trying to regain the ease of the previous conversation.

"She is, but the downside is that she's so damn curious. All I hear all day is, 'Why? Why? Why?' and sometimes I just feel like screaming, 'I don't know why, goddamn it!' It's hard enough answering adult versions of that question, never mind a three-year-old's."

"I don't know," I said. "When you're a kid, it seems OK to expect enthusiastic and uncomplicated answers to your questions."

"Maybe, and maybe when we grow up we just silence that wonderful curiosity and praise it as self-control. Do you have any kids, Paula?"

"Me? What, are you kidding? I got F's in self-control."

She laughed. "It's hard to raise them, especially since I don't want to raise Sara the way my parents raised me: nice, quiet, obedient Italian Catholic girl makes for a dull adult."

"Oh, I don't believe that," I said, because it seemed like something one said. "Besides, you've probably more than made up for it. Still are, for all I know."

"Yeah, right," she said, but it seemed to please her.

"But I know what you mean," I continued. "I grew up with the same Old World see 'em but don't hear 'em, especially if they're girls, mentality. And look at me now!" I made an exaggerated sweeping gesture.

"I am," she said, resting her hand on her chin.

I looked down at my Virgin Mary and raised it to finally take a drink, but she clicked against it with her glass before it reached my lips. "Here's to nice Catholic girls," she said.

The next day I asked her, "So if your husband's a big-time lawyer, why are you working here at night?"

"So I can spend all the money I make here buying new shoes," she answered as she stuck her feet out from under her chair and wiggled a shiny pair of black leather high heels that I'd actually seen before and remembered her calling her "Wicked Witch of the West pumps."

I noticed she didn't say anything to me the rest of the evening. Except for perfunctory hellos and goodbyes, she didn't say much the rest of the week either, or play any of her hideous music. She also didn't make any suggestions to anyone to go out after work.

But on Friday, everyone—including Christine—acted as if our usual group date was on. I went to the bathroom while they headed for the elevator. While I was in the stall, the bathroom door opened and someone walked in. I took my time tucking in my shirt and blowing my nose—bladder shyness extended to everything with me. Once I finally did come out, Christine was leaning against the vanity.

"There you are," she said. Tonight she was wearing simple black jeans, black boots, and a white shirt, but until I saw her there waiting for me, I hadn't really noticed. She stood leaning with her arms straight out beside her, which opened her shirt at the undone second button, the material below pulled tightly against her breasts.

"We thought you'd disappeared," she said as I calmly

walked over to wash my hands at the sink closest to her. She turned slightly toward me so her shirt touched me. I knew I could've had a better view if I'd wanted, but the one I had in the mirror was just fine. I was so close I could have kissed the smooth, pale skin below her neck with barely a movement of my head.

"You are coming tonight, aren't you, Paula?" Hearing my name was enough to guarantee it.

"Do you always wear your shirt like that?" I asked, looking down at my hands for a moment as I washed them, wondering what the hell I was getting myself into but getting into it anyway. She edged closer so that now I felt the press of form beneath the shirt. I looked up. Staring straight ahead, I could see in the mirror how close our faces were, and I imagined what, in different light, her skin would look next to mine.

I reached away from her for a paper towel and dried my hands slowly. I tossed the crumpled towel in the trash and leaned on my palms to stare once again in the mirror. My hand did not touch hers but stayed within that infinitesimal distance across which the air conducts the electricity of the skin. There was no difference now between touching and not touching. I may as well have had my whole body stretched out beside hers; I may as well have been running my hands across her skin. As I turned to kiss her, I felt a little pang at knowing we'd never be as innocent as childhood friends.

THE CALLING

Anne Seale

I'm rubbing hard with my old cotton nightie at the bottom of the bed, when the doorbell chimes. *Jeez,* I say to myself, *I'm just getting into this—it'll take forever to get back in the mood!*

I give a final swipe to the maple footboard, put the lid on the polish, and stow it and the rag under the kitchen sink on my way to the door.

I peep through the peephole. The woman standing there looks vaguely familiar. Her head is bowed, her attention centered on a piece of paper in her hand. I don't open the door right away, hoping she'll look up. She finally does, staring me directly in the peephole. I pull back my eyeball and unlatch the three deadbolts.

"Hi there," she says. "Are you Allie…"—she glances at the paper, which is actually a 3-by-5 card—"Prevoznik?" She pronounces it pretty well for a first try.

"That's me," I say, enjoying the sweet round face wrapped in ebony curls.

"I'm Yolanda Fry. I'm with Lick."

"Lick?"

She nods, sending me a smile, the kind that is often followed by a wink.

"Which...lick would that be?" I ask.

"You haven't heard of us? We're a lesbian group..."

By the time she finishes the "n" of "lesbian," I have whisked her from the apartment building hallway into my living room. I stick my head out before closing the door to make sure none of my neighbors are lurking about, or even worse, my mother on one of her mercy food drops. All clear.

Please sit down," I say, indicating the sofa. I take the recliner, not an easy thing to do since the mechanism broke during my recent move and now it's always in recline mode.

When she's settled, Yolanda says, "LLIC is an acronym for Lackawaukee Lesbians in Coalition. We're sort of a new group, formed last winter. We're very *active*. Haven't you read about us in *GIB*? Or don't you subscribe?"

Another acronym—*Gay Inner-City Bulletin*—and no, I don't subscribe. I don't trust plain brown wrappers. "I've been out of town for a couple of years, just moved back," I tell her. "And let me warn you, if you're looking for a donation, I'm not working."

She smiles again—what a smile! "No donations. In fact, I know you're not working. Kitty Ricardo told me. That's why I'm here."

"Kitty Ricardo? *That's* where I saw you, at Kitty's birthday party!" I was in Kitty's dining room, hanging by a bowl of Chee-tos, trashing politicians with a woman I'd just met. She made a clever pun on Bush's name, and when I threw back my head to laugh I spied a striking honey-brown face across the room, a face I'd like to see more of. I wound up the conversation as soon as I could but had no luck finding the owner of the face. Grabbing a fresh beer, I put the whole thing out of my mind.

And here's that face now, beaming at me right across my own coffee table. What a great world!

"You saw me at that party?" Yolanda says. "I was there for only a minute, to give Kitty her gift and make my apologies. My lover and I were having a disagreement, and I wasn't in a party mood."

Lover? I hope I don't look as disappointed as I feel, but just in case I slide out of the recliner and head for the kitchen, muttering something about coffee.

"Coffee? Lovely!" she says. "I've been out and about all morning."

By the time I get back with two steaming mugs, I've recovered enough to ask, "Who's your lover? Maybe I know her."

She's leafing through my latest issue of *Alternative Animal Husbandry*. "I doubt you know her, but you may have heard of her. Sylvia Sidewinder? She's a singer, mostly cabaret, but she does some theater. Did you see Stage Left's production of *Gypsy* last year?"

"No."

"That's right, you were out of town."

I hand her one of the mugs, offering to fetch sugar and milk. She shakes her head, sips, and sighs huskily. "Black, strong, and hot. *Just* the way I like it."

My kneecaps turn to Jell-O. Narrowly avoiding the sharp corner of the glass coffee table, I drop on the sofa next to her, partly on top of her actually. "Me too." I say, working my way to the next cushion.

"So, Allie…" she says, pulling her skirt from under me, "back to why I'm here. I'm Executive Director of LLIC, and there's way too much work for me right now, with the upcoming festival and all. So the board agreed to my hiring a temporary assistant. I asked around, and Kitty suggested I talk to you. She said you're having a hard time finding work in your field. What is your field?"

"Pig massage."

She stares at me in amazement. "That's a field?" she asks, then covers her mouth with her free hand. "Oh, I'm sorry."

I pat her knee in forgiveness. We pig massagers are a thick-skinned bunch. "The technical term is Livestock Reiki. For the past several years I was employed by a friend who had a farm about 70 miles west of here. I worked with all the animals, but my favorites were the pigs. They're very intelligent, you know, pigs. Affectionate too, always nuzzling you with their cute little snouts."

Yolanda tries not to wrinkle her nose. "Why did you leave?"

"I had to. My friend took up with a city woman and sold the farm to a guy who terminated my position. He didn't care about the emotional well-being of the little fellows at all. He saw them as"—I blink back tears—"just so much pork!"

It's her turn to pat my knee, after which she sets her mug on the end table so she can give me a big squeeze. "If it's any comfort, I'm a vegetarian," she croons in my ear.

I squeeze back. "I can't tell you how much that means to me." I choose not to tell her I have a chop thawing for supper.

She finally pulls away and straightens her blazer. "So, do you keyboard?" And that's how I got to be Yolanda Fry's temporary assistant at LLIC. (Please don't tell my mother it doesn't stand for Lackawaukee Ladies' Integrated Charities.)

Every weekday from 9 to 5—although I arrive at 8:30 in order to be with Yolanda every possible minute—I occupy a chair and desk in the small anteroom of her office on the second floor of an old building in a not-too-bad section of town. My job is to answer the phone, manage Mr. Coffee, and enter stuff in LLIC's antique Packard Bell, a donation from a board member who probably took a huge tax deduction. I also run errands with Yolanda, and sometimes we even stop for lunch. I'm in hog heaven.

Most of our tasks have to do with the planning of the first ever Lackawaukee Lesbian Autumn Festival of Fun—shortened, of course, to LLAFF. Yolanda has booked the Art Center of Castanetta Catholic College for Women, which is a real coup, in my opinion. Castanetta's a pretty conservative institution, at least it was when I earned my degree in biology there several years ago.

It's not that big a school, so it makes me pretty nervous to be walking around the Art Center taking notes as Yolanda says loudly, "We'll put the Bisexual Dating Exchange table here, next to the Radical Witches' tarot-reading booth." If a professor I know comes by, I hold the notebook in front of my face, as if I am extremely near-sighted.

The only thing I really hate about my job is answering the office phone when Yolanda's lover, Sylvia, calls. I answer cordially, as always, "LLIC, Allie speaking, how may I help you?"

"Yeah," a voice says in a distinctly uncordial tone. "Gimme Yo."

The first time it happened, I didn't understand, and asked, "Give you my what?"

If Yolanda happens to be out of the office, Sylvia gets all whiny, "Well, where *is* she?" As if I'd tell her.

From comments Yolanda has let fall, I know that she and Sylvia have had a stormy on-again, off-again relationship for six years or so. They're currently on-again, which makes it hard for me, because, as you've guessed, I've fallen for Yolanda in a big way. I work my tail off to earn her grateful smiles and shoulder pats. I can't wait for her goodbye hugs at the end of each day. Then I go to my lonely apartment, and Yolanda goes home to Sylvia. Damn.

The Wednesday morning before festival weekend, Yolanda and I are at the college, going over arrangements with the sound technician for the stage show that's going to be the grand finale. The best local lesbian talent is set to perform, and for emcee, we have hired no one less prestigious than comedian Teri Winkle, who is coming all the way from Albany. It's going to be quite a show!

When the sound business is finished and the tech has gone, Yolanda and I walk the perimeter of the deserted auditorium, discussing crowd management. Then, noticing it's lunchtime, we take two seats, front-row center. I unwrap the sprout-burgers and carrot juice we purchased on the way over, and we feast while discussing the upcoming show, our favorite performers, and the wonders of lesbian life in general.

I bring up the dreaded Sylvia Sidewinder, inquiring why she isn't on the program if she's supposed to be such a hot-shot singer (although I don't exactly word it that way).

Yolanda frowns. "Sylvia doesn't perform at lesbian functions."

"She doesn't?"

"No. She won't show her face in any kind of lesbian environment. Haven't you wondered why she never comes to the office, why you've never had a glimpse of her in all these weeks?"

"No." I was happy that I hadn't.

"Somebody might see her, she says, and her career in straight cabaret would be over."

"That's ridiculous!"

"I know! That's what we were arguing about the night of Kitty's party. I begged her to come with me, but she wouldn't." Her shoulders slump.

I squeeze her hand. "It must be difficult for you, being such an *out* person."

"It is!" she says in such a tragic tone that I can't stand it. Laying my sandwich on the next seat, I put my arms around her and massage some spots where I used to rub the shoats to comfort them when they were taken from their mamas.

After a while I feel her muscles relax, so I pull my head back to see how she's doing. What I find are two eyes full of lust and wanting. I then memorize the location of the spot I've been rubbing.

Yolanda pulls me close and kisses me hard. Her tongue darts in and out of my mouth. I suck on it.

Somewhere in a corner of my brain that's still working, a bunch of cells are doing cartwheels, screaming, "The woman has finally come to her senses! Down with Sylvia. Up with Allie!"

My hand runs up Yolanda's thigh, under the hem of the short skirt that's been driving me mad all day. She groans against my mouth and scrunches down in the seat, legs open, granting me full access. The crotch of her panties is damp to the touch.

Wrenching my mouth from the suction we've built, I kneel in front of her and work the panties down, applying my tongue, still tingling from the kiss, to her steamy mound. Her clit is hard. I flick at it.

"Allie, baby," she whispers, "give it to me."

Increasing the pressure, I move my head in a circular motion. Her fluids run down my chin and onto the seat. She nods her hips against me, making each stroke a long one. Twenty or so strokes later (who's counting?), she comes in a river of juices, making it tough for me to breathe. Still, I hang on, in hope of a second coming.

"Excuse me? Excu-u-use me?"

I know that voice. Last time I heard it, it was barking out a benediction at my graduation ceremony, fiercely commanding God to *Bless! This! Class!* It's Sister Omniscience, Dean of Students.

I jump up and automatically stand at attention. My chin is dripping. Yolanda hands me a paper napkin and coolly pulls her skirt over the wet spot.

"Excu-use me?" Sister says again. "Would you care to tell me what right you have to be in here, doing...*that?*"

"We have a perfect right to be here, Sister. I'm Yolanda Fry, the coordinator of LLIC, the group who has rented the Center for a festival on Saturday. We're here today finalizing details."

"Oh, is *that* what you're doing," Sister O says with a smirk, then turns to me. "And who might you be?"

"Bella Karenski," I mumble without looking up, praying for my departed Aunt Bella's forgiveness for besmirching her good name. Yolanda, standing, gives me the *who?* look.

Sister O stares at me like she's seen me before and is trying to place my face. Finally she gives up. "I know all about LLIC." She spits it out. "I can't believe you *lezz*-bians were able to coerce Sister Charisma into letting you use the Center for your sinful goings-on. Wait until I tell her and our esteemed president what I saw here today. They'll cook your festival goose, I wager." She flounces up the aisle and out of the auditorium, leaving a great silence in her wake.

All the way back to the office, Yolanda rants and raves about nuns in general, and Sister Omniscience in particular. She says that Sister O is no doubt a closet dyke, because the worst 'phobes always are. I hope if she's right, Sister O will never be outed. She'd taint our image.

Then Yolanda tells me that what happened between us this afternoon was a big mistake, and I shouldn't mention it to anyone, ever. I nod, too miserable to speak.

Back in the office, I plunge myself into my work, which consists of dealing with the dozen or so phone messages that accumulated while we were gone. Half of them are from Sylvia, who immediately calls again. I put her through to Yolanda without giving the phone a rude gesture, for once.

The next morning, like Johnny Cash, I dress in black. I walk into the office at 9 sharp, early no more, wearing a black vest over a black shirt, black jeans held up with black suspenders, and black boots. My underwear and socks are white cotton, but they don't show.

If Yolanda notices my suit of mourning, she gives no sign.

The phone rings at 9:15, and the caller identifies herself as Sister Charisma, Castanetta Catholic College's Community Coordinator. "May I speak to Miss Yolanda Fry, please?" she says, not sounding happy.

Two and three-quarters minutes later, according to my Radio Shack sports watch, the little light on the phone goes out. Then it goes right on again, and this time Yolanda talks for four minutes, 13 seconds. Another minute, and she strides out of her office, bag over shoulder, pausing to announce, "The Castanetta Board of Directors is meeting in an hour. Sister Charisma thinks they are going to cancel our contract. I'm on my way to pick up Veda." Veda is LLIC's attorney.

After she leaves, I bury my face in my hands. This is terrible! I may be upset with Yolanda, but I care very much about this festival, into which I have invested so much time, energy, and enthusiasm. Also, I feel responsible for what happened in the college auditorium yesterday. I should have kept my hands to myself. I know how potent those pressure points can be.

I can't sit still. I pace the area in front of my desk. I do deep knee bends and a few jumping jacks. Finally I reach over, switch on the answering machine, and run out the door, locking it after me.

I avoid the main entrance to the college administration building, circling until I find a back door that admits me onto a small landing. I figure the board would meet on a higher floor rather than a lower, so I start climbing the stairs, wondering what on earth I'm doing here.

Hearing voices, I stop, poking my head slightly above second-floor level. Seven or eight women, half of them wearing habits, are gathered in front of a double doorway in the middle of a wide hall, conversing in low tones. Some hold dainty teacups balanced on saucers. This *has* to be the board—drinks for the college hoi polloi are served in Styrofoam.

"Ah, here they are," one of the women says loudly. All eyes turn to the wide staircase opposite me where three nuns in matching habits rise slowly over the horizon, step by solemn step. Sisters Omniscience and Charisma flank a tiny Sister Percepta, president of the college. When they reach the top, there are greetings and hugs, then all of them disappear through the double doorway, taking their china cups with them. Nobody bothers to shut the doors.

I finish my climb, pausing at the top to listen. Someone in

the room is speaking, but I can't make out the words. Staying near the wall, I tiptoe closer, cursing the fact that I am wearing leather-soled boots instead of my usual soft sneakers.

As I reach the doorway, I hear, "And now let us hear what Sister Omniscience has to say."

A chair scrapes. I peek around the door frame. Sister O stands at the foot of a shiny conference table. The rest of them are seated around it, gazing at her expectantly.

Sister O clears her throat. "As I told my dear friend and colleague President Sister Percepta," she waves at the tiny nun, who answers with a nod, "I was passing through the Art Center yesterday at noon when I noticed that the auditorium lights were on. Remembering Sister Percepta's admonition that we turn off unused lights wherever we find them," another wave, another nod, "I entered the auditorium to ascertain whether the lights were, indeed, in use. And what did I see?" She looks around, but nobody says, "What?"

She goes on anyway. "I found two *lezz*-bians, members of that LLIC group who coerced Sister Charisma"—she has no wave for Sister Charisma—Sister O.into letting them use the Art Center this weekend for their nefarious affair."

Sister Charisma glances around frantically. "I had no idea what that second 'L' stood for. Truly!"

Sister O sends her a pained look and goes on. "Those two *lezz*-bians were engaging in *sinful and illicit sexual conduct,* right in our own auditorium. I can't tell you how stunned and disgusted I was."

I step back in case I might mutter, stomp my foot, or otherwise call attention to myself, pushing heavily into a nun who has come up behind me. "Excu-use me?" she says. It must be the new school motto.

"Sure, no problem." I step out of her way and turn my attention back to the gathering.

Instead of passing, however, she grabs my arm and pulls me to the staircase. "I don't know who you are," she hisses, "but I am sure you have no business spying on our board."

"Oh, I do!" I say cheerfully. "I'm the one they're talking about."

"Really? You can explain that to Security." She tightens her grip and tries to force me down the steps.

An explosion goes off in my brain. All of a sudden I know why I am here and what I have to do. My mission is to save LLAFF!

I wrest my arm from her hands and run into the boardroom, not stopping until I am standing beside Sister Omniscience. She looks at me, does the placing-your-face routine again, then says, "Aha!" She turns to her audience. "This is one of those fornicating *lezz*-bians!"

I pull myself to my full height, which is still an inch or so shy of Sister O's, and speak directly to the board. "Yes, I was in the auditorium yesterday, but Sister Omniscience misread the situation. I was merely comforting my friend, who had just confided something upsetting to me, something of a personal nature."

Sister O snorts. "Oh, really? And did this *comforting* necessitate thrusting your tongue against your friend's lower anatomy?"

The board gasps in unison. The Police Nun, who has been watching from the doorway, staggers to a chair.

"I did not thrust my tongue against her lower anatomy," I proclaim. It's true. At that point, Yolanda was thrusting her lower anatomy against my tongue. "But yes, I am a lesbian, and proud of it."

I can't believe I just said that, old closeted me. However, there was no going back, so I went on. "I am a lesbian, and I am also a graduate of Castanetta College, class of '88, cum laude. I'm proud of that too. And if you think I'm the only lesbian to ever graduate from this institution, let me assure you, I am not!" I knew there was at least one other, my dorm mate Sheila.

"By the way,"—I raise an eyebrow and stab the air with a finger—"Castanetta's lesbians are among our *most financially supportive* alumni!" I couldn't prove this, of course, but they couldn't disprove it either. I personally had never sent the college a postgraduate dime.

"And," I go on, "if you think a breach of your contract with LLIC would not be widely publicized, think *again*." I see Sister Percepta's eyebrows go up an eighth of an inch. "However, there will be *no* breach of contract. Honor and righteousness will prevail." I stab my fist into the air. "LLAFF will go on!"

There's a burst of applause from the direction of the doorway. I turn my head to see Yolanda and Veda standing just inside, smiling and clapping. I try to smile back, but I'm shaking too hard and my knees are buckling. The burst of manic energy has taken its toll.

A woman to my right stands and puts her arm around my waist. "That was wonderful, babe," she says in my ear. "I'm Nan Troupe, the college's attorney. I'll take it from here." She delivers me into Yolanda's arms.

As Yolanda and Veda support me through the double doors, I look back at Nan Troupe. I can't believe I hadn't noticed her at the table. She has that strong, no-nonsense, take-charge...you know, that *dyke* look. Confident that LLAFF is safe in her hands, my mind moves on to other matters, like wondering if she's busy tonight.

Another woman follows us out. "Allie!" she calls. "Allie Prevoznik!" It takes a minute to identify her—I haven't seen her for years. It's my mother's next-door neighbor, Mrs. Horner. We engage in a short conversation about my mother's health, which I'm sure will worsen as soon as Mrs. Horner gets home. Satisfied that she has fulfilled her social obligation, she returns to the board room. Police Nun pulls the doors shut behind her.

Yolanda, Veda, and I lean against the wall to wait. They

tell me several times how wonderful I was in there. Yolanda stares at me lasciviously, but I deliberately look away. Been there, done that.

I ask Veda if she knows Nan Troupe. She says they are personal friends as well as fellow attorneys and goes on for a long time about Nan's intelligence, impeccable ethics, and general worthiness, finishing with, "And can you believe she's single?"

I try not to smile.

Then she says, "Do I understand, Allie, that you're not a professional activist? You really should think about it—you're a dynamic speaker, and that totally black outfit makes such a statement! Why don't you come see me? I'll put you in touch with the right people."

I start to say oh, no, I couldn't. Then I stop to consider how euphoric and turned-on I felt in that room a few minutes ago. I also consider the fact that my temporary position with LLIC expires Saturday with the end of the festival. I consider that there's no need for me to stay in the closet any longer. If Mrs. Horner doesn't tell my mother what happened, I'm going to.

The final consideration—that association with Veda may well lead to association with the fascinating and *single* Nan Troupe—is the deciding one.

I turn to Veda, slip my thumbs under my black suspenders and say, "How about Monday?"

A sense of righteousness and destiny flows through me, and for the first time despite my Catholic upbringing, I understand what is meant by a "calling."

Fools Rush In

Lisa DeSantiago

"AAYYEE love to love you bay-be..." My hand comes down hard on the snooze button of the "Betty Davis Eyes" alarm clock my friend Sebastian just couldn't live without. It's 7:30, and all I want is ten more minutes of sleep. Pulling the covers over my head, I catch the smell of her: sweet and musky. I hug my pillow, disappointed to be waking up alone. Knowing that Sebastian can't afford any more therapy, I make a mental note to wash the sheets before leaving. Thoughts of my recent exploits consume my ten minutes. The eyes of Betty Davis click open once more: *"AAYYEE love to love you bay-be...AAYY"* —must get to the radio before I feel the urge to buy platforms and a polyester pantsuit—both of which, I'm sure, Sebastian has in his closet. Mercifully, disco is finally dead, and I swing my legs over the edge of the bed, cursing my publisher for wanting to do breakfast instead of brunch. My body rebels with the grunts of my foremothers as it tries to embrace the idea of getting up. "Come on, old woman." I rise slowly, testing the ability of first one and then the other leg to hold its share of my weight before shuffling through the rest of

Sebastian's own personal Hollywood Boulevard, avoiding the stares of Clark Gable, Marlon Brando, and Dorothy holding Toto. "Jesus, when did I get this old?"

"About the same time you started talking to yourself, I suspect."

"Who asked you?"

"You did."

Though I'm never sure who wins these arguments, I'm seriously considering getting a parrot to referee. The kitchen is black and white and chrome, with just a splash of red to keep one from getting vertigo. When I find the coffeepot, I'm happy to see that the coffee is already ground and in the filter. "Sebastian, you're a fine hostess." I push the "on" button and will my legs to propel me toward the bathroom.

Sebastian's bathroom is nothing short of palatial. The floor is a beautiful light-gray marble with a mosaic of a naked Greek Olympian in the middle. The sunken tub is more than adequate to accommodate the 6-foot-1 diva, and the vanity holds more makeup than the Lancôme counter at Fields. Across the top of the mirror in a very fine script is etched, "Don't Hate Me Because I'm Beautiful." I splash my face with cold water and laugh because the face that stares back at me from this mirror is definitely not the face of the youthful imp who possessed my body just hours before. This face has laugh lines. These eyes have crow's feet. This hair is beginning to show more salt than pepper, and this body had no business doing what it did last night. "Coffee. I need coffee," I mumble. "A big pot of coffee and a big vat of Ben Gay."

I smile at the Betty Boop coffee mug smiling back at me from the kitchen counter. "No offense, Betty baby, but you're a little too perky for me this morning." I open the cabinet to discover James Dean, Marilyn Monroe, Veronica Lake, and others all staring back at me. I close the door quickly, deciding that Betty Boop is the least disturbing because she's the only one who isn't dead. When I fill Betty with coffee the words "Careful I'm Hot" appear across her forehead. A note that had been tucked under Betty Boop unfolds itself. I pick it up and adjust my arm length for focus.

Good Morning, Professor,

DAMN, WOMAN! You wore me out. This should have happened years ago. Now I'll never get you out of my head. Sorry I couldn't make you breakfast, but I have practice this morning. Looking forward to a repeat performance. Don't you dare leave town before I can reclaim my good name. I'll call you.

Love,
Flips

P.S. Are mine the only knees that are weak?

"Yeah, yeah, yeah and the check is in the mail," I reply, sipping my coffee and rereading the note. "Speaking of knees, what the hell did mine do last night and why the hell did they think they could do it?" I take my coffee and the note into the living room. Sebastian's condo has a fabulous view. The living room has an entire wall of glass that looks out over Lake Michigan toward downtown. Lucky for me, he's touring the country in his one-man show, "From Dumpling to Diva." So for this weekend the view is mine. I collapse into a huge leather chair, lay the note open on the end table, rub my knees slowly in a clockwise motion. My mind wanders back to the last thing Sebastian told me before we kiss-kissed good-bye: "Honey, if you can't get laid in this place, you may as well sew it up. And if you do get laid, clean the sheets."

"Well, Sebastian, you were right. This view is an aphrodisiac," I drawl out, reversing the direction of my rubbing. I read the note again, picking out my favorite parts. "I wore her out. Imagine that," I say proudly to myself, side-stepping the fact that she's probably sweating it out at a full soccer practice while I sit here recovering from getting coffee.

As much as I'd like to, I can't fool myself. My sustained vigor had nothing to do with eating right and proper exercise, though it might've had a little to do with being celibate for two years. Prior to last night I was sure my pent-up sexual energy could power Las Vegas. I was tired of looking for love in all the wrong places. I was tired of looking for love at all. There was no way my body was going to let my mind talk me out of this one. Flips's body could make a nun question her vows, and I'm far from being a nun. Besides, how much safer can you get? By this time tomorrow I'll be in Miami. No strings attached. "Damn, she was limber," I hear myself say.

"No shit, Sherlock. You're lucky you're not in the emergency room," I hear myself answer.

"I think I need a dog. Everyone talks to their dog. Plus a dog will never leave you, even if a younger, prettier dog comes around."

I sit back to enjoy the view, secure in my sanity for the time being. Images of last night overwhelm me. The Chicago skyline pales in comparison. It's funny to think of how pure chance had dropped this goddess into my lap...

I'd been scheduled to do a book signing in Chicago and was looking forward to touching base with some old friends and catching a night game at Wrigley. Before having fun, though, I'd have to spend an afternoon at my friend Lucille's bookstore, discussing my happy dysfunctional childhood and signing: "To What's-your-name, Thanks, J. Margoles." My given name is Julietta, but the only person who calls me that is my mother.

We'd just decided to close up shop when I looked up. "Professor, you look great." Her familiar eyes took me in, entirely. I thought I'd melt. "I am so glad I caught you. I was afraid I'd be too late. Damn! You look great," she repeated, not bothering to adjust her stare. Phyllis Waterman played soccer for my ex at the University of Florida-Miami. Dirt, grass stains, and shin pads had never been enough to hide that body, and this day wasn't any different. There she stood: 5-foot-8 inches of well-toned, well-tanned muscle in soccer shorts and cleats. Normally a pair of muddy cleats on my good friend Lucille's hand-waxed, high-glossed hardwood floors would have bothered the shit out of her—that is, if she'd been able to stop gawking.

I can't say that I wasn't gawking as well, but I was able to stop thinking of running my hands through her thick black hair long enough to retreat to the safety of my professor persona. "You usually are, Ms. Waterman," I scolded, turning my back to her and continuing to pack up the remaining books. "Late, that is."

"I'm not in your class anymore, Professor. Call me Flips." Her hot breath flowed over the back of my neck. She was way too close.

"You are absolutely right, Flips." I stood straight up in an attempt to find some air. "I suppose you can call me Dr. Margoles." We were standing face to face, and she looked as if she had just been put in time-out. Quickly, I scribbled something in the jacket of one of my books and handed it to her. "I'm kidding," I reassured her. "Call me J. We're both grown-ups, right?" I sounded more certain than I felt.

"Yeah, right. Kewl. Ya wanna get some coffee, maybe?" she asked, before opening the cover and reading what I had written. Her smile lit up the room—or maybe the overhead light, the one with the short, had just flicked on again. Before I could stop her, she hugged me. Not a sorority girl kinda hug either. This was a full body contact, you-make-my-knees-weak sorta hug. My arms didn't want to let go. "It's been so long," she said, squeezing tighter. "Let's get some coffee and talk, OK?"

The contact was broken but not the spell; before my mind knew what my mouth was doing, I answered, "Yeah, right. Cool. Let's get more than coffee, though. I'm famished."

"Exactly what I was thinking." She spoke far too quickly, a sly smile sneaking across her face. Alarms went off in all my erogenous zones, and I barely heard her when she said, "This is really nice, what you wrote."

"Well, yeah, that's why I'm here. I write nice things." I threw the rest of the books in the box, not caring which end was up. "Can we go now?" I was certain that if I didn't sit soon, my wobbly knees would give away the prurient nature of my thoughts. I said my goodbyes to Lucille and left her still recovering from the sight of such a vision.

As I followed Flips out the door I stared. It had been hard not to stare four years ago when I was solidly entrenched in a relationship. Now, after the death of said relationship, and after the reality of my two-year vow of celibacy, it was impossible. I was happy to discover that lesbian bed-death was not an irreversible disease.

We walked along the lakefront. We walked as close as two women can walk without attracting attention. We talked about sports and politics. We talked about why she moved to Chicago and why I left. At times I would just watch her lips move. I couldn't tell you what she said. I was floating on air. It was May, and the air smelled of spring. Actually it smelled of *smelt*—but in Chicago, smelt means spring. As soon as we hit the boundaries of New Town—or Boys' Town, or whatever you want to call it—Flips took my hand. We walked hand in hand for two blocks before Flips steered me into a neighborhood diner. The diner screamed of great cheeseburgers, greasy fries, and strong coffee. The decor, a tribute to Chicago sports teams and their fans. I loved it. "Great place," I said as I stared in awe at the autographed picture of the '69 Cubs, the Billy Williams jersey, the Michael Jordan Nikes. Flips had to drag me away.

"I'm glad you like it. Next time I'll bring blinders." Flips let me slide into the booth first, then gestured to a lady behind the counter. "Dottie, can you bring us two coffees? Thanks, babe."

"Sure thing, sweetie," Dottie replied, looking happy to oblige.

Flips slid into the booth next to me. She either didn't know or didn't care what the smell of her was doing to me. It's a curse. I have always loved the smell of an athlete after she's just played ball. It makes me crazy. It makes me forget for a moment that a lot of women love the smell of an athlete after she's just played ball. You'd think I would learn from my mistakes.

"Is someone joining us, or do you always crowd your dinner companions?" I asked, trying to ignore the involuntary movement of my body toward hers.

"Only when the companion is the one who got away," she answered, sliding her arm across the back of the booth. "Besides, we need somewhere to put our coats."

"But we don't have any coats," I corrected. I was doing my damnedest to keep my thigh right where it was, to wait until hers came to me.

"I know we don't have any coats, but we're in Chicago. I bet you that when we leave here, we will need coats."

"That's a sucker bet. Anyone who has ever lived here would know that."

"Precisely. This way when we need them we'll have some place to put them. Get it?" With this said, she placed her hand over the hand that was holding my thigh in place, and all hell broke loose below.

"Got it," I managed to squeak out, unable to stop my thighs from doing a toned-down version of the Charleston.

"Good. Let's eat." She removed her hand in order to take her coffee from Dottie.

"Here you go," Dottie cooed as she leaned over far too much to place my coffee in front of me.

"Thanks, Dot," Flips mumbled toward Dottie's Wonderbra. "I think we'll both have cheeseburgers and fries, if you don't mind."

On her way back up I glimpsed what Flips had just had a faceful of. Dottie had what one might call *ample* breasts, which she managed to place in the vicinity of Flips's face at least three times while serving coffee. "Why, I don't mind at all, sweetie," she answered as her left hand lingered on Flips's shoulder. "I'll bring you some fresh cream too. I know you hate the stuff that's been sitting around for a while." She flashed me a snotty smirk and turned to go adjust her pasties, I assumed.

"Well, she can just forget about her tip," I spat as I watched her swish her firm young ass back to the kitchen.

"One might say that you were jealous, Professor." Flips's arm was firmly on my shoulders now. "I hope you don't mind cheeseburgers? I remembered that you liked them." While I was glaring at Dottie, Flips was looking at me. It was nice, and disconcerting. My insides felt like a can of Coke that had just rolled down the stairs.

"Wait a minute. Did you just call me jealous?" I fumed. "Jealousy is a useless emotion that screams of insecurity." My passion comes in many forms, and something had to give. Since a physical release was out of the question, Flips was going to have to deal with what she got.

Flips pulled away. "I just meant that a few years ago you didn't even know I was alive." Now there was definite space between all parts of our bodies—not so much space that I couldn't feel her heat, but space nonetheless. The kind of space I wanted gone.

"What do you mean, I didn't know you were alive? I'm not dead, you know." It took all I had to keep myself from jumping her right then and there. "Jesus, Flips! You're a goddess in soccer shorts! What woman wouldn't know you were alive?"

"Maybe a woman with a lover?" She was closing the space between us again. Her hand touched my hair.

"Maybe a professor with tenure?" I shot back. "A professor shouldn't get involved with her students." Flips was so close her breast pressed against my shoulder.

"That's bullshit, J. I wasn't your student until you stopped coming around." Hearing her say "J" made me *feel*. It had been so long, and I wasn't sure I was ready to feel yet. "How many literature classes do you think a fourth-year premed student needs?"

I couldn't respond. I was locked in the gaze of her blue eyes.

"I took your class so I could see you. Don't tell me you never knew." She leaned in closer, as close as the laws of physics would allow. "I wrote poems, but I was only brave enough to send you the one that made the school review. You never read it, did you?" Her eyes challenged me. Her full lips teased me.

I broke free of her gaze. "OK, so you're a smart goddess in soccer shorts. What's your point?"

"You're avoiding the question."

"What question?"

"You didn't read it, did you?"

"I didn't say that, did I?" I held her face between my hands. Remembering the words, I closed my eyes. "you burn in my heart / without knowledge / your aura excites / my senses / without malice / i see all that you are / without recognition / i hunger for the heat / of your skin / without relief / my mind knows your touch / without your consent / i / fell in / Love" I opened my eyes and kissed her lips, once, softly. "How could you think I wouldn't read it? I knew exactly how you were feeling. I just didn't know, or I didn't want to know, that you were feeling it for me."

It was Flips's turn to do the Charleston. She told Dottie to make those burgers to go. We couldn't sit still. It seemed like an eternity before our order was up. Flips paid the bill and threw a tip on the table and said, "Let's go." She grabbed my hand and led me outside.

The spring air did nothing to cool off my insides. "Where to, *mi amor*? I'm starving."

Flips wrapped me in her arms, pronouncing to the world,

"I love it when you speak Spanish. I love you when you speak Spanish. I love Spanish." She began to swing me around, which made me warmer—but people were starting to stare.

"So I take it we're going to Spain?"

"I don't care where we go as long as it's close," she whispered in my ear as she returned me to earth.

"I'm staying a block away." Our pace bordered on a trot, which didn't leave enough time for me to worry that Flips had just said, in a roundabout way, that she loved me—but only when I'm speaking Spanish, so I figured I was safe. The young always confuse lust with love. As far as I was concerned, I was about to use and be used. Sebastian would be so proud. The ride up the elevator was excruciating, though I'm sure the Sister and the two Girl Scouts didn't sense a thing.

Flips took the keys from me after I failed three times to open the door. "Here, let me." Her control was extraordinary, I thought, as she slid the key slowly into its hole. We fell through the door, slamming it closed with our bodies, tearing and ripping at each other's clothing. Dinner would have to wait.

We each came twice before we hit the shower, where I discovered that I could, indeed, get off while standing, but only if I have a young, nubile soccer player holding me up. Sebastian's bed was converted into a jungle gym. I attained positions that would make the author of the *Kama Sutra* blush. I discovered muscles I never knew I had. I reveled in the touch of her. Flips was a finely tuned instrument, and I was going to Carnegie Hall. "Coma" is the only word to describe how I slept.

"Damn, no wonder I hurt. No wonder I'm starving," I remark to the empty apartment. I get up to look for what's left of dinner. A pickle and a couple of French fries are all that survived our late-night feeding frenzy. I eat the pickle to take the edge off. Remembering that I have a date with a plate of steak and eggs in a little while, I dispose of the fries. In the shower I try hard to forget how much I miss having someone wash my back and how much I hate the business end of writing. "Hey, free food is free food," I keep repeating as I pick out an outfit: a pair of faded but not torn jeans—after all, this is a business breakfast—my purple dashiki, wool socks, and a pair of well-worn Birkenstocks. I have to choose another leather necklace, because the necklace I had on last night got chewed off and spit across the room. By whom, I'll never tell. The African goddess in bone seems to enhance that "day-after glow."

Ann Sather's Restaurant is a three-block walk, and I'm looking forward to stretching my legs. When I arrive Pat is already seated, drinking coffee and munching on a cinnamon roll. Pat is a large woman. Some people see her as intimidating. I just see her as Pat, my good friend, who would squash me like a grape if she ever felt I needed it. "Hey, Pat," I say as I lean over and kiss her cheek. She kisses mine in return.

"Hey, J. What the hell happened to you? You look like shit."

So much for my day-after glow, I think to myself. I can always count on Pat to be straight-up. "If I told you I'd have to kill myself." I take the seat next to her, hoping that my cryptic answer will satisfy her curiosity.

"Well, it's about time!" She snickers, leans over, and shoves my shoulder like a teammate in a locker room.

"You don't have to be so happy, Pat. It's not that big a deal." I adjust from the shove and regain my balance.

"But it is, Blanche, it is. We were starting to think we'd lost you to your quest to restore your virginity."

"Screw you, Pat" is all I can come back with.

"Love to," Pat says quickly, "now that the seal's been broken."

"Yeah, right, rub a lamp." I tease, knowing Pat won't take offense. We have been friends far too long for it to ever be sexual and she knows it, but that doesn't stop her from trying. As far as I'm concerned, she wouldn't be Pat if she didn't try.

"I hope you don't mind, but I invited my niece." Before I

can protest, Pat flags down the waitress. "She loves your books. Makes me mail her a copy of the new stuff before it hits the bookstores."

"Wow, a real fan. I'd love to meet her." We place our orders and are pleasantly surprised when our plates arrive 15 minutes later. Just as I'm about to dig into my steak and eggs, Pat stands up and waves frantically at the door. "Over here, Phil."

"Phil? I thought this was your niece," I say. I strain to see, but the waitress assigned to the table in front of us blocks my view.

"It is my niece, dork. Phil is short for Phyllis." The fact that Pat has stopped waving tells me that Phil or Phyllis is close. My mind attempts to wrap itself around the possibility. *Phil is short for Phyllis* reverberates in my brain.

"No way, it can't be—Flips! Hey, how are you?"

"Hey, Professor." Flips kisses Pat, then leans over to kiss me. My insides jump in response to her touch. "Long time no see, Professor." She winks at me as she straightens up. I feel her stare as she takes the seat Pat holds out for her. I quickly start in on my steak and eggs.

"I didn't know you two knew each other," Pat pouts.

"Briefly," I answer before Flips can open her mouth. "Besides, I didn't know she was your niece. Funny how these things forget to be mentioned." I glare across the table, only to be mocked by Flips's mischievous grin.

"Why didn't you tell me, Phil?" Pat picks at Flips's hair, removing one blade of grass after another.

"I didn't tell you because I wasn't sure if Professor Margoles—"

"Call me J, please," I interrupted, wanting just to hear her say my name again.

"J, it is. Anyhow, I didn't think she would remember me." Flips makes a feeble attempt at brushing grass stains from her jersey.

Seemingly satisfied with Flips's answer, Pat starts to fuss like a mother hen. "You know, my brother would kill me if he knew I let you come into a restaurant dressed like this."

"Daddy doesn't like my uniform because he's afraid his girlfriends might."

"Enough said, Phyllis." Pat is old-school. "What he doesn't know won't kill him, I suppose." She decided years ago to ignore her family's homophobic tendencies. Apparently, Flips has decided to do the opposite.

"Here! Here!" I toast, raising my glass of orange juice in an effort to break the tension. Flips and Pat join in and we all share an uncomfortable laugh.

Flips orders enough food to feed a small country while Pat and I eat and discuss the sale of the book and how many more appearances I can make before the summer session begins. Nothing we haven't discussed before. It's clear to me that this "meeting" is just an excuse for Pat to have breakfast with an old friend on company time. As we continue to talk, Flips proceeds to lick every platter clean—including mine. *Good,* I think. *If Flips keeps her mouth full, Pat will never know that her niece and I have shared more than just an interest in books.* Forty minutes later, Pat leaves, apologizing for having to cut our visit short.

"It's about time. I thought she'd never leave," Flips utters through a mouthful of hash browns. "Are you surprised, J?"

"Surprised would be one way of looking at it. Confused would be another." I'm elated and angry at the same time. I don't know whether to feel manipulated or appreciated. "What are you doing, Flips?"

"I'm doing what I should have done years ago. I'm trying to convince you to look at me, not through me."

I can't handle the sincerity in her eyes, and I'm glad when the waitress comes to clear the mound of plates in front of Flips.

"Let's be honest here, Flips. I live in Miami. I just don't see what's in it for you besides big phone bills." I fidget with the salt shaker, hoping this conversation ends before I come up with a way to fit her into my carry-on bag.

Flips refuses to be ignored. She reaches across the table and takes my hand. Everything inside me screams, "Pull away!" but I can't. Her eyes hold mine captive. "What's in it for me, J, is you. Maybe you don't want to hear it, but I fell in love with you the first time I saw you on the sidelines reading O. Henry."

She's right. I didn't want to hear it, but she said it anyway. Our eyes remain locked. My mind whirls. Desperate for a way out, I take the most obvious route: "You didn't fall in love. You fell in lust. I'm going to be 42, Flips. You're still in your 20s." I can see that she wants to protest; but instead she just holds my hand tighter. "One day you'll meet some pretty young thing who reads O. Henry too, and you'll see the difference. What we had last night was fabulous. Let's just keep it at that, OK? I don't mind being one of your conquests."

"Why would I conquer what I want to embrace?" She releases my hand and grabs hold of my heart. "I don't care how old you are—you can't tell me what I'm feeling when you won't even accept what you're feeling. I love you, and you love me, but I won't beg, J. Life's too short."

My mind attempts to grasp what Flips has just said, when suddenly we're interrupted. "Dr. Waterman. It's so nice to see you again. Did you get Jessica's card? She was so happy when you told her she could play soccer again."

"Mrs. Abrito, hello." Flips stands to shake the woman's hand. "Tell Jessica thank you for the card and to keep up the hard work. If she sticks to her exercise routine she shouldn't have any problems with that knee."

"I certainly will. I can see you're busy, so I'll let you be. Have the potato pancakes; they're wonderful. Bye." When the woman leaves, my mind is still processing what she said. *Dr. Waterman?*

"Wow, it's weird hearing someone call you "doctor." I'm

impressed. I still see you as that cute, cocky soccer goddess."
What I thought would be an opening for lighter conversation
becomes an opportunity for Flips to cut and run.

"And you always will, J. That's our problem. I've grown
up, and you've grown cautious." She leans over and kisses me
softly on the lips. "So I guess we'll do it your way. Goodbye."

I watch as she walks out the door, doing my best to convince myself that this is for the best. *Well, you got what you
wanted. No strings attached, remember?* I take the long way
back to Sebastian's.

My sleep is restless. I keep waking up before I can dream,
afraid my subconscious might give me answers I don't want
to hear. I spend all night and most of this morning making
pro and con lists: all the reasons Flips and I should get
involved and all the reasons Flips and I shouldn't get
involved. Time after time the cons win, and yet I can't stop
making the lists. This is ludicrous, I decide. I write Sebastian
a thank you note and lock the door behind me. The cab ride
to O'Hare is scary, but I make it there with just enough time
to stand in line for an hour to have my bags checked. Every
time I see someone with thick black hair I turn. Maybe it's
just fallout from sleeping in Sebastian's Hollywood Hotel that
has me looking for Flips—just like in the movies. The hero
appears right before you get on the plane, or the hero stops
the plane by driving a bus in front of it, or—better yet—when
you take your seat you find that the seat directly in front of
you is occupied by your soul mate. Of course, the guy next to
you sees how in love you are and gives up his seat, and you
all live happily ever after.

The gate to the jetway closes behind me, and there's still
no sign of Flips. The flight attendant hurries me to my seat
and helps me with my carry-on. The pilot announces that
we'll be landing in Miami in approximately three hours. I
decide to try and get some sleep, but only after I'm sure the
plane has left the ground and the the seat in front of me is still

not occupied by a cranky toddler. Sleep evades me and Tennyson taunts me: "It is better to have loved and lost than never to have loved at all." I question whether my decision to keep my heart safe was a wise one. I question why, if my heart is so safe, does it hurt so much? Why, if I made the right decision, am I kicking myself now? "Life is nothing without risk," I say aloud, scaring the lady next to me. The peanut gallery in the back of my brain gets up and cheers. I make up my mind to put my heart at rest—or at risk, whichever, I don't care. Love is the food of life, my *abuela* always said.

I decide to take the next flight back to Chicago, and my head spins with the idea of allowing myself to feel love again—and to feel Flips again. That is, if she'll have me. It is, after all, a woman's prerogative to change her mind. For the remainder of the flight I worry. I worry that there won't be any more flights to Chicago today. I worry that when I get back I won't have the words. I worry that Flips will be cohabiting with a candy-striper. I worry that I'll get hit by a taxi and be paralyzed because I was looking up at the Sears Tower.

I am in such a hurry when the plane touches down that I have to hurdle two senior citizens and a baby stroller to avoid collisions. I can't decide whether to get my bags or my tickets first. Ahead of me the crowd waits for the passengers to come out. I'm not expecting anyone and I see the crowd as a deterrent to my mission. I turn my shoulder to slide past the guy in front of me. I see an opening between two soldiers and their duffel bags and I take it, disrupting a mother and child reunion in the process.

"What's your hurry?" I hear someone behind me say.

If you only knew, I think, *you wouldn't ask*. I want to tell this person, "I'm in love, that's my hurry. I'm trying to get back to Chicago to tell her, that's my hurry. I'm a fool, that's my hurry." Just as I turn to proclaim my justifications, all the change in the jacket I'm carrying falls out. I stoop to start collecting and miss the opportunity to share with the world—or at least with the person behind me—what I'm feeling. I reach for another quarter that has landed near a pair of white Converse high-tops.

"What took you so long?" It is the same voice that asked what my hurry was. It's a familiar voice. I look up, and there she is. Just like in the movies.

"How the hell did you get here?" I ask from my stooped position, trying hard not to give away the fact that my knees don't work like they used to.

"Mommy's a pilot, remember?" She offers her hand to assist me. "Let's go home."

"Oh, you think it's that easy?"

"No, I just think I'm that lucky."

I wrap my arm around her waist to pull her close, not willing to let her go again. "Let's go. I've got to call my mother and tell her I'm dating a doctor before the rates go up."

AIRPORT

Melissa Walker

The sky is denim, 6 A.M. I have your body cradled in my arms,
feeling its cool touch against my hips. Your smell of passion,
of sweat, of the strawberry ice cream you had after dinner.
Stupid industrial city. I am fabricating a net like a spider. It is
not even cold, the air conditioner barely keeping up with my
speed. I leave the bed, slowly, not to wake you. I want you
sleeping, quiet, semidead, semiconscious.

I walk to the window. Life is underfoot—people slowly
recovering their insanity. I don't know what city this is, or
what country. We have been traveling too much, and I decide
we need to settle down, buy a house, build a fence, get a dog.
I don't want to be a nomad anymore. My feet are cemented
in your heart, in your arms, in your body—penetration that
goes beyond gender. I sit naked by the window, my skin glued
to the cheap brown leather that makes this chair. You move.
I stop. Inertia not to create sparkles. I hear you sighing and
changing sides in bed, looking for your spot in this cheap
motel room. Distant from me, you sleep, dreaming of a date
with a complete stranger. I smile, because it can be me. I

cannot turn my head to see your smile or the flowery sheets. It is 6:18 A.M. I believe it to be Sunday.

The last time I checked the calendar, we were crossing Tennessee. You were singing, looking out the window, and you did not see me crying. Your hair thrown to the wind, your jeans dusty—we have been traveling too much. You had your bare feet laid on the board, your right hand caressing the wind, and the radio was so loud. I did not know you know Mary Chapin Carpenter. But you sang out loud, while I cried, the tears evaporating before peeking out from under my glasses. Damn car, we need to fix the air conditioner.

You turned your head to me and laughed because I was still wearing that stupid hat you made me buy in New Orleans. I turned to you and laughed, because you still wore my tattoo and your smile. No one around us. We are the only kind of semilife in a range of miles.

"I am thirsty."

"I cannot see any stores, you will have to wait."

"What happened to the Gatorade?"

"I drank it all the last time we stopped."

You shook your head and looked outside again, and I wondered if your eyes do not like what they see inside the car anymore. Your hand reached for my leg; I was wrong again.

"Do you think brandy will quench my thirst?"

"You might aggravate your ulcer. Besides, we don't have any brandy."

"It was just a thought."

You think a lot. That is why I love you.

In the hotel now I watch the train going by. Remind me never to get a second-floor room again. I want to stick to the ground I know. Your body. Your labia. You move in bed and part your legs knowingly, ever-so-wisely. I smile. The phone rings.

"It's 6:30. You asked me to wake you up?"

"Thanks."

"Breakfast is opened, in the room close to the pool."

"I didn't know we had a pool."

I stand watching you, your eyelids closed, and I am thirsty. I reach for the bottle of brandy, feeling it burning down my throat. Half-drunk. Completely satisfied. I hope you can repeat what you did last night some other day when I cannot feel or ache. I reach for you; I want to touch your back, the morning shadow playing tricks on your marble skin. You stretch. I retract my hand. Your voice is husky.

"What time is it?"

"6:30. Go back to sleep."

"I thought we were leaving early."

"I want to stay a little longer."

You roll back, exposing your ass, making something sparkle in me. I drown it in one more sip of brandy. I hate it when you turn me into this, a vicious lesbian who cannot keep her hands away from a pussy. A bull dyke pimping you around—I hate it when I pimp you around. I hate it when you make me feel this butch, when you are this vulnerable, this innocent, when I am half-drunk and awake. I hate it when you make me think of the box of toys we have back home: Legos and multicolored dildos. I hate to feel this lascivious. I blame it on you, and when I tell you this you shake your head laughing, because you know it is all about me. Everything is all about me with me. And with you. And I hate to have you this subservient, even more in moments like this when I need you so bad, when I want you to hold me close and let me be sick.

More brandy.

Approaching the window, the world outside becoming even farther away from me, I watch as people pass by, tired and sleepy faces, not many cars. I can see the whole town from this window, the whole country. There is not even a lake around here, I will have to swim in your eyes. I want to go swimming, but I don't trust that pool. We need to find a lake, a beautiful one. Later, you will tell me we cannot just swim naked in the first lake we find. I will hate you for that.

I feel like nothing, like crumpled paper in a basket case, discarded poetry, used Post-it note, like trash. I light up a cigarette, easing the burn from the brandy with the ailment of the smoke. You get fussy in bed, rubbing your nose. I cannot open this window, it is stuck or locked. I put the cigarette down in an anxious movement, filling up the ashtray even more. I take a look at the paper beside it, my calligraphy, our pain, the last words scribbled in a way I know I lost them forever, because I had you sucking me while I traced them. I was trying to write us a love story, I was trying to make it beautiful, I was trying to throw poetry into your body, but you sucked it out of mine. Back then I did not mind; I did not mind at all. I take the pencil in my hand, the graphite not as sharp as I want it to be, blunt blade effortlessly cutting this paper, sugar pills for Valium in this pretend suicide. I pace around the rooms in my head, ignoring locked doors, falling into common places, plunging down a river, touching the ground, emerging in need for air to find your mouth over mine, saliva sweet as honey, bitter as you are. I run your taste off with brandy. I cannot do you tonight.

"How long until we get home?"
"I don't know."
You pass me by, not knowing I have no home, not knowing I do not know you, not knowing we are strangers. I hear the click in the bathroom door, and the way you turn on the faucet. You are ready for a bath. You come back in the room, go through the pile of clothes on the floor. I think you say something about needing to wash your jeans. I think I reply that it doesn't make any difference—they'd only get dirty again.

"It's the fucking air conditioner. We have to keep the window open or we'll bake. Too much dust."

I shake my head, agreeing. You lock yourself in the bathroom again. I pretend I am writing, but the sound of the water touched by your body, the smell of the cheap soap, the sight of your eyes closed take over my head. I put the pencil down and light a cigarette up. Outside, the day has just started. I miss your hand in mine, the butterflies, the novelty. I miss the nation of your mind, the feeling of home in your heart. You don't know this yet, but I am exiling myself from you. I think I wanted to be punished. Later, you will say I am turning into a submissive dominatrix. I will tell you to go to hell.

"I am starving."

"Breakfast is in the room close to the pool."

"I didn't know they have a pool."

"They do. It's next to the breakfast room."

"We don't have suits anyway."

"We could go naked—I don't think they'd mind."

You turn your head to me, bend, putting on your jeans. Your legs disappearing into the denim of the sky, to be devoured later by dust, by red dust, by the red of my eyes. I look outside, I look east, and I wonder if we should have taken a plane. But you told me you like to drive, and off we went. I thought we were going to have fun. The past nine days, though, nothingness. All I have is you. We keep on forgetting to get a camera. I have you, and the stupid hat you made me buy in New Orleans. I love you for that.

You kneel next to me, resting your head in my breasts. I wrap you up to go, your blond hair caressing my brown nipples, your breath removing the air from inside my lungs.

"Are you coming?"

"I'm not hungry. I'm feeling sick."

"You didn't sleep at all, did you?" I shake my head. "I'll bring you some coffee."

I see as you leave the room, closing the door not to let me out. Captive, a prisoner inside the walls of this hotel room. I miss your body so much I feel pain coming, and tears coming, and I want to pretend you went to India, and I write, I write, I write, I write… When you come back to the room, a cup of coffee in hand, you find me crying, still naked, lying in bed because I needed your scent. I needed your touch. You sit next to me and bring me into the cabin by your arms; I'm surrounded by the marble pillars of your arms. We change places. We swap roles.

"Why didn't you tell me you needed to cry?"

"Because you would have stayed."

I feel your eyes down my soul, searching for my spirits, and you find blood, and guts, and the strawberry ice cream we ate after dinner last night. You dry my tears with your mouth.

"I love you."

I shake my head, my eyes glued to the gray sky now. Fucking industrial city. Pollution inside my head.

"I know. Just don't love me too much."

MY HEART IN HER HAND

Amie M. Evans

She held my heart in her hand. I could see it beating in a regular rhythm. I had hoped, at the very least, it would be pounding—hard and fast. But no. It was beating rather normally. *Beat. Pause. Beat. Pause.* Almost as if it didn't know it was no longer connected to its owner—*my* body—didn't care it wasn't a part of an interdependent relationship, a fine-tuned system in which each separate unit relies on the others to continue functioning. No, my heart seemed to be oblivious to the fact that she'd ripped it out of my chest—leaving a large gaping hole—held it in one of her hands as if it were a blue-ribbon-winning cat, for all the world to see. My heart seemed to be getting along just fine without me. *Beat. Pause. Beat. Pause.*

My mind knew in an abstract, academic way that my heart had been torn from my body. It briefly pondered the fact, and then adjusted system controls to function without the heart. My mind, in all honesty, was never exactly sure what purpose the heart served to the body as a whole. It viewed the heart as a weak link, and in hindsight, perhaps my mind was correct.

So the adjustments to bypass the heart, for my mind at least, were easy, quick. I cannot say the same for the rest of me. It had been, after all, a relatively painless extraction. So much so that my mind had been unaware the operation was even underway until my eyes actually saw her standing there with my heart in her hand. *Beat. Pause. Beat. Pause.*

I was surprised at its actual size. I hadn't realized it was so large or that it would leave such a big hole if removed. Not that I had ever considered the possibility of it being removed, since, as I understood it, my heart belonged to me. I'd planned very carefully not to get rid of it. I'd also taken extreme measures to prevent anyone from getting too close to it. Although very strong, it was also very fragile if handled incorrectly. I didn't want to have it broken again. Repairing it the first time was hard enough, and insurance was too expensive. It looked like any other heart—a reddish blue-purple in color, with thick, almost white muscle masses; openings to move blood in and others to move blood out. Which, I might add, it seemed to be doing just fine in her hand—my heart, that is, moving blood. *Beat. Pause. Beat. Pause.*

My heart had betrayed me. Worst of all, it hadn't even bothered to give me a clue, a sign, a hint that it was thinking about betrayal. It was a traitor. A mean, malicious, no-good traitor. My heart apparently had been plotting behind my back. It had ideas of its own that it hadn't bothered to share with the group, which was probably a smart move on my heart's part, since the group would have rejected any plan that involved giving it away to anyone—especially to Ms. I-Need-More-Space.

But I am ahead of my story. Let me start at the beginning, before my heart went freelance, before this woman with the piercing blue eyes reached into my chest and pulled it out. Back then, things were simple—really simple—and while maintaining a consistent status quo often created havoc in the lesser organs, the system as a whole worked well. It required very little servicing—just routine adjustments. It had a regular pattern and was predictable—not in a boring way, but in a comfortable I-am-really-good-at-what-I-do-so-anything-you-throw-at-me-I-can-handle kind of way. Aw, but that was before mutiny on the bounty happened and my heart went AWOL with this she-Casanova.

Our first date was like every other first date I've had except she didn't kiss me. She didn't even try to kiss me. Even after I'd taken public transportation to meet her at her job, leaving my house an hour before I would have had to if I'd taken my car, which I didn't do so she'd drive me home and kiss me good night. Nope, no kiss. What's more, she was cocky enough to announce she *would* kiss me but she had a cold sore. Considerate, since who wants to get herpes simplex one from a first date? But it showed she was assuming: 1) I'd let her kiss me; 2) I'd want to be kissed by her; and 3) the kissing was her responsibility. All three facts, of course, turned me on and made me more frustrated than if she had just not kissed me and left it at that.

We went to dinner at an Irish pub; but first, before we went to dinner, she interrogated me: "Drink? Smoke? Eat red meat?" All perfectly innocent questions on the surface, especially when one is trying to figure out where to take a first date—which she hadn't, apparently, done before I showed up—but also deadly lesbian taboos seething with potential trouble, trick questions to the trained eyes—which mine were.

Consider this: 51% of the lesbian population is in rehab for alcohol abuse, 60% is antismoking as part of the scent-sensitivity movement, and 30–70%—no one is actually sure how many—are vegetarians (the difference from the actual and the estimate is lesbians pretending to be vegetarian in order to not appear unsympathetic to animal oppression, but eating meat when alone or with other meat-eaters). Add in the fact that many of my sisters have very thin skin when it comes to the aforementioned issues, and these questions, asked just seconds after only a "hello" has been exchanged, could potentially make or break my getting laid. And, after all, that's what I was doing there—trying to get laid. This was all about sex. I was ready, willing, and able to eat tofu, drink soda, and go without a cigarette until I got home if it meant getting laid. In a nutshell, I would have lied if I'd known what answers she wanted, where she stood on these issues, but I didn't know. I didn't know because, well, I'd barely talked to this woman before.

We'd had one phone conversation that lasted almost, but not quite, 20 minutes, and a follow-up call to confirm the date and time we would meet for dinner. Prior to either of these calls, she had waited on me at the pet store about six times without ever noticing I was actually alive or female. When I walked into that same pet store for our first date, she had no idea who I was. Well, she knew I was coming, but she didn't know who exactly was coming. Anyone could have walked in and announced they were me and she would have believed them. After two weeks of trying to get her attention and purchasing more cat toys than my cats could play with in a lifetime, I'd sent her a red pepper plant with a very forward card and my phone number.

She called.

We made a date, and here I was, standing at the top of the three steps in the entrance of *my* pet store, where I bought *my* cat food, being interrogated on three of the four lesbian deal-breakers without a clue as to how to answer or where else I could buy my cat food if this date were to implode.

So, I told the truth, which worked out since she was actually relieved that I smoked and drank, and while I didn't eat red meat, I didn't care if she did. Bring on the fatted calf; if it means that you'll fuck me, I'll eat it.

She took me to this Irish pub in Boston. OK, she gets an F for originality, but an A for sexual tension. We spent the entire dinner talking around, over, and near without actually addressing the fourth lesbian deal-breaker—sex. More specifically, S/M vs. vanilla sex and antipenetration vs. penetration. There was so much free-floating sexual energy at our table, I didn't care if we *were* in an Irish pub in Boston. She did everything but actually say she was into S/M. She oozed sex. I was sure she'd take me on with the same intense passion she was directing at her food—and at avoiding mention of certain lesbians having problems with some types of sexual activities. The whole time talking about how she was a Scorpio and how scorpions were the astrological sign of sex and death.

Be still my heart. This hot punk dyke was single, had a regular job, was into S/M, and smoked. Not to mention, she had blond hair and blue eyes. What more could I want from a three-month fling? Which is exactly what she was going to be—three months, hot and heavy, four to five times a week. I was new to Boston—there were places I wanted to have sex, sights I hadn't seen, and she was going to be my personal Duck Tour.

She drove me home. We sat in her car. Silence. Chatter. Silence. I was waiting for *the* kiss. *The* good night kiss, maybe even *the* good night grope. I was waiting. And instead of the kiss, she gives me: "I'd kiss you, but I have a cold sore."

All right, so she threw me off my game by not kissing me, but that was nothing at all compared to what would follow. I called her the next day to tell her I'd had fun and to see if she wanted to meet up that afternoon. This is the point at which I should have said: "This woman is not your typical dyke." In my experience, lesbians get in as many dates as possible as quickly as they can to determine if there is any potential for a possible relationship and, if there isn't, to end the dating process. She, however, expressed a concern that while she'd also had a great time, we'd just seen each other and she couldn't possibly do anything again until next week.

I checked my copy of *The Official Guide to Lesbian Dating* to make sure I hadn't mixed up the call-the-day-after rule. And sure enough, right after rule number 2 (It is acceptable to date your ex's ex once removed) and right before rule number 4 (It is assumed that sex is an indication of commitment unless otherwise clearly stated before the sex occurs.) was rule number 3 (It is expected that you call the day after the first date to set up the second date, if the second date was not prearranged at the end of the first date). It was clear to me that I had followed the rules and that no date had been prearranged. What wasn't clear to me was whether maybe, just maybe, this dyke didn't have the rule book.

Our second date—one week after our first date—was uneventful, more of the same. I arranged for our third date to be at my apartment—two and a half weeks after our first date, and one and a half weeks after our second date. I planned everything to get that kiss and, more important, to be able to say "no" to her sexual advances. I packed my roommate off to her girlfriend's for the evening; I left my bedroom—which was located off the kitchen—door open, lights dimmed, bed made, candles burning; and I didn't wear the dress I'd planned on wearing because my roommate insisted it would make me look like Betty Crocker. Instead I wore jeans and a T-shirt. I looked like a good dyke. I made my grandmother's rosemary chicken with warm-from-the-oven sourdough bread and fancy salad. We ate by candlelight. I played blues. Not just any blues, but Betsy Smith—hot, sultry, sexy blues. I didn't make her do the dishes after dinner. For this I got a hug. A hug! She didn't even try to cop a feel while she was giving it to me. Her hands stayed on my upper back the whole time. As far as I was concerned, her hug might as well have been a handshake.

A good portion of our three months was gone and she hadn't even kissed me—hadn't even tried to kiss me, much less tried to get into my pants. By this time I've normally said "no" for a week and a half to sexual advances before starting in on the nonstop fucking. What was she doing? Was she crazy? Who the hell did she think she was?

By our fourth date, I was back on my game—or at least I thought I was. What normally took me 15 minutes to figure out had taken me three dates—three weeks. She was good, but I was better. Well, actually, it was an accident that allowed me to figure it out. The *it* would be: "How do I get this woman to need me more than she needs to breathe; how do I make myself something she must have in an obsessive way; and how do I get her to want to see me so much she'll come when I call—no matter what—for at least three months?"

I showed up at the knock on my door in a vintage blue taffeta dress—off the shoulders—with a rhinestone brooch at my cleavage and combat boots. I have to admit, I actually thought this would be our last date. I was sure she wasn't interested and the dress would be the final straw. It would push her from "not interested" to "I never want to see this woman again." At this point, I didn't care if it was our last date. I couldn't figure out what was wrong with her; but if she wasn't going to be a good dyke and try to get into my pants, I wasn't going to be a good dyke and wear them.

She drove. We went to the same Irish pub. I was anxious, a little afraid to look at her; after all, dykes don't normally wear blue taffeta to Irish pubs. We ordered. Our beers came. I tentatively looked up at her, certain she'd have that "How do I end this date fast?" look on her face. She squirmed in her seat as she told me how good I looked. Her eyes sparkled as they flashed from the table to me sneaking looks.

Click. I felt it. I heard it. In fact, I could smell it. That free-floating sexual tension had pulled itself together and was focusing itself in one concentrated beam in the area of my brooch.

Yes. Yes, there was interest. Yes, there was still hope that I'd get laid by this hot little pet store number. I decided at that moment to restart the three-month time limit, reclaiming in high-femme tradition the month we'd lost to her standoffishness and my dyke denim. I also made a note to wear more dresses with this dyke.

Back at my cleared-of-roommate apartment, we stood in my bedroom and chatted. I could feel the moisture collecting in my panties. I could feel the electric charge in the air. I was still planning on saying "no" to sex, if she ever got around to kissing me, that is. I leaned against the wall, titled my head to the side—but she still didn't kiss me. I squirmed. I leaned closer to her as she leaned against my dresser. Nothing. Both of us avoided the bed like it wasn't the only piece of furniture in the room designed for sitting. Then after one and a half hours of sexually charged conversation, she announced she had to leave.

I walked her to the door, and as my foot hit the last step in the common area she turned to give me what I was sure would be another good night hug. Her lips were on mine and her tongue was in my mouth before I knew what was going on, before my brain had time to register that she was finally giving me *the* good night kiss I'd been waiting for. She'd sucked the air out of me, shocked, and surprised me in a pleasant way. Her teeth bit with just the right amount of pressure in my neck, sending tingles down my spine. Then I was standing by myself—a free agent, disoriented, confused, staring at her like a schoolgirl. I hadn't even kissed her back. I suggested setting up the next date right then.

That's when I got the verbal warning.

I'd freaked her out by calling her too soon after our first date. Freaked her out? I was beginning to think moving to Boston had been a huge mistake. This was our fourth date and she hadn't even tried to get into my pants. Who exactly had the right in this situation to be freaked out? Not her, I was sure.

She only wanted to date and too many lesbians didn't understand what dating meant. I couldn't agree more. Dating was all I was interested in, but what I wanted to know was did her definition of dating include sex?

She was not interested in a "relationship." Who said anything about a relationship? I have a relationship with my cat, my ex, and my dentist. All I wanted from her was sex and someone to open the car door. And opening the car door was optional.

She needed space, lots of space. She didn't even see her friends more than once a week. Who cares about how often she sees her friends, her friends didn't want to have rough sex with her for three months before cutting her loose again.

She finally kissed me and now she needed more space.

I could accommodate her.

I'll show her freaked out.

I instituted what my roommate and I would lovingly refer to as "the Asshole Plan." The Asshole Plan, commemorated by the fancy divider from her Turkish Delight cigarette pack, enhanced with the words "The Brand Assholes Smoke" written in black marker and displayed for almost two weeks on my refrigerator, consisted of me not calling her at all—ever again. I waited ten days for her to call me.

Which was fine; I had the pieces of a friendship with a 23-year-old, and I toyed with the idea of sleeping with her to put it back in order, and I had three other woman to date—one of whom I was actually having sex with and two others with strong potential for the three-month program.

By the tenth day I announced I was no longer taking phone calls from anyone—especially Ms. I-Need-More-Space.

I was obsessed, beside myself, consumed. My roommate, who in traditional high lesbian dysfunction was one of my ex-lovers, started making up lyrics to popular songs about Ms. Brand-Assholes-Smoke and singing them nonstop around the house. She was overjoyed to see me flopping about like a fish out of water. I should have clued in to the fact that any woman *not* dating my ex, yet giving her so much pleasure, was more than likely going to be trouble for me. I should have bailed on this one right then and there, but no, the unit was on overload and only absolutely necessary systems were functioning. I had no time to analyze what was going on. I was too busy masturbating to Blue Eyes's image, trying to act like I didn't care if she ever called me again, like I hadn't been marking the days on my calendar with red ink.

All right, so this casual sex relationship was like no other I'd ever had. I am not the chaser; I am the chase. I do not sit at home wondering where the hell she is and why she hasn't called. I do not wait. I do not long for sexual contact. I am the sayer of "no," the stopper of sex. I am the tease. I am the builder of tension.

She'd completely thrown *me* off my game. *My* game. She was playing me, and I think she was really enjoying it. It was, I admit, a new kind of challenge. I had to come up with all kinds of new skills and tactics to deal with the twists and turns she put in my path. This, or she, kept my undivided attention and, I have to admit, her verbal warning made me want her more than I'd ever wanted anyone. She felt like a puzzle I had not yet encountered, much less solved.

Then she called, inviting me over to her house. Her housemates, she informed me, were away. The plan was I'd meet her at her house Friday at 7:15 P.M. and we'd go to dinner. I packed a small bag of essentials, including clothes for the next morning, and put it in the truck of my car. A girl can never be too prepared. I arrived at 7:15 P.M. She arrived at 7:17 P.M. She jumped from her car into mine and we went to dinner at the same Irish pub as before. I drove. I got a good night kiss, and I never even saw the inside of her house.

I called on Saturday while she was at work and left a message: "Don't be freaked out, since Sunday is actually the start of the new week, perhaps I can come over with a pizza and watch wrestling with you and your dog."

Yes, wrestling. She was a big wrestling fan. I'd done more trying things than watch "professional" wrestling with a dog in order to get laid. This would be easy. Something she hadn't been since the beginning.

She called back and agreed.

I showed up with a large pizza and a six-pack of beer in hand. Dressed in a cute, short flared dress that "puffed" when I sat down—the overnight bag still in the trunk of my car—I was certain tonight would be the night. In the living room there was a TV, a sofa, and a huge pit bull. I determined the sofa was long enough for us to lie down on and the dog could be sent into the other room and locked out. It was perfect.

We ate as we chatted about our days. Her feet up on the coffee table, her arms crossed with her thumbs hooked under her arms, she looked good enough to eat. She slipped her arm around me. She smelled like spices and myrrh. Her tongue was soft and warm in my mouth, her hands firm on my shoulders as she pulled me into her.

Did you know there is a story line in professional wrestling? Neither did I. There are characters with complex histories and enemies and allies. Yes, we watched wrestling and then she sent me home, but not before we sprawled out on the sofa, her on top of me, and made out. She did manage to grope my breasts and push her leg hard between mine, creating a pleasant friction. But nonetheless, I was sent home wet and wanting. Something about her nose running.

I should have known things weren't what they seemed when my 25-year-old girl-toy turned out to be a 42-year-old homeowner. But I never pay attention to warnings until it's too late. She was charming in her nontraditional approach to dating, and I was starting to grow fond of her nerdy qualities. She knew the Latin names of lizards. I usually referred to them as simply "look at the [insert color] lizard." I had no idea that they had names in Latin as well as English, or that anyone outside of a lizard farm would know these names. I was also growing attached to the idea that I was really dating a 13-year-old boy with breasts. She gave her dog beer while they watched "professional" wrestling and ate popcorn together on the sofa. But it was clear to me that she was a mature adult. She was giving off increasing levels of sexual energy and she actually knew who both Patrick Califia *and* Andrea Dworkin were. She was wise and sly and completely unaware of what she was doing to me with her baby blues and her inaccessibility. Or was she?

I think the first clear sign came in early February, but I ignored it or—more correctly—refused to acknowledge it. We'd progressed into seeing each other three or four times a week, although never two days in a row. We started the traditional sleeping over two nights a week, and sex was great. If I'd paid attention I would have realized that she'd done it. Somehow when I wasn't looking she'd captured my heart. Now she's got it. I can only hope she takes good care of it. I can hear it. *Beat. Pause. Beat. Pause.*

Reunion

Juliet Sarkessian

Judith, she practiced in her head, *I want to thank you for saving my life.* Alicia wondered if she still called herself Judith. Maybe these days she went by Judy, although it did not suit her as well. A lot about a person can change in ten years, though, a name being the least of it.

As Alicia's plane approached Newark airport, the dingy air grew thicker until it was almost a fog. The flight from Boston was a short one. Nevertheless, she wouldn't have taken it if she had not seen Judith's name among those classmates who were signed up for the reunion "festivities." Alicia had missed the first reunion five years back, having no reason to return to the scene of so many unpleasant memories. This time, though, she had a reason.

The image of Judith came back to her, as vivid as if she had seen her yesterday: kohl smudged thickly around the eyes, soft breasts bouncing under a thin peasant blouse, hips swinging, skirt swirling as she passed. Alicia could almost hear the click of Judith's thick high-heeled boots against the wood floor of the school hall.

Judith was a transfer student, the only one in the senior class of their suburban New Jersey high school. As "fresh meat," she was a popular topic of the boys' conversations, bits and pieces of which Alicia had overheard in passing. More than one boy claimed to have "done" her. Alicia didn't know if their stories were true. She had seen the way Judith acted with boys, and the way she looked at them. Inviting, but with a warning behind that teasing smile. Alicia could imagine Judith punching a guy if he went too far. She rather liked the image and played it over and over in her head. Punch, punch, and the guy would fall backward to the ground with a thud. Judith would walk away triumphant, stepping over the body with a contemptuous backward glance.

There was another Judith who had played a role in Alicia's life, although that Judith only existed in a picture book. When she was eight, Alicia had come upon a reproduction of *Judith and Her Maidservant* by Artemisia Gentileschi. Alicia was fascinated by this portrait of two robust women who seemed to be on a secret mission. It was dark, and they stood close together, their faces turned sharply to the right, as if they had been interrupted by footsteps. Alicia had wondered what they were planning. Then she saw the straw basket one of the women held in the crook of her arm. In it was the severed head of a man, nearly obscured by shadows. The women must have killed him. Alicia knew killing was wrong, but she figured this had to be an exception. The man was clearly bad. The women were strong and brave. All this she knew from looking at the painting. It was then Alicia decided she wanted to be an artist.

Fortunately, Alicia had talent, and by the time she reached high school she was spending all her free time in the art room. It was there she met Judith, a sculptor who favored slim and elegant figures in contemplative poses. One afternoon they were alone in the art room together—Alicia working on an abstract still life, Judith at the sculptor's wheel shaping a lump of clay into the bust of a child. Alicia's eyes dropped to Judith's thighs, which strained against the canvas of her worn army pants as she sat on the stool. It was hard not to look. Everything about Judith screamed "sex," at least for Alicia. Alicia had known she was gay since she was 13. Even before that she had a crush on Elizabeth Montgomery and would race home every day to watch ancient reruns of *Bewitched*. She'd also had a special friend in fifth grade. They'd hold hands walking home and cuddle during sleep-overs. As she entered puberty, her crushes became more romantic. Perhaps because of that, she found herself shying away from friendships with most other girls. When she was younger she had gotten on well with boys, but now they wanted too much from her, so she stayed away from them too. It was not her choice to be a loner, but that's how it ended up. Sometimes she thought it would be better if she told people she was gay, but she didn't want to scare off the few friends she had. *I'll bet I could tell Judith,* she thought. Judith seemed cool about everything.

"Shit!" Judith shouted, startling Alicia from her reverie. Judith sprang from her chair and dashed to the kiln in the back room. A moment later she returned, holding a small, pale-green female nude. The figure was in a reclining position, her head resting on an outstretched arm.

"It's beautiful," Alicia said timidly.

Judith sat behind the sculptor's wheel with a grumpy sigh and looked disdainfully at the figure. "Her boobs are way too big. She looks ridiculous, like a Playboy bunny. And the color is wrong. Left it in the kiln too long."

"I think it's great. It's the color of my room." Alicia regretted the words the moment they left her mouth. Surely Judith didn't care about the color of her room.

Judith smiled sweetly, her bow-shaped mouth the color of a June plum. "Take it then," she offered, extending the figure toward Alicia. "To match your room."

Alicia approached hesitantly. "Thanks."

"I see why you like green." Judith tossed her head back, shaking the long, golden-brown hair from her shoulder. Her dangling silver earrings tinkled like small wind chimes. "Your eyes. They're the color of emeralds. How unusual."

Alicia felt her cheeks turn hot. Judith seemed to be flirting, but was that possible? Alicia mumbled another "thank you," and went back to her seat.

That night, while getting ready for bed, Alicia replayed her conversation with Judith. She tried to focus on what Judith had said about her eyes, tossed off in that seductively mellow tone. No one had ever complimented her before, except her parents, and that didn't count. Alicia looked at her reflection in the mirror over her dresser. Maybe her eyes were kind of pretty, but what about the rest of her? She looked at the little clay woman, which now rested on her dresser. Its shape bore an uncanny resemblance to Alicia's. Judith had said the woman looked ridiculous. Did that mean Alicia looked ridiculous? But Judith had also said the figure looked like a Playboy bunny, and weren't they supposed to be attractive? It was all so confusing. Alicia had received so many conflicting messages about what kind of breasts were desirable. "The French believe the perfect-size breast fits in a wine glass," she had read in one fashion magazine. There was no need to break into her parents' liquor cabinet to know she did not meet that standard. On the other hand, so many actresses and models were getting implants. Yet those fake breasts—unnaturally high and bouncy—didn't look like Alicia's. Hers were torpedo-shaped and hung low on her chest. But maybe some people found that attractive. Alicia had no way of knowing, as she had never been naked around anyone. The best she could hope for was that when it did happen, it would be OK.

The following day, Alicia took her baby-sitting money and went shopping. Usually she didn't care about what she wore, but Judith's "Playboy" comment had made her sensitive. She tried on a number of loose shirts, hoping to disguise her figure, but they only made her look pregnant. Eventually she decided on a couple of tunic-length sweaters, she and wore one to school the next day. "Neat sweater," Judith commented casually when they saw each other in the art room. "You should wear it to Joe Butterfield's party this weekend. "

Alicia made a noncommittal sound.

"You're coming, right?"

"Maybe," Alicia answered.

"Come on. It'll be fun."

Alicia rarely went to parties, especially those given by the popular crowd. They always made her feel uncomfortable, since she didn't fit in with any of the school cliques. But if Judith was going, she would too. She had already been invited by Orrie, a dorky guy who had a crush on her. Ordinarily she wouldn't have gone with him, but he had a car. The drive there was awkward. Orrie was making small talk. Alicia responded enough to seem polite but not encouraging. As soon as they arrived, Alicia ditched him to look for Judith. Dozens of kids stood on the front lawn, milling around a keg. Inside the music was blasting, but no one was dancing. Dopers lay sprawled on couches and the rug, eyes half closed, cigarettes dangling from their grimy fingers. The parents must have been away, because Alicia couldn't imagine any adult allowing this.

Alicia found Judith over by the stereo, flipping through a stack of cassettes. She looked great in a burgundy thrift-store blazer and black velvet jeans. "You're here!" Judith exclaimed, letting the tapes scatter on the table. "Let's go outside." Judith grabbed her hand. Mesmerized, Alicia followed, thinking, *She's holding my hand. I can't believe she's holding my hand.*

They joined the kids around the keg. "Do you want a beer?" Judith asked as she let Alicia's hand drop.

Alicia nodded and they approached the two guys guarding

the keg. From the way they were stumbling around, it seemed like they had drunk most of it themselves.

"Hey, girls," said one of them with a leer, "give us a kiss and we'll give you a glass."

Judith smiled. "Give us a glass and we won't tell everyone we saw you behind the house sucking each other's dicks."

As she and Judith walked away, Alicia began to giggle. "Did you really see them do that?"

"Shit, no." Judith took a sip of her beer. "I just love to watch them squirm." Now Judith giggled too, sending beer foam up her nose. That made both of them laugh harder. "Come on," Judith said once they settled down. "Let's find some weed."

Alicia didn't really smoke pot. She had tried it a few times, but all it did was make her cough. Nevertheless, she followed Judith, not wanting to break the gossamer thread that now connected them.

There was a group of kids standing in a semicircle in front of a tree, passing a joint. Judith stepped into the circle, with Alicia tagging behind. When the joint reached them, Judith took a long toke, then offered the crumpled roach to Alicia. She shook her head. Judith raised an eyebrow in surprise, then passed the stub along to the next person. After that, no one paid attention to Alicia. She hung back from the crowd, shadowing Judith. Hunched in her coat, she watched ghostly clouds of frozen breath escape from the mouths of her classmates. Obscured by the night, she felt safe and empowered by her invisibility. This, together with the buzz from the beer, gave her the courage to reach out and touch Judith's leg. She was prepared to drop her hand immediately if Judith reacted negatively, but she didn't. She didn't react at all. Alicia began to caress the side of Judith's velvet-encased thigh, first with her fingertips, then with her whole palm. It was the first time Alicia had touched another girl. It felt like a miracle.

Judith didn't look at Alicia or talk to her while this was

happening, but when the group broke up Judith took her into the woods behind the house. They stood close, facing each other, not saying anything. The only sound was the crunch of dead leaves under Alicia's feet as she shifted her weight nervously from one leg to the other. She wasn't sure what was going to happen until Judith leaned forward and kissed her. Alicia had been kissed by a boy before, but it was nothing like this. Judith's mouth was the softest, warmest thing Alicia could imagine. And unlike the boy, who had rammed his thick, clumsy tongue against hers, Judith only let the tip of hers slip between Alicia's lips. That little tongue in Alicia's mouth made her want so much more. Not just more of Judith, but more of life.

Judith unbuttoned her blouse. The white, gauzy material fell away to reveal breasts that were creamy, firm, and perfectly round. There was no doubt they would fit in a wine glass. Alicia was surprised and flattered that Judith would expose her tender flesh to the cold just for her. She wanted to make Judith warm, to cover her breasts with her hands, but her hands were too cold. So she put her mouth on one. Everything after that was a blur. She did not remember when they stopped, how they parted, or how she got home. What she did remember was lying in bed that night feeling she had discovered a world more fantastic than any she had read about as a child. *So,* she thought, *this is what adults have been hiding. This is the big secret.* It wasn't about doing something messy and unpleasant in the back of a car. It was about the sensuousness of lips, and thighs, and breasts, and the wonder of finding someone who wanted to share those things with you.

For the next two weeks, Alicia lived in paradise. Every day after school, she and Judith would meet in a recessed doorway at the back of the gym and make out for what seemed like an eternity but was never long enough for Alicia. They had to jump apart frequently, when they heard voices or other sounds, but that was part of the excitement. It was like riding a roller coaster. Fun, but scary. The most nerve-racking part was not knowing what Judith felt for her. They didn't talk about that kind of stuff. Alicia did notice, though, that Judith acted weird when they were around other people—like there was nothing special between them. Even when they were alone, Judith wasn't as affectionate as Alicia would have liked. Then again, Alicia wasn't sure what she had the right to expect.

One afternoon, Judith suggested they go to her house after school. Alicia readily accepted. Judith lived in a part of town Alicia had never been to. Unlike Alicia's neighborhood of sprawling rancher, here the homes were crowded together, with only a tiny patch of land in front of each. When they entered the house, the first thing Alicia noticed was how low the ceiling was. They came in through the living room, which was furnished with a modest TV, tweedy couch, patched vinyl recliner, and an old stereo on a rickety bookcase. A small, square dining room was overpowered by a large table and china cabinet of dark, scratched wood. Alicia had the feeling the furniture belonged to a dead person. The kitchen was better, modern and bright, though the wallpaper was peeling in one corner. Alicia stood by the entrance as Judith walked up to the stove. "Want some tea?"

"Sure." This was the part Alicia hated. She wanted to put her arms around Judith and kiss her. But Judith was acting like they had never touched and never would.

"Are your parents home?" Alicia asked, even though it was clear they weren't.

"My mom's still at work. My dad lives in Washington."

Oh, divorced—like the parents of everyone else at school. Sometimes it made Alicia feel uncool that *her* parents were still together. But secretly she was glad. "You used to live in Washington, right?" Alicia hoped that if they talked about something personal, it might thaw the chill that had settled between them.

The teapot began to whistle. Judith turned off the gas. "Used to live there, and wish I still did."

Alicia felt like someone had sliced her with a razor. She watched Judith's expression as she took two mugs from an overhead cabinet, placed them on the counter between the stove and sink, and filled them with hot water. Judith seemed completely placid. Perhaps she hadn't intended to hurt Alicia. But Alicia knew she couldn't mean much to Judith if she wished she had never moved here. All of a sudden, Judith jumped back from the counter, her face filled with disgust. "Ewww!"

Alicia approached the counter. "What's the matter?"

"Nothing, nothing," Judith insisted, dumping the contents of the two mugs down the kitchen drain. The tea bags hit the drain with a wet "whap." Floating around them Alicia could see dozens of tiny drowned roaches.

Judith pulled Alicia away from the sink, her face red with embarrassment. "Let's go to my room."

When they got to Judith's room, Alicia wanted to look around, but all she could see was Judith undressing. Alicia didn't know if she was supposed to watch her or avert her eyes, so she did some of both. Her heart thumped as Judith peeled her black leotard to her waist. She hadn't seen Judith's breasts since the night at the party, though she had touched them a bit over her clothes when they made out at school. They were as incredible as Alicia had remembered, perfect in form and color. It would be wonderful to paint her someday. Judith unzipped her pants. When they dropped to the floor, she shimmied out of her leotard, pulling her underpants down with it. Judith sat on the edge of her bed, stark naked. "Come here."

Alicia approached hesitantly, afraid that at any moment Judith might change her mind. As they kissed, Judith took Alicia's hand and pressed it between her thighs. The moment Alicia slipped into Judith, she felt like a drug had been injected into her brain. It was so tight and warm there, and Alicia could feel little pads of muscles all around. Even more intense was the visual image of Judith, gorgeously naked, legs spread, groaning and biting her lip in response to the thrusts of Alicia's finger. Alicia couldn't believe Judith was letting her do this. She knelt and placed her mouth a few inches above her finger, mostly guessing what to do. She must have guessed wrong, because Judith quickly dropped a hand to her head, and said, "Gently, like a cat lapping milk." Alicia did her best, and within a few minutes Judith was squirming and pressing her nails into Alicia's shoulder. Then Alicia felt a powerful muscle contraction. Judith's thighs closed and she pulled away.

Alicia remained where she was, crouched at the edge of Judith's bed. Heat flowed through her body like a river of lava. She wanted Judith to touch her. She rose and took off her T-shirt. Under it was a white satin bra, one she had picked out shyly in a department store with the hope that something like this might happen. She stood expectantly in front of Judith, but all Judith did was bend down and pick up her clothes. "You know, my mom is going to be home soon. But, uh, thanks for coming over."

Alicia went numb. "Did I do something wrong?"

"No, I just didn't realize how late it was." Judith pulled on her clothes hastily. "You should get dressed too," she advised, with a pointed look at Alicia's chest.

Feeling suddenly naked, Alicia fumbled to get her shirt back on. The room smelled like sex. So did Alicia's fingers. She wiped them on her jeans.

"I'll see you tomorrow in school, then?"

"Yeah, sure," Judith replied.

Alicia leaned over to kiss her. Judith accepted the kiss but did not kiss back. Alicia left the bedroom and found her way out of the house.

Alicia missed her bus stop on the way home because she was crying and couldn't see the road. *Why wouldn't she touch me?* she asked herself over and over. But she knew the answer. When she got home, she stripped off her shirt and bra and stood in front of the mirror. Her boobs were "ridiculous," just like those of the little clay woman Judith didn't want. Judith didn't want her either. No one ever would. She picked up the figurine and tossed it in the trash.

After that day, Judith did all she could to avoid Alicia, even rescheduling her time in the art room. When they did cross paths, Judith barely acknowledged her, and they never spoke about what happened. When they graduated later that year, Alicia left New Jersey to attend the Rhode Island School of Design and did not see Judith again.

Despite the brevity of their relationship, Judith's rejection had a lasting impact on Alicia. She panicked at the idea of anyone seeing her naked. Sex was usually manageable, as long as it was in the dark. Morning, though, was a problem. If she woke up first, she'd pull on her shirt. Otherwise, she'd hide her body with the sheet. Of course, she knew her lovers could feel how big she was, but she rationalized that feeling was not as bad as seeing. She tried everything she could to decrease her breast size, to no avail. She lost weight, but she could not lose it there. Minimizer bras were unhealthy and uncomfortable; sports bras were ugly and uncomfortable. Not that anyone complained about the way she looked. One girlfriend, Sidonie, even claimed to like large breasts and lavished quite a bit of attention on Alicia's. When they made love, Alicia would sometimes be lulled into a momentary sense of attractiveness. Then she would see herself in the mirror. It made her want to yell at Sidonie, to call her a liar. But how could she curse her lover for complimenting her? She would simply have to learn to live with the way she looked. There was no other choice.

Then one day another possibility presented itself. Alicia worked in the art department of a trade publication for interior designers. She assisted with the layout of the pages, figuring how to best juxtapose an advertisement for faucets with text on antiquing in Anchorage. Not exactly what she had in mind when she was an art student, but it was (usually) not unpleasant and it paid the rent. Alicia was on friendly terms with most of her coworkers, so when the receptionist, Melissa, returned to the office after a two-week vacation, Alicia stopped by her desk to say hello. The first thing Alicia noticed was that Melissa was wearing a blouse that buttoned down the front. That would not be remarkable for most women, but Melissa had a figure like Alicia's, which virtually ruled out such blouses unless bulging buttons were the look you were going for. The buttons on Melissa's blouse, however, lay perfectly flat. Then Alicia realized why. Where once there were mountains, two tiny hillocks now rested. All week long Alicia was dying to ask Melissa about it. Then, when they were alone in the ladies' room together, she decided to pop the question. "You know, since you came back from vacation you look really great. Did you lose weight or something?"

"Yeah, about 20 pounds off my chest!" Melissa exclaimed enthusiastically.

"But how?"

"The wonders of modern surgery. You go in, they put you under, and within a few weeks you're a new woman. I'm doing things I've never been able to before, like exercising normally. Hell, walking down the street is a completely different experience. I'm full of energy, and I look great!" She smiled, as if pleased at her own lack of modesty. "We're talking boobs of a 16-year-old. Except I didn't look this good at 16."

"Did it hurt?"

"Amazingly not." Melissa paused and in a discreet voice asked, "Is it something you're considering?"

"Oh, I couldn't possibly afford that."

"Insurance will pay for it. Just stress how much back pain you have." Melissa fished a business card out of her pocketbook. "Call my doctor. You won't regret it."

Alicia made an appointment with Dr. Carlin, but she did not expect to be making a decision any time in the near future. Surgery was a serious matter, to be considered carefully over a long period of time. But when the doc, a slim, flat-chested woman in an Armani suit, showed Alicia "before" and "after" pictures, she was sold. After picking out what size she wanted—a nice B cup—Alicia met with the doctor's assistant and set a date. It was as easy as that.

Alicia had a few bouts of uncertainty, but she didn't change her mind, even in the face of her mother's disappointment—"Honey, you have such a lovely figure"—and concerns about scarring. What caused her the most anxiety were the pictures she had to have taken in advance of the surgery, the "before" part of the before and after. Alicia found herself topless in a big room, bright lights pointed at her tits, having to pose in the most inartful positions imaginable. The only way Alicia lived through that humiliation was to tell herself that the medical photographer was used to seeing disfigured bodies. Anyway, it didn't matter if her body disgusted the photographer, because in a few weeks she would be beautiful.

Her mother insisted on flying out for the operation. Alicia told her it wasn't necessary, but she was glad to have the company. Since her relationship with Sidonie had ended over a year ago, she hadn't been involved with anyone. Although she had friends, none were close enough that she could ask them to stay through the surgery. While the operation wasn't supposed to be dangerous, Alicia didn't want to be alone when she woke up. It didn't help matters when the anesthesiologist brought her papers to sign in pre-op acknowledging the risk of death in surgery. Alicia's attempt at levity, "Please try not to kill me," did not elicit even a smile. Following that exchange, Alicia underwent one of the strangest experiences of her life. She had to stand motionless while Dr. Carlin drew big black lines on her breasts with a magic marker. Afterward she was wheeled into the operating room, placed on a table, and hooked up to an IV. She was out before Dr. Carlin even came into the room.

When she woke up in the recovery room, the first thing she did was look down at her chest. Her breasts looked the same. Maybe they were swollen from the surgery. She fell asleep again, and when she woke up she was in her hospital room. Her mother was standing on one side of the bed, holding her hand. Dr. Carlin was seated on the other side. There was another doctor in the room too. Alicia wondered why they were there. Was a boob job such a big deal?

"Alicia, I didn't do the reduction," Dr. Carlin explained in a soothing voice that was a departure from her usual brisk tone.

"Huh?" Alicia asked, still groggy. "Why not?"

"When we opened you up, we found something we hadn't expected." The doctor shifted in the chair. "There was a mass of cells. It turned out to be cancer. But," she added hastily, "it was a small mass, so your prognosis is very good."

Alicia wished she had her glasses. The doctor was blurry and not making any sense. "I don't understand. You just gave me like a hundred exams."

"It was too small to detect manually. But that's good. It means it probably hasn't spread."

Her mom stroked her head. "Everything's going to be fine, honey." Alicia could tell she was trying not to cry.

"But it's gone now, right? You took it out."

"No, we needed your consent first, and we have to do further tests. That's what Dr. Janklow is here for, to talk to you about treatment options."

Treatment options. Fuck. Alicia closed her eyes. The lingering anesthesia made her nauseous and irritable.

"Take them off," she said in a hoarse whisper. "Just take them off."

The morning sun warmed Alicia's face as she sat behind the steering wheel of her parents' car, a thermos of coffee cradled between her legs. The day was bright and clear, reminding her of when, as a child, her parents would drive the family to Sandy Hook, or one of the other shore points, to spend the afternoon at the beach. She was tempted to change her route, blow off the reunion, and head for sand and sea. Other than Judith, there wasn't anyone there she wanted to see. She wasn't even sure she wanted to see Judith. It was more something she felt she had to do.

The first thing she'd do would be to steer Judith away from the crowd so they could speak privately. She'd start with the line she had been practicing. "Judith, I want to thank you for saving my life." Judith would look at her strangely, like she had misheard. After all, how could Judith have saved her life when they hadn't seen each other for ten years? At this point, Alicia would casually take off her jacket, and Judith would see her perky new breasts: small, round, and snug in a cornflower-blue T-shirt. Judith would notice how different they looked but wouldn't comment. No one ever did. Then Alicia would say, "You know the way you treated me, when we were together? How you made me feel ugly and unlovable. At the time, I didn't see any silver lining, but wouldn't you know, there was one." Judith would be feeling pretty uncomfortable by now, unprepared for this. Perhaps Judith would try to fumble some explanation or halfhearted apology, but Alicia would brush it off cheerfully and continue. "You see, you made me hate my body so much that finally, after years of misery, I decided to have it surgically altered." A little melodramatic maybe. She'd have to work on that part. But the next bit was the trickiest, because she was not sure what tone she should adopt. She could play it cavalier, like it was all a big joke: "Due to your inspiration, I went in for a boob job, and guess what? I had cancer. So thanks for playing a part in my early detection plan!" Or she could be more serious: "When they opened me up they found cancer. Because it was early, they were able to get it all. So in an indirect way, you're responsible for me being alive."

Perhaps she would wait and see how Judith acted when they saw each other before deciding which approach to take. Anyway, she had run out of time to work on her speech, having reached her destination. A large banner with the legend "Welcome Class of 1990!" hung from two trees on a suburban lawn. She wasn't crazy about the idea of a cookout—it seemed kind of hokey. It was preferable, though, to the other event scheduled for the weekend, a semiformal dinner and dance. Seeing a bunch of predominantly straight white people jerking around to Top 40 hits from the '80s was more than she could stand.

Alicia parked her car and followed a general din of voices around to the back of the house. A wooden gate opened to a sprawling yard. There were a good number of people there, most of whom she didn't recognize. There were lots of children too, which she hadn't anticipated. She suddenly regretted not bringing Connie, her girlfriend of the past few months. She and Connie were still building their relationship, though, and she hadn't been ready to expose all of her past. Still, it irked Alicia that everyone here would assume she was single. Poor, pitiful Alicia. We always knew she'd end up alone. Of course she could tell them about Connie, but most of them wouldn't understand, or if they did, they'd act repulsed or, worse, titillated. Not that Alicia cared, but sometimes she got bored with educating people. It would be so much easier if she could simply wear a pin that said, "I'm a dyke. Deal with it or keep moving." Of course, she did plan to tell Judith about Connie. Not in an obvious way. Just slip her name into the conversation a few times, casually, until Judith asked who she was. Then Alicia would say, "Oh,

I'm sorry, we've been together so long that I assume everyone knows her. She's my partner." No, that sounds too businesslike. "She's my lover." Romantic, but a little ostentatious. "Girlfriend?" Too sophomoric. "Wife." OK, a huge exaggeration, but it had a nice ring to it. "We have a town house together in Boston, with a yard for our golden retriever. And we just found out Connie's pregnant!" Alicia enjoyed the fantasy, and not only as a way to prove to Judith how happy she was. The idea of permanence had taken on great significance in her life. She knew a relapse was always possible. If that happened, she wanted someone by her side. It was too early to know if Connie would be that someone, but Alicia was hopeful.

Not seeing Judith among the crowd, Alicia walked over to a folding table heavy with soda bottles and poured herself a glass. Nearby people were grilling burgers, hot dogs, and ears of corn, but Alicia was too nervous to eat. She noticed an adjoining table with name tags, arranged in alphabetical order. Judith's tag was there, confirming she had not yet arrived. Alicia's tag was there too. She picked it up, considered wearing it, then returned it to the table. She didn't particularly care if anyone knew who she was, other than Judith, who surely wouldn't need a name tag to recognize her. Scanning the lawn, she saw a few people she remembered and didn't hate. She walked over to where they were standing and joined the conversation. It was the usual stuff. Where are you living, what do you do, married, kids, etc. People moved around in a kind of round robin. One or two new people would approach a group, others would leave. Alicia was surprised to find that most of her classmates, even ones who were jerks in high school, seemed to have turned into decent people.

Almost an hour had passed since Alicia had arrived, and she was becoming anxious. Maybe something had come up at the last minute and Judith had changed her plans. Or maybe she found out that Alicia was going to be there and didn't want to see her. Alicia decided to wait another ten minutes before giving up. Just then Judith appeared at the gate. Alicia recognized her immediately, even though her hair was now much shorter, stopping right below her ears. Following her was a very ordinary, somewhat older man, holding the hand of a small boy. At first, Alicia did not realize the man and boy belonged with Judith. But then Judith stopped to fix the collar of the boy's shirt, and said something to the man.

Alicia was momentarily disoriented. This was Judith's family? But then what had she expected, that Judith would roar in on a motorcycle with some biker chick by her side? Now it all made sense. Judith was straight. It explained why she had acted the way she did. Her lack of desire had nothing to do with Alicia's breasts. It had nothing to do with Alicia at all. Of course, this raised the question of why Judith had become sexually involved with her. Maybe Judith needed someone to admire her, to make her feel wanted. Someone who was safe and couldn't hurt her. Alicia remembered that last day they had been together in Judith's house. Not in the bedroom, but before, in the kitchen. How embarrassed Judith had been about the roaches in the teapot. Judith, always so strong and self-assured, was suddenly vulnerable and scared, the new girl in town desperate for a friend. Maybe that's what she had needed from Alicia. Maybe the sex was purely for Alicia's benefit, the only gift Judith felt she had to give. A new feeling began to grow in Alicia, one she had never had for Judith—compassion. Alicia knew there was nothing left for her to say to Judith. The speech she had been practicing was for a person who didn't exist, at least outside of Alicia's imagination. The same was true for the anger she had been harboring all these years. Silently, she apologized to Judith, then slipped undetected around the outside of the crowd and through the gate. It seemed she would get her day at the beach after all.

Nena Eskridge

Paula ran her hand down the back of her lover's neck and along her spine, sending her into a giggly frenzy.

"Stop," Katherine said, laughing. "That tickles."

"You smell nice," Paula cooed. "Like chocolate." Paula reached up to Katherine's smooth shoulder and flipped her onto her back. Now eye to eye, Paula gave her a long, soft kiss.

Katherine pulled away. "I have to go." Paula put her mouth back on Katherine's, this time parting Katherine's lips with her tongue. Again Katherine broke away. "You're gonna get me fired."

Paula was about to burst at the seams. Her eyes, her mouth, her entire body ached from holding back. She moved down Katherine's body and sucked hungrily on her breast.

Katherine fell back into her pillow. "OK, five more minutes." She took Paula's fingers into her mouth, then moved them to her crotch, parted her lips, and inserted one of Paula's slippery fingers. Paula wiggled around inside Katherine, who felt as warm and snug as a satin glove. But it was all happening too fast. Paula wanted the moment to last, so she pulled back.

"Deeper," Katherine protested. Paula couldn't resist and eagerly obliged, plunging a second finger in, her mouth lingering nearby for its turn.

Katherine moaned as she took Paula's wrist and shoved her in further, pulled out, then back in. "Faster," Katherine groaned. Paula obeyed—in and out until she knew Katherine was ready, then she pulled her hand away and quickly covered Katherine with her mouth. Paula was in heaven.

"Paula... Paula..."

Paula's eyes shot open to Katherine in a nurse's uniform, standing over her, shaking her awake.

"You were calling me," Katherine chirped too cheerfully.

"I was?" A sudden panic washed over her. "What did I say?" Paula wiped away the stream of drool that connected her lip to the pillow beneath her aching head.

"You were screaming my name and moaning like a moose. Got to admit, that's a first." Katherine laughed as she moved across the room and snapped open the curtains, making the room too bright. "Much better, don't you think?"

"Not really. I have a headache." Paula rubbed her temples.

"That would explain the moose call. Want some Tylenol?" Katherine moved back to the bed.

"Yes, thanks."

Katherine dumped two capsules into her hand. Paula popped them into her mouth and chased them with a glass of water.

"Need help getting dressed?"

"Dressed?" Her eyes were still groggy with sleep.

"I told you you'd be home in time for Christmas." Katherine smiled.

Paula stared at her blankly.

"Silly, you're being discharged today."

The memory came rushing back so fast it made Paula's head throb harder. "Oh, yeah."

Katherine squeezed her hand. "Why the long face?"

"I forgot, that's all." She couldn't decide whether she was glad or sad.

Katherine shook her finger in the air. "You need to watch your fluids. Otherwise you'll end up right back here."

At the sight of Katherine's waving finger, Paula suddenly had a flash of the dream she'd been shaken from. She quickly averted her gaze as her face turned crimson.

Katherine's voice turned serious. "No kidding. You have to start taking better care of yourself. Do you have family you can stay with?"

"I can take care of myself. Have been for a long time." Paula wanted desperately to look Katherine in the eye—a grateful gaze, nothing more. She had no idea where the dream had come from and felt terrible about her uncontrolled rampage.

"So what do you have planned for the holidays?" Katherine asked as she took Paula's dress from the closet.

"Spending time with my son, I hope."

"Your son? I didn't know you were married." Katherine draped the dress over the back of an ugly orange chair next to the bed.

"I'm not anymore. We broke up a long time ago."

"I'm going through that myself."

"Sorry."

"Don't be. I couldn't be happier."

"Oh. Then congratulations, I guess." Paula watched Katherine place the rest of her clothing on the chair.

"How old's your son?"

"Five. He lives with his father."

"Why?" Katherine's tone was disapproving.

"He sued for custody and won. That's the short version."

"Because of your HIV status?" Paula nodded. "What a bunch of bull. With all the new advances in treatment, there's no reason you can't live a totally normal life."

"Yeah, well, tell his father that."

"Give me his phone number and I will."

Paula laughed, which felt strange. She couldn't remember the last time she'd had anything to laugh about.

"Being gay didn't help." Paula waited anxiously for Katherine's response.

"Oh," was all Katherine said.

"Unfortunately, I was married at the time I figured it out. When I told Howie, he left and took Shelby with him."

The room fell quiet, but only for a second. Katherine quickly rebounded. "So what? People don't lose their kids for that anymore. You should go back to court and fight it."

Paula often fantasized about getting Shelby back, but she knew she didn't have the strength to undertake such a massive battle, not again. The irony was that there was nothing she loved more than being a mother. It got her up and out on those mornings that she otherwise would have spent in bed. For that she would always be grateful to Shelby. But her fighting days were over.

"Well," Katherine interjected, "I'm sure you're a great mother. Any judge should be able to see that. And if your son's half as sweet as you, then the world's a better place." Katherine moved back to Paula, gave her a quick but firm hug, and was gone. Paula opened her mouth to call her back. To thank her for the only kindness she'd known in a very long time. For treating her like she was both ordinary and extraordinary at the same time. To thank her for the dream. Her day would be better for it. Hell, maybe the rest of her life. She wanted to call her back, but didn't.

Paula sat in the diner until 5 o'clock before it occurred to her they might not show. The disappointment exploded in the pit of her stomach like a hot can of soda. Four o'clock on Christmas Eve was what Howie had promised, she was sure of it. Paula didn't have the energy to get up and leave, so she remained seated, staring out the window, watching the snow build a pointy fortress atop a fire hydrant. She'd stay until the fortress fell.

Howie took nearly everything when he split: her money, her CDs, the car. Everything except the habit. That he left behind. They had tried many times to get clean. But doing it together was like trying to kick the flu with a dozen sick kids in the house. When one of them wasn't using, the other one was. But now they were both clean. How he managed to escape unscathed and healthy was a mystery to Paula—just one more on a long list of unknowns.

Paula opened her purse, took out two neatly wrapped gifts, and put them on the table next to her glass of water. When Paula was a child it snowed a lot. But since Shelby was born there hadn't been a single flake. This would be his first. She couldn't wait to show him how to construct the perfect snowball. Not too hard, not too soft, packed with just enough slush to inflict a painful sting without the threat of skull fracture. She laughed out loud as she imagined her son's look of wonder and admiration at the sight of one of her beauties. The man sitting in the adjoining booth gave her a curious look but remained firmly rooted in his seat, hunkered over his dead cup of coffee and folded newspaper.

Paula looked up at the clock on the restaurant wall and was angry when she saw the time. *Katherine's right. I should go get Shelby back,* she thought. She had no idea how much time she had left. And if she wanted to leave him with at least a few good memories of her, she'd have to hurry up and create some.

Paula jerked back from her daydream when someone slipped outside and knocked the snow fortress off the fire hydrant. "Shit!" she screamed through the glass. "You ruined it!" The passerby didn't hear, but everyone in the diner did. Sometimes she couldn't tell the difference between actual words and thoughts, but these words were real and hard as handballs bouncing off the walls, echoing through her head. And every eye in the house was on her. Normally she wouldn't have the nerve to face them, but today she was feeling feisty. So she turned to her waiting audience and said coolly, "Take a picture why don't you." The man in the booth behind her gathered his things and left. The other patrons returned to their coffee and conversation.

The waiter appeared at Paula's table. "Lady, you gonna be ordering any more water?"

Paula responded, but not to anyone in particular. "He said they'd be here at 4. I'm sure that's what he said."

"Yeah, well, it ain't 4 o'clock. It's time for my dinner rush. So if you're gonna eat, fine, if not..." He left without finishing the sentence.

Paula sighed at the thought of the long ride back on the bus. She picked up the two gifts on the table and tucked them carefully into her purse. She pulled her frayed collar snugly around her neck as she moved to the front door and stepped out into the bitter cold. She glimpsed the bus stop in the distance through the thick blanket of falling snow, but turned suddenly and went the other way. She wanted to walk. To feel the sting of cold against her face. It masked the dull throb of her breaking heart. That, and she didn't want to be alone on Christmas Eve. But she had no place to go. Across the street she noticed one of her old haunts—a bar she frequented back in her partying days. Liquor was against doctor's orders. It didn't mix well with her meds. But she was tired of always being responsible. She wanted to feel lovable, sexy, and virus-free, if only for a little while. So Paula ran across the street, ducked inside, and took a seat at the bar.

"What can I do you for?"

Paula looked up from her frozen stupor to a pretty bartender with crystal-blue eyes and a room full of rowdy customers.

"A double shot of anything."

The bartender topped off a glass and slid it in front of Paula just as someone took the seat next to her.

"Paula?"

Paula turned to a woman she didn't recognize.

"I can't believe it!" The woman shouted. Her voice suddenly sounded familiar. "It's me, Katherine."

Paula's eyes widened. Out of her nurse's uniform, Katherine looked like any other stranger.

"What are you doing here?" Paula asked sternly.

"Having a drink, obviously," Katherine shot back playfully.

"No, I mean what are you doing in a gay bar?"

"Gee, I don't know, like, maybe I'm a lesbian and this is where lesbians go!" Paula's mouth dropped open.

"I come here all the time," Katherine continued with a wink. "Now that I'm single." Unexpectedly, Katherine's butt slid off the slippery vinyl seat and she nearly tumbled. "Oops, guess I'm a little buzzed. Been sipping margaritas for the past two hours waiting for a date that never showed. Stood up on Christmas Eve, how pathetic." Katherine carefully perched herself back on her seat. "So, how you feeling lately?" she asked in her best nurse's voice.

"Fine," Paula lied. "Other than I sort of got stood up too."

"Oh, that is too funny! We can sit here and be pathetic together!"

Paula came into the bar to surround herself with anonymity, not pity. She wanted to escape her sorrow, just for the evening. And now she was sitting next to Katherine, oozing with compassion, making it impossible for Paula to forget. Perhaps she couldn't do much about her dismal life, but she could surely walk away from a pity-packed conversation with Katherine. "I need to go," she said as she got to her feet and dropped a few bills on the bar.

"Did I say something...?" Katherine asked gently.

Paula didn't have an answer, so she simply turned and walked away. It felt good to get out of the hot, smoke-filled room into the crisp clear night. She stopped just outside the door, her head reeling.

"What did I do wrong?" Paula spun around to Katherine standing behind her. "I haven't been out on the prowl for a long time," Katherine confessed. "Guess I've lost my touch."

Paula's tongue searched for the right words, but didn't find them. "On the prowl?" was all she could manage.

"When you were in the hospital, couldn't you tell I had a crush on you?" Paula's eyes landed firmly on Katherine's. "I knew you could tell!"

As the words sunk in, a tiny surge of confidence ignited in Paula. "Would you like to walk with me for a while? Maybe stop for some coffee?"

A smile spread across Katherine's face. "Absolutely." She stepped onto the frozen sidewalk toward Paula, and her feet suddenly shot out from under her. Paula managed to catch Katherine in her arms before she hit the pavement. They were face-to-face, lips inches apart.

"Are you all right?" Paula asked, wide-eyed.

Katherine moved in close and whispered into Paula's ear, "I guess it's your turn to take care of me." Katherine's warm breath tickled Paula's ear, making her laugh.

"You smell nice," Paula announced brazenly. "Like chocolate."

Katherine gently brushed her hand against Paula's cheek. "That's the sweetest thing anyone's ever said to me." She reluctantly peeled herself from Paula's arms but slipped on the ice again, nearly taking them both down. They laughed like schoolkids, trying to steady each other as their feet played wibble-wobble on the patch of ice. Eventually they made it to safe and salted ground.

The snow was still falling. Velvety drifts covered the heaps of trash lining the streets, giving them a gentler look. Katherine looped her arm through Paula's and snuggled into her. Paula snuggled back, and together they vanished into the kindness of the soft white city.

Kyle Walker

"Tissue?" Darby offered.

"Do I look like I'm going to cry?" Marigold asked.

"In case you feel something coming up," Darby explained.

"You mean like my lunch?"

Darby laughed. "It's been known to happen."

"Really?" Marigold couldn't imagine throwing up in front of anyone, much less a therapist. She took a handful of Kleenex. "Just a precaution," she told Darby.

"So do you want to tell me why you're here?"

"I seem to have had…that is, there was an incident…you see," she said, "I'm brand-new at this, and apparently quite terrible. Laughable, in fact."

"At what?"

"Being gay."

"Really?"

"Well, let's say *realizing* it."

"And you think you're not doing well at it."

Marigold reached for the tissues then, and used them to hide her face as well as wipe her tears. She put one wet handful in the wastebasket and started on a dry one. Darby got up from her chair, and sat next to Marigold on her couch. She patted Mari's back and stroked her hand. Half a wastebasket full of tissues later, her sobs gave way to long, hiccuping breaths.

She didn't want to look at Darby. She felt very broken and old.

"Hey," the therapist said gently. Marigold decided that if she was ever going to be able to look anyone in the eye again, she might as well start with this woman, who was paid to listen, to heal, not to judge. She had an assured, no-nonsense air that Mari found comforting.

"Somebody treated you badly." It wasn't a question. Marigold nodded. As a storyteller, she liked to start at the beginning. However, she wasn't quite sure where the beginning was.

"I met this woman…" she finally said.

Marigold had been at a bar for a reading by an author whose work she published, when she was jostled. A lithe young woman apologized, then started talking as though they knew each other. Marigold hated when that happened. She knew lots of people: between her job as an editor, her teaching at the New School, and the literary events she attended, she was always being approached by someone who wanted a job or a book contract. Strangers were invariably pleasant when they were writers and found she could help them.

Marigold didn't mind; it was part of being an editor, but there were so *many* of them. *Who is this?* she thought. *I can't imagine not remembering her.* She tried to bluff her way through. But it was hard to follow the conversation because she found herself looking at the woman, not listening to her.

Terry, that was her name, had an aggressive energy and underlined her words with quick, staccato movements. She spoke with her hands, which were pale and slender, and touched Mari for emphasis, and stood at a distance Mari usually found invasive.

But she was drawn in by Terry, who had the look of a biker yet was unmistakably feminine. She wore her hair in a cocky pompadour and had the chiseled, fine features to bring it off. Mari had met some young butch girls. She'd published a number of lesbian authors, and their readings tended to bring out vivacious types, many looking for a mentor or a date, or both.

Terry unzipped her leather jacket, and Marigold saw she was wearing a tight black T-shirt. She stretched out her arms and threw back her shoulders, and she wasn't wearing a bra. Mari had always noticed women's breasts (in an artistic sense), and she saw that Terry's were small but nicely shaped.

"Do you write?" Terry asked. "Or are you more of a literary midwife?"

"That's an elemental way of putting it," Mari replied, finishing her gin and tonic. "But I've birthed a few pieces myself."

"Not a virgin, then?" Terry asked, nudging her.

"Not for *ages,*" Mari replied, enjoying the subtext.

"What's it like?" Terry asked suddenly, almost childlike.

"It's lovely," Mari replied, warming to her eagerness. "The recognition is nice...but the creation is what's special."

"Oh..." Terry didn't seem to believe it. "I'm still waiting, myself. To be recognized. I was in college upstate, but I dropped out and came to the city to, you know, *live.* And play bass."

Lately they were all in bands. Most of them played bass and had an almost-finished novel, or a chapbook with a title like *My Kuntry.* Mari liked the new wave of young women in New York in the early '90s, with short hair and bad attitudes and big black boots. There was something sweet about them.

She'd had long hair and long skirts and written humorless poetry when she came to New York in the early '80s with a degree in Irish studies and a stack of singer-songwriter vinyl. She thought these girls must have a much better time.

It was time for the reading, from a book that was not called *My Kuntry*. Mari was proud of her author, who'd produced a breathtaking collection of stories. Mari had helped her shape and order them, and she'd worked with the author on her presentation (she had a tendency to mumble).

At the story's end, the crowd applauded with cheers and "Bravas" (Mari loved readings in bars, they loosened the audience up). She waited for the crowd to disperse and was touched and pleased to see the writer coming over.

"This woman made me a writer!" she cried as she hugged Mari. Her partner scowled.

Terry took it all in. She tagged along for another drink and was still there as the writer's partner pulled her out the door, still singing Mari's praises.

"She likes you," Terry observed.

"I'm a good editor," Mari said. "She *should* like me."

"No, she *likes* you…that's why her girlfriend doesn't," Terry said. "You could have her in a minute."

"I beg your pardon?"

"Or would that offend your ethics or something?" Terry inquired.

"No…I'm afraid you've…" Why did people always assume she was a lesbian? Or that the men she dated were gay? She'd had a run where most of them were, but that was just New York, wasn't it?

"Don't tell me you haven't thought about it! I mean, she's hot and talented…"

"No, I haven't thought about it," Marigold snapped. "I am not interested in her that way."

"Not your type?" Terry asked.

"My type is male," Marigold declared.

"All right," said Terry, with a smirk, zipping her jacket. Marigold hated it when lesbians were amused by her.

"Talent does turns me on," she said. "I fall in love with people's work."

"I suppose you could take a good book to bed," Terry replied. The streetlight cast her in a satiny glow. "You could go home and get wild with a good book...though it would probably get the pages all gooey."

"I didn't know you were a comedian," Marigold replied, hating that she was blushing, that her eyes were stinging.

"Sometimes the truth is funny," Terry replied, brushing her hair back. "Sometimes it's a smack in the head. Can I get you a cab?"

"What?" Marigold couldn't stop looking at her. Even without makeup, her lips were very, very red.

"It's late. You're a little loaded," She stepped into the street, put her fingers in her mouth, and whistled. When a cab pulled up, she held the door for Marigold, who suddenly blurted: "Can I drop you someplace?"

"No, I live in Brooklyn." Marigold didn't want her to disappear. Didn't want to have to go looking for her.

"Would you like me to read your work?" she offered. Terry lifted her chin, looked pleased.

"If you want..." she began.

"Where to?" the driver asked. Now Marigold was in familiar territory.

"Don't play hard to get when an editor asks to see your work," she said. "This is my card. Send me something. Send me your best piece."

"And then you might fall in love?"

Marigold didn't answer. As the cab pulled away, it took all the willpower she had not to turn around and look.

Terry called, not the next day but the one after. Marigold had been trying to persuade herself that she had not felt what she had felt. It was something else, a kind of bond that one had with a friend, a companion, a meeting of the minds.

At night, when she dreamt, she knew it was not Terry's mind she wanted to meet. She had been with men. She had even been engaged to a graduate student in California. Somehow they had stayed on opposite sides of the country. Her work was her love. Her friends gave her the sustenance she needed. She had a full, active life and treasured her privacy and independence.

Except at this very moment, and for the last two days, she had not been able to stop thinking about Terry's breasts, and her hands, and her mouth. It wasn't even thinking. It was just flashes that came, unbidden, oh, several hundred times a day. And at night, she dreamed. *She was bathing with Terry, washing her with thick, lathery soap, pressing her wet body against...*

"This is Mari Myers," she said, grateful for the phone's interruption.

"Wow, you sound so professional," Terry said. Marigold felt a pang at how young she sounded. A sweet girl. With sweet eyes and lips and *LET'S NOT GO THERE...*

"Hi! Terry? Do you have something for me?"

"You sound kind of stressed...are you busy?" Terry asked uncertainly.

"No more than usual," Mari replied. She could hear the edge in her voice.

"It's not a good time..."

"I can talk now," Mari insisted, walking around her desk to shut the office door. "I'm glad you called."

"I...I'm not sure what I should show you," Terry said, and Mari found her stammer endearing. "I have a bunch of stories...I mean, I'm not even sure they're stories. They're these...things I've written."

This is where she would usually have told the writer to sell herself, act like a pro; you only get one chance with an editor, so make the most of it. She'd been told she could frighten young writers. She wondered where her snap had gone.

"What if we met outside the office, someplace quiet, and you can show me what you have, and I'll take a look at your work. Would you like that?" She spoke in a low, encouraging tone.

"Yeah!" Terry replied, and a wave of excitement coursed over Mari. "I would appreciate that...I mean, thank you!"

They arranged to meet at a café near Mari's office the next evening, and when she hung up her hands were shaking. Her thoughts, which had always been like a carefully tended, well-laid-out garden, suddenly burst into wildflowers overspilling their borders and designs.

I want her, I want her, I want her. I want to lick her and kiss her and find out what the hair feels like between her legs. I want to bite her on the neck and kiss her toes and chew on her earlobe. Marigold gently thumped her head against her desk trying to derail that train of thought, but it was no good.

The next night, she got there early. She'd brought along a manuscript to read, so she didn't look as if she was waiting for a train, or a bus, or a lover. Before she left work, she'd put on gold hoop earrings and a dusting of makeup and refreshed her perfume. She'd worn a full linen skirt and sleeveless top, sexy-preppy, she hoped. Her hair, which she usually pulled back, she let flow over her shoulders. She drank a glass of wine.

Terry was late. Soon it was almost 7, and as Marigold was ready to leave, she turned up.

"I had to finish," she explained as she sat down and placed a bulky envelope in front of Mari. "I was looking at my stuff, and I couldn't find anything I liked, so I sat down and wrote something new."

That was something Mari could forgive. She smiled, and let her eyes linger on Terry's fine features, her dark brows, and her hands, literally ink-stained. She had obviously tried to dress for the occasion, in khakis and a white shirt, unbuttoned pleasingly far down. She'd slicked back her hair with pomade, and it shone darkly smooth.

"You look nice," Marigold told her, and Terry gazed in another direction.

"I want to do this the right way."

"So far, so good," Marigold said. "What do you need from me? How can I help you? What can I tell you?"

"I didn't come to New York to be unknown," Terry said, and Marigold liked her intensity. She never minded ambition as long as there was something to back it up. "There's so much I see, stories I want to tell. It's just so hard…the ideas spinning around in my head, getting them down."

"Yes, it's hard," Marigold agreed. "Even if you're talented, it takes persistence, and hard work, and walking through the door at the right moment."

"Maybe I did that?"

"We'll see."

Mari picked up the envelope and pulled out a sheaf of pages, some fresh printed, the others dog-eared and with scribbled inserts in childlike handwriting.

Terry used phonetic and unconventional spellings; Mari hated that. To her it was an affectation that smacked of high school. Still, there were markets for that style, and for some it was an experiment in form. Not a very successful one, in most cases.

It was hard to get a feel for Terry's voice, since everything she had was fragmentary. However, there was a style to it, if a rough one; and some nice moments on subjects like coming out to her parents, moving to New York. She turned to the newest pages:

She was not the sort of woman I usually noticed: I go for young, dark girls who wear leather, chicks who can really fuck u up, unless I beat them 2 it. This one was not like that. She was tall and older, maybe 30, dressed like uptown. The downtown dive was not the kind of place u'd find her unless there was something like a reading going on.

There was, a reading, I mean, from a book by this chick I sort of knew, sort of liked, had made out with in a bathroom. In this bar. Her girlfriend didn't know. That was why I went: I like the menace of secrets. They're interesting, especially when you hold them close, knowing they might explode in your face. They're also hot.

This woman I saw looked like she had a secret. The way she held herself so close, the way she pretended 2 b all relaxed and shit when there was a tight little nut inside, a hard kernel I wanted 2 crack. How could I tell this? I just could. I'm psychic sometimes. So I pretended I knew her, which is a good way to tell a lot about someone; if they're a no-bullshit type, they'll call u on it, nail u for the little conjob hustler u r. If they've got a little tact, they'll try to figure out who u r and how they know u.

This 1 was good, slippery, smart. I liked watching her, as she took me one way and another, and finally realized we'd never met, and decided 2 ignore it. I like 2 c how far a certain amount of denial can go. Or maybe she just had just the ability 2 hop a ride without knowing where it's going. I can respect that.

Red hair. She had long red hair, her real color? Everybody's getting red hair now. I'll probably get it one of these days. Just 2 c how it looks. But black works for me at the moment, and the effect is good with my white white whitegirl skin. I look like alienvampireElvis. I liked the thought of my black and her red 2gether. I wanted 2 c if she was a true redhead.

Would she let me kiss her and do all kinds of things 2 her with her uptown suit on the floor and me still in my biker boots and her crying and calling my name as she came about a million times?

"What happens next?" Marigold asked.

"That's all I wrote," Terry replied. "What do you think?"

"I think you need to keep going." *Go home with me.*

"Beg your pardon?" Terry asked. Mari realized she must have thought the last bit out loud.

"I want to see more...of you. I mean, of your work."

"Could you fall in love with it?" Terry asked, not as the cocky biker girl. She was very vulnerable. Almost naked. Mari so wanted to see her naked.

"Quite possibly," Mari told her. Terry's face lit up; she took Mari's hand.

"Thank you. I really mean that! You're the first person who's ever given me the slightest bit of encouragement."

"*What happens next?*" Mari insisted.

"I guess...I'd better go home and write it. I mean, shouldn't I?" Terry swept up her papers. She pulled out a pen and began to jot notes on her hand. She leaned in and gave Mari a kiss somewhere around the left eyebrow. Then she was gone. Mari tried to pinpoint the moment she'd out-smarted herself.

They met regularly at cafés, bars and Mari's living room. Terry loved Marigold's apartment and found excuses to linger, hinting that her own situation was not as comfortable. Mari lent her books Terry should read. She line-edited Terry's pieces and gave her texts and articles on technique. Their sessions stretched into evenings, and they ordered takeout and had wide-ranging conversations about their lives and experiences.

Mari found these times tantalizing and frustrating. There was Terry, her blouse unbuttoned a little lower every time, inches away, her hair falling in her eyes, as she pushed it out of the way with the back of her hand, a gesture that made Mari's heart clench. Sometimes, when Terry read something personal, her eyes filled with tears. Once, they spilled over, and Mari brushed them away. She let her hand linger on Terry's cheek, and Terry leaned into it.

The writing was also frustrating. Terry didn't seem to be able to revise. She kept writing new pieces, as fragmentary as the first ones, still showing flashes of insight and style, but never growing into anything complete.

"You might want to take a workshop," Mari suggested. "To ground yourself in narrative technique. It's important to master the basics."

"Then I'd be just like everyone else!" Terry snapped.

"No, you're like everyone else *now*," Mari replied. "Like thousands of sensitive artists who can't bear to channel their passion into a form...a musician who won't read music, a painter who won't learn to draw."

"I don't need to read music," Terry replied. "I *feel* it. When you confine yourself to...*notes*...you lose the real emotion. Might as well spread your legs for money, for all it means."

"There's a certain level of competence expected if you want to reach an audience other than yourself," Mari replied. "Being a professional doesn't mean being a whore." She'd had this argument with many writers; the ones who listened didn't automatically have a career, but at least they knew how to write a sentence. Others had walked away to publish their own broadsides and chapbooks, produce their own performances. They'd cut their own paths, and she respected them for that.

"I'm not saying my way is the *one* way, or even the right way for you," Marigold said. "You're the only one who knows what you want to say and how to say it. But from what you've told me, you want mainstream success, with book contracts and reviews and readings and all the accoutrements of a literary star, if there is such a thing. Though I wonder if you realize those are side effects of your work, not the goal to work for."

"*Accoutrements?* What kind of fucking word is that?"

"French," Mari replied. "If I've read you wrong, please

correct me. But you want to be some kind of star, and you know you want it."

"Bit of a snob, aren't you? Using words like that, telling me what to do, especially when you won't admit what *you* want!" Terry leapt from the couch.

"Yes, I'm a snob," said Mari, who usually let Terry's rude remarks slide. "I have certain standards and judge artists by whether or not they're capable of meeting them. That's pretty much a textbook definition of a snob. You want what you think I can give you, but I can't! You have to work for it."

"What do you think I've been *doing* all this time?" Terry said, almost crying. "I keep trying, and it's never good enough for you. You could make it good; you could get me into magazines and get me an advance. You *could* open the door for me, but you *won't*. What do I have to do?"

"I can't give you a craft," Marigold said. She grabbed Terry's hand and tried to pull her back.

"No!" Terry said, wriggling away. "I don't get what I want, you don't get what you want."

"I don't know what you're talking about."

Terry didn't reply but threw herself on the couch, on top of Marigold. She pressed their bodies together, and her face was closer than it had ever been.

"*This* is what you want, stupid," she hissed and fastened her mouth to Marigold's. *Yes, it is,* Marigold thought. She opened her mouth and felt Terry's hard tongue going in deep. She put her arms around Terry, who stopped kissing just as quickly as she'd started and sat back up. She ripped Marigold's blouse open, and buttons ricocheted around the room. She unhooked Marigold's bra with the practice of a frat boy, and began to squeeze Mari's breasts, lowering her mouth first to one, then the other.

"Oh, please...yes," Mari managed. Terry suckled and nuzzled and bit, drawing her teeth over the exposed skin, raising red marks. It felt good. Terry unzipped Mari's pants and roughly pulled them down, and tore at her panties. She thrust a finger into Mari's pussy and drew it back, wet.

"You know what you want," Terry told her. "Say it!"

"I want you, Terry." It was a relief to finally admit it.

"Tell me what you want me to do!"

"I want you to touch me. I want you to make love to me."

"Yeah," she said, thrusting her fingers inside Mari. "You like it inside? You like it hard?" Mari pushed onto Terry's hand, desperate for her touch, feeling her go deeper. No one, nothing had ever filled her this way.

"Ride me, baby! I'll go in you so hard…" Terry told her.

"Let me kiss you," Mari groaned.

Terry bit Mari's lips, stuck her tongue in Mari's mouth, and Mari sucked it hard. She would explode. She would turn inside out. She would… She let out a howl that came from a place she had never been, a sound she didn't know she could make. Then she started crying.

"That was good, baby. You came good," Terry said, suddenly gentle. She gathered Mari in her arms and kissed her. Mari was so relaxed she could barely form words.

"You were right. I wanted this."

"Tell me something I don't know," Terry said, proud of herself.

"You make love…forcefully," she mused.

"You like that?" Terry touched one of the red marks on Mari's chest.

"I do," she said. "I like the passion…the commitment."

"Well, that's what you like about writing too," Terry said, getting up. "You want to feel it down to the bone."

Mari couldn't name what she wanted, but she hoped Terry could teach her. "Do you want me to make love to you?" she asked shyly.

"Not tonight," Terry replied. "I have to work." She was tending bar downtown.

"Do you want me to meet you when you get off?" Mari asked. "I'll take you out to breakfast."

"As payment for having serviced milady?"

"Why do you have to be like that?" Mari said, as the words raked across her naked psyche. "That was...special. Something I'd never experienced before."

"And you'll do it again many times, with many women, some of them a lot nicer than I am," Terry said. "You didn't know how to get out of the closet; I pulled the door open."

"Surely it was more than that?" Mari asked. Terry was just being macho, hiding behind her butch facade.

"Don't call me Shirley," Terry said with a grin. "You can decide what it was worth to you." She was gone before Mari could catch her breath. She looked around and saw the mess they'd made: papers were scattered on the floor, her blouse was ruined. One of her shoes had made contact with a lamp that had fallen on the floor, its shade bent at an odd angle. She wondered how long it would take for her to straighten up; if she would ever be able to.

All the time she'd fantasized about Terry, the months she'd told herself they were friends, mentor and student, she could keep the reality at bay. She'd never *actually* made love to a woman, or been touched by one romantically. Until an hour ago, she was still on the straight and narrow. The boring, the unassailable, the accepted norm.

Her crotch ached with the reality that she'd never been as excited as when Terry was touching her, that every other experience she'd had paled beside this one. It was three-dimensional, Technicolor, after a lifetime of black-and-white.

She looked at a stain on the carpet from spilled wine. She could get it cleaned. She couldn't excise the last few hours, or the last few months.

She is mean, hard, a hustler, someone who can hurt me, who probably will. Why do I want someone like that? Why do I want her more than ever? Why do I want her to come back, and to do it all over again, harder and faster and deeper?

Mari touched herself where Terry's hands had been. She squeezed her clit, and stroked it, and wished she had something to fill her pussy. She imagined lips locked hard on her nipples, which stood erect. In a moment, she came again, and then she realized that the sofa cushion was quite wet.

Terry didn't come back. She didn't call, didn't make any contact. Mari grew frantic. She'd never been this possessed by the need to see someone. She'd always thought that friends of hers who'd gotten obsessed with a lover were a little unbalanced, and chalked it up to hormones. *I've been a judgmental bitch. I certainly haven't appreciated the position they were in.* She had no idea she could be so thoroughly torn from her moorings, unable to believe or trust anything she knew about herself. *Terry, Terry, Terry* ran through her mind all day and night. She resolved not to chase her, but by the end of the week her resolve was shot.

She went to the bar where Terry worked. She'd brought Terry's writing with her, a reminder that they still had some business together, they still had a bond. Terry was, of course, late.

Three gin and tonics later, she was convinced that it was all a misunderstanding and Terry would greet her with open arms. They would pick up where they left off.

Terry sauntered in, her arm around a young girl with bright pink hair who wore a housedress and combat boots. She spotted Mari, and her grin faded. She kissed the girl and asked her to go down the street to buy a sandwich.

"What are you doing here?" she demanded.

"You left some things at my place. I thought I'd see what you wanted me to do with them."

"Why don't you burn them?" Terry asked. "You don't think my writing is worth anything."

"If I thought that, I wouldn't have spent the last couple

months working with you," Mari said. "There was a reason for it."

"I think we found the reason," Terry said, snatching the envelope. "You got what you wanted, and I got screwed."

"Do you really think that?" Mari asked. "I care for you, Terry. More than just care for you... And I think you have potential. Can't we talk about that?"

"Well, then, why don't we determine the price?" Terry asked. "How many times do I have to fuck you to get a story in a magazine? What will it take for me to get a book contract? Name your terms, sweetheart!" The way she said "sweetheart," she might have been saying "bitch."

"You don't...you don't feel the same way about me that I feel about you," Marigold said, discovering one more thing she'd been fooling herself about. "I thought that piece you wrote...the first one you showed me..."

"You're so smart...you can't even tell a piece of fiction," Terry scoffed.

"I thought you wanted me..."

"At first. I thought you were kind of interesting, but you're not my type at all," Terry replied. "You're so *old*. Older than you really are, even."

"I thought there was...we had a friendship, a feeling that drew us together."

"Us? There *is* no US!"

Terry stood up so fast, the bar stool fell over, and people turned to look at them. Marigold let her hair fall in front of her face and looked down at her drink.

"The only thing I want from you, you won't give me," Terry said. "Whether it's because you're just a cunt, or you really believe those stupid ideas about technique and doing it over and over and over, I don't know. I just know you don't have anything to give me, so you're a waste of my time."

"Can you keep your voice down?" Terry didn't mind the scene she was making. She knew there were women looking at her. She swept her hand through her hair. Her look were haughty, and she stared down her long, straight nose at Marigold, who thought it was like being ridiculed by the star jock of the football team. Even as Terry humiliated her, Marigold wanted her.

It had been almost two months, and Marigold still couldn't cope. She found herself missing work, unable to concentrate on manuscripts. She'd left many hang-ups on Terry's machine and even stood outside the bar, but hadn't gone in. If she could have traded something for Terry's love—no, for her attention—she would have. Except when it came down to it, Terry wasn't good enough. Mari couldn't sell or place anything she'd written.

"Publishing is a business," she explained to the therapist she'd finally decided to see, this Darby who listened. "If I had tried to pass her off as an accomplished writer, I wouldn't have had a job *or* Terry." She felt exhausted, but lighter. It was a relief to tell someone what had happened; she'd kept the details from even her closest friends. It was just too embarrassing. It was one thing to come out to people as a result of a moving epiphany and passionate love affair, another to have been shouted down publicly by a 22-year-old who'd left her doubting her appeal to anyone.

She'd found Darby through the Gay and Lesbian Center. They'd given her several names, and Darby took her insurance.

"That girl is going to get hers one day," Darby said. "In fact, she needs her ass kicked now." Marigold liked that. It was the sort of thing she wanted to hear. She thought she should have gone in for therapy weeks ago.

"Thank you!" Marigold said with a sigh, putting her hand on Darby's. "Or is taking my side part of the therapeutic process?"

"No, not really," Darby said. "But when a beautiful woman like you is treated like dirt it bothers me. That girl played you.

You're lucky she decided to walk when she did, because you could have ended up with her moving in, you supporting her, her mind-fucking you."

"She did a pretty good job of that anyway," Marigold said, wondering if she'd ever get back on her feet again. "I saw her, and I fell and fell and fell. Knowing I'm capable of that scares the daylights out of me. How can I ever trust my own judgment again?"

"Please don't give up," Darby said softly. "I know it's hard. Those girls are so attractive, and so awful, with their swaggers and their leather jackets."

"You sound like you knew a bad girl," Marigold said. She took another look at Darby. "No: You *were* one."

Darby nodded. She had a gleam in her eye Mari took for pride.

"Do you still have a leather jacket?" Marigold inquired.

"Of course."

"Why do I want a bad girl?" Mari asked angrily.

"Because we're fun," Darby told her, grinning. "We're all the things you aren't supposed to say or do, and the ones your mama told you not to go with. We are the most exciting thing that ever happened to you."

"But do you have to be such JERKS?" Marigold exploded.

"Not all of us," Darby said. "Under the crap, we really are pushovers, and very romantic. When we're done making asses of ourselves, we can clean up nicely. Terry might have been the right person for you, but at the wrong time of her life. She certainly got to you like no one else. Something about her pulled you into a deeper realization of who you are, pardon the jargon. And that's good. Though it sure doesn't feel like it right now, does it?"

Mari felt a sudden urge to rest her head on Darby's shoulder. "No it doesn't!" she sighed.

"You were in love for the first time. What experience did you have to go by? None! You're a very smart lady. You'll learn from this and find there are women out there who would be honored to treat you right. Please believe that!" She spoke with such sincerity that Marigold wanted to believe her.

"I don't know if I have the guts to try again," she confessed.

"I hope you will," Darby said quietly. She went to her desk and began to write. "This is the number of another therapist who takes your insurance," she said. "I think you should give her a call. She's quite good."

"But what about *you*?" Marigold said, stunned. "I want *you*. I thought we were really connecting."

"We *are* connecting. And I want you. But not as a patient."

"Oh." Marigold was speechless. She had to admit she was drawn to Darby. And all of that fumfering around and lying to herself about Terry had only been a waste of time. But the last time she had been so moved had been…Terry. Was she being naive, self-destructive? And yet Darby had calmed her, given her answers and insight, and made it a point not to be manipulative.

"I need to ask you a personal question." she began. Darby tensed. "How bad are you, exactly?"

"So bad that I'm very good for you," Darby told her. She stood there, one hand in her pants pocket, radiating goodness and longing and a lot of other things Mari wanted to know. She forgave herself for being fooled the first time.

Terry was a kid, she thought. *Darby is a woman.*

She held out her hand. Darby took it and pulled her close. They moved easily into an embrace that felt as though they had been, and would be, doing it for a long time.

Not Ever Destined to Be Classic

Michelle Sawyer

Greenwich Village. Birthplace of the American Beat Society. Original home of the "come crash at my pad" crowd. Romantic. Eclectic. Funky. Unpredictable. Multicultural. Each corner you turn unveils something. And it all looks so harmless and fag-happy and pink, with dozens of places to find a good bottle of wine and black cats sleeping in the sunlight of the flower shop windows.

The Village is, however, the place to get mugged. Everybody says it's the city, you know, downtown Manhattan, where all the shit is—and don't get me wrong, downtown Manhattan does have its shit. Pre-Rudy Times Square was no place to fuck with, let me tell you. But the Village is far more dangerous, I think, for those who don't live there. Deceptive. The streets twist and turn and spin you around like you're drunk. I once found a tourist, happily intrigued, following a trail of red footprints. "Where does this lead?" asked the man, bearded, cardiganed, camera in hand. I couldn't say. And, of course, I didn't dare tell him that the footprints were not in red paint but blood, baked into a patch of light-colored sidewalk. I didn't dare tell him that the path he was following was more than likely someone's last. I didn't dare tell him Jack Kerouac had died quite some time ago. For in New York, even death is art. And in the Village, it's best to keep secrets.

But with all of its odd curves and dark stairwells, Greenwich Village is the place to be if you're...well...a lesbian. And I hardly think that tiny Piqua, Ohio, was ready for their prized Piqua Peach Queen of 1977 to come bopping out of the closet. I moved to the Village in my early 20s and stayed. Straight people live here too. Take my friend Trish, for instance, who came here to check up on me and met Hal, with whom she became totally infatuated, married, and had two girls with great teeth (Hal's an orthodontist). Trish has known me since long before I was the Peach Queen. As kids we skipped rocks across my aunt's pond and had tea parties. As teens we skipped school, listened to Led Zeppelin, and dared each other to inject ourselves with insulin shots we stole out of my grandmother's purse. Trish was the first person I came out to, as she sat stoned and giggling uncontrollably under the tampon machine in our high school bathroom, and when I started to cry she stomped out her joint and hugged me and told me it was OK. To be gay, that is.

Trish is dying now. Liver cancer. She found out six months ago.

That's when I started having the dreams again, dreams of being locked in a basement with no light. And that's also when my asthma came back. And that's also when I stopped jogging every day and instead started drinking every day, and it was this particular hobby that spawned a recent injury: After a tequila-soaked evening at Pete's Down the Street, I overcorrected after missing one of my front steps and toppled down to the sidewalk to land square on my ass—to my amusement (at the time). The next morning, however, my left ankle was the size of a baby's head. Sprained, but in a peculiar manner—most twisted ankles turn inward; a "high sprain," however, was achieved by twisting the foot outward, thus tearing a long list of ligaments, some of which might never heal entirely; others would take weeks. A "high sprain." Sounds like an award—or a cocktail.

Crutches were a bit unnecessary; no, instead they gave me this Velcro-belted, neon-blue nylon deal—a shoe, I guess, to wear over my cast—with hospital-white rubber tread. I immediately dubbed it "das boot." The fit made me claustrophobic, I couldn't walk for shit, and it was so goddamned ugly I thought I'd die. And the pain! Even with an enviable stash of Percocet at hand, the pain was absolutely unbearable. Luckily, one of my employees was nice enough to loan me a cane made out of a petrified—and seriously stretched—bull penis. Me, a bull dyke? It is to laugh.

"Steve got it for me on eBay. For our anniversary," said Allen, surprisingly stoic as he passed the enormous phallus to my waiting hands. I had rarely seen him sans smile since I'd met and hired him a few years before. This was, apparently, a somber occasion and, of course, a very special cane. I attempted to put forth an air of...reverence?

"Thank you, Allen." I fondled the cane at its handle, which seemed the safest place to touch, as it was wrapped in a braided cloth tape at the curve. The shaft itself resembled approximately 28 inches of beef jerky, dry and veiny and made of not-so-mysterious beef parts usually slung to the scrap heap at the slaughterhouse. "I suppose this sort of thing is very...rare."

"Actually, no." Allen seemed embarrassed. "I used to think so myself until I stumbled upon this very item for sale in a Vivian Pring catalog."

Known throughout the East as the queen of cheap mail order, the name Vivian Pring was synonymous with monogrammed silver-plate Christmas ornaments and made-in-Korea vinyl moccasins. Vivian Pring sold the kind of shit that wasn't at all funky, just junky, and the very thought of his betrothed's love offering originating from such a tacky place obviously didn't set well with Allen.

"It was Larry Hagman's! I got it through a celebrity auction!" Steve scampered out from behind his desk, clipping a potted palm with his shoulder as he made his way over to us. "Two years ago, after he got the new liver, he sold some of his...you know...ephemera. And this!"

And, well, that made sense. With a new liver, one would never have room for a bull penis in one's life. I made a mental note to pass this rule de etiquette on to Trish, should she ever be in the position.

"Together three years and he presents me with this." Allen rolled his eyes. "One would have expected a set of crystal."

"It's a genuine bull penis," Steve said. "From the head bull at the Southfork Ranch. Perhaps he used it to keep Sue Ellen Ewing in line."

"Perhaps," I nodded, turning it over and over in my hands, looking for some mark of beauty or interest or...something.

"Anyway, it should help you get around until that ankle heals up. It's quite supportive. There's a metal rod that runs the length of it." Allen tugged nervously at the thin knot of his silk tie. A "pimp knot," he'd always called it, careful to craft a tiny dimple in its center with the tips of his soft, nimble fingers. "I know the crutches are a drag."

"Why, that's very sweet of you." A metal rod? I wondered if it could be removed to leave the bull penis hollow. I imagined somehow rigging a Super Soaker to the cane, a Super Soaker loaded with...warm cream? Let some tourist elbow me on the street and I'd give them a sticky blast! "It's lovely, really. A lovely thought. I'll be proud to use it."

So there I was, this tragic, crippled figure, hobbling out my front door with J.R. Ewing's petrified bull penis in one hand and my Prada bag in the other. Tiny Tim in a gray Armani suit—the one that makes me look like Sigourney Weaver in

Working Girl. All this cloaked warmly in my shin-length monstrosity of a coat, a man's coat tailored nicely to fit my lanky frame, its black cashmere impenetrable to harsh New York winter winds—a treasure I'd awarded myself on a visit to Barneys in those happier days when I actually gave a damn about how I looked.

The news of Trish's impending doom had changed me. I'd lost just enough weight to be under suspicion. (My secretary came right out and asked me one day if I had, as she called it, "the virus," to which I'd cheerfully informed her that no, I didn't, as I always made my vibrators use protection.) Gray hairs were popping up through the Auburn #5 more frequently, and I'd been leaving them. Gray suit, gray hair, gray world... And then she came.

Joseph, my regular driver, never minded blocking a lane of traffic to park and properly escort me to the cab. Joseph, however, was away on vacation, leaving me in the incapable hands of Giuseppe, a nervous dwarf who barely spoke English and who insisted upon pulling his cab into actual parking spaces—no matter how much of a tip I offered. And so, with enough prescription drugs in my body to eliminate any pain I might experience throughout the next millennium, I gimped my pitiful self down the front steps and was steeling for the agonizing hike to the car when, dear God, along she came.

Black hair, and I do mean *black,* like *Elvis* black. Big, soft brown eyes. Rollerblades. A bright blue backpack. Foreign maybe. *Romanian? Cambodian? Cher?*

Whatever her nationality, the girl was startlingly beautiful. And young. Probably didn't even own a heating pad. Definitely hadn't even entertained the thought of making that first demoralizing purchase of Lancôme Wrinkle Recovery Cream. She snapped her gum loudly and proudly and just as I was envisioning her on the cover of the first lesbian Harlequin romance novel...*SMACK!* This guy trotted up behind her, slammed her headfirst into my wrought iron fence, and took off with her backpack. In an instant she wiped out on the sidewalk, landing in a crumpled, though not entirely unattractive, heap. I knelt down, nearly falling myself—no thanks to das boot—and gently touched her face with my fingertips. Her eyes fluttered open. I smiled in relief. She stared up at me with an innocence that turned to panic as she reached up to touch the blood that had run down the side of her cheek.

"It's all right," I said, surprised at myself for sounding so soothing and maternal. "You've just got a little cut. A bump and a cut."

I pulled her hand away from her face and held it in mine. It had been a cool morning already, but it began to rain and was just fucking icy. I slipped off my coat and covered her with it. A few people gathered, probably tourists, but most everyone kept right on with their city pace. Assholes. Someone had called an ambulance.

Dismissing the diminutive Giuseppe, I decided to ride along with her in case the police needed a witness, as if it would make a difference. And though I sat, arms folded, freezing my ass off, I couldn't help but be taken aback by her beauty. Not in a lustful, perverse, I-wonder-what-she-looks-like-naked sort of way. Not at all. Well, not entirely. It's just that she looked so...sweet. And soft. Like we all look when we're young and still believe in things.

"You wear Chanel No. 5," she said, grinning up at me. *Snap!* Again with the gum.

"Why, yes, I do," I said, flattered, you know, excited that such a pretty young thing would not only recognize but comment on my signature fragrance. I glanced up at my reflection in the window. Not bad for my age. Late 30s or early 40s or whatever I was telling myself that day. A little hagged out, a bit rode hard and put up wet, as they say, but then so was Madonna.

"My mom wears Chanel No. 5," she remarked.

I laughed to myself. "Figures."

"You're smoking again," Trish said. "You wheeze in your sleep."

I jerked awake, already feeling the kinks from my nap in a standard-issue hospital-room chair. Trish looked good, considering. Sometimes I wished she'd look worse so it wouldn't seem so unreal that she had cancer.

"Oh, you're awake," I said, shaking and shivering, my clothes still damp enough to cling.

"No shit," she said, straightening her bedclothes. Good old anal Trish. Chronic hand-washer. Organizer of my silverware drawer. Light of my life. "What happened to you? You're all wrinkled."

"Got caught in the rain," I said. "Some guy shoved a girl headfirst into my fence this morning and stole her backpack."

"No kiddin'!"

"Yeah, I, you know...I rode with her to the hospital." I lowered my gaze. "Filled out the police report and everything. Not like it'll do any good, but..."

"Mm-hmm." Trish smirked. "So did you ask her out?"

"Oh, no. No, no. She's just a kid. 23...24..."

"Pretty?"

"Ravishing," I admitted, then blushed.

"I love it! There's hope for you yet!" Trish pointed toward my cane. "What the hell is that?"

"Oh, this old thing? It's a petrified bull penis."

"Oh, yeah, well, now that I see it, how could I not have known?"

"It's also a cane," I said. "I sprained my ankle. Princess Grace strikes again."

"It isn't broken?" Trish wrinkled her brow.

I shook my head. "A high sprain."

"Sounds like such an achievement."

"It happens when you bend the foot outward, and it hurts like nobody's business." I moaned and rubbed my calf, then I threw my hand to my forehead. "I'll never play the violin again!"

"Tripping over empty tequila bottles?"

I casually flipped her off.

"I would have brought you something," I said, ever-so-slyly changing the subject from my rampant alcohol consumption to my unlimited generosity. "I just didn't know what you needed."

"Well, hey..." She snapped her fingers. "I could use a new liver! Maybe a magazine..."

"Well, hey..." I snapped my fingers. "I saw one in the gift shop, but didn't know if it was your size..."

I laid my head on the mattress beside Trish's hand and started to cry. Nothing unusual. I tried to be strong about the whole situation, but sometimes the unfairness of it all was overwhelming. During each visit there came a point where I just cracked. She tousled my hair.

"Mace?"

I didn't answer. I had no answers for anything. Nothing made sense. She had a beautiful family. She had a life.

"Ma-cy?" she said softly and singsongy. "Macy's Thanksgiving Day Parade?"

I closed my eyes and took a deep breath.

"Little friend?" she whispered. "Are you home?"

"I'm fine."

"C'mon, girlie. Don't be so weepy. This whole 'My Best Friend Is Dying' thing is turning into a bad made-for-TV movie."

"Starring Tori Spelling," I responded, blowing my nose.

"Yeah." Trish snorted. "As you." She reached over to check my forehead. "You're sick, missy."

"On the verge." I nodded. "Feel like I'm coming down with something."

"It's no wonder. You probably haven't eaten a decent meal since I've been in here."

"Yeah, well, I gotta go." Standing, I tried my best to straighten out the wrinkles in my suit. "Last thing you need right now is to catch a cold from me. Don't worry, Trish. I'm a big girl."

"I know, but when you come in here looking like 'Liza, fresh from the club,' I can't help it." She waved. "Go home and go to bed, for crying out loud."

"I will. I love you."

"You should."

"Wow." I slapped my forehead. "You are so Jewish."

"Don't smoke!" she called after me as I walked into the corridor. "You've got asthma, remember? And stop hitting the sauce so hard! You look like shit…"

I could still hear Trish when I stepped onto the elevator. Six floors down, my dark-haired sorority princess had been stitched up and exited stage left. That was that.

Case closed.

"Just missed her," the admissions clerk chirped.

"Story of my life," I said. " 'Just missed her.' Maybe I'll have that tattooed on my ass."

I decided to stop by Pete's on the way home. No tough decision, no big surprise, as I'd been stopping at Pete's every day for the last six months, consuming enough tequila shots to encircle the Earth. It usually started at 5:45 P.M., right after work, but today, as I'd called in citing a "personal emergency," the process could start a little earlier.

It was 3, this time, when I took my first sip of Cuervo on ice from the big glass. The bartender knew it was a waste of time for both of us if she gave me a regulation shot size. The tumbler she placed before me would last all evening, generally, and allow me to become gently smashed in my quiet little corner. But while I reveled in my privacy and, admittedly, self-absorption, I was hardly oblivious to the goings-on around me. The standard butches ogled and swaggered around the standard femmes. The selection of pretty youths trickled in from the club crowds, dancing loosely to the Alanis Morissette tunes they'd selected on the jukebox. I sipped my Cuervo in my corner and wondered where I was supposed to fit in, how I had slipped out of my comfortable pocket of living in this odd, gay world.

In the '80s I had ruled Pete's with a wide-smiling self-confidence and a passion for playing pool. I'd listened to Blondie and had worn a lot of black (which, in retrospect, probably made me look like a member of *The Avengers*, but it must've worked, somehow: I never went home alone). I'd worked at a travel agency and had been able to go anywhere in the world...cheaply. I'd sniffed cocaine when I felt like it and had felt virtually unafraid of almost anything. With the exception of commitment.

I sat and thought of all this in my corner. At 40-plus, I was now wearing designer clothes. I owned my own successful travel agency in the Village, and its success had enabled me to buy my apartment building. I had been very lucky over the years and it showed, and I was at a time in my life when I should have been enjoying the vague air of sophistication I had achieved. Yacht clubs. Rolex watches. Polo ponies. Such things—appearances, frivolities—meant nothing, however. Well, almost nothing. The only person I had ever shared my secrets with was dying, and all the trips to Barneys in the world couldn't change that fact.

I lit a cigarette and examined my nails...*time to schedule a manicure*...and felt that sinking weight in my heart and my stomach again. Selfish or not, the feeling was very real. Without Trish, my life would be eternally fucked. How dare she have cancer? How dare she die?

"God, how long has it been?" a throaty voice asked from behind me. "Two years, maybe?"

I turned, and the voice was that of Naomi. Tall, but not as tall as I. Short blond hair. She was a singer I had met a few years back in Manhattan. Yet another reminder of my bad judgment, for the whiplash of our "relationship" left me waking up to find all cash, credit cards, and personal checks missing from my handbag in a crummy hotel room. "Sorry" was all that was written on a piece of paper I found on the TV. At least she apologized.

"My, my...the ghost of Christmas past." I was aware of my slurred speech—but, hey, who was I trying to impress?

"You're drunk," she stated, and looked at me with...pity? "You never used to drink before 6."

"Yeah, well, I use alcohol to cope with people *stealing* from me. You know, I swore if I *ever* saw your thieving ass again, I'd..."

"You'd what?" She smirked, gesturing toward the bull penis. "Chase me with your cane? Shit, Macy, what happened to you? You used to have a sense of humor." She sat down, facing me. "What do you say I buy you a drink? Huh? Let bygones be bygones. Come on, Macy. We had a lot of fun together."

"If you call hours of orgasms fun, well..." I shrugged. "Yes, I guess we did have fun together."

Naomi smiled, reaching across the table to touch my hand.

"I'm sorry," she said.

"I know," I responded curtly. "I got the note."

What happened shortly thereafter I can't explain, as I consider myself a fairly logical person and my actions were totally devoid of any logic whatsoever. I was instantly angry upon seeing Naomi, but the anger stirred other emotions within me. No, not in my heart, but, well, in other places. It was just like I remembered...more of a game than sex. But it was a physically satisfying game, the details of which I'll not divulge (well, except for how she found my G spot without a map by using her middle finger and a soup spoon and, hence, made me come five or six times). Anyway, I wasn't proud of myself as I lay alone on the edge of the bed. My strange surrender had not been out of any true passion, but more of exhaustion. I had felt just as drained and spent before our desperate little tryst as I did after it.

It was 4 A.M. when I awoke, trembling like a junkie as I sat up and swung my legs over the side of the bed. I coughed and my chest felt as if it would explode. Sick. Sick. Sick.

"Naomi, where's my coat?" I asked, my voice deep and hoarse.

Nothing.

I grabbed her shoulder and shook her. She moaned.

"Naomi, where the fuck is my coat?" Then I remembered...the girl, the gum-cracker. She had it.

I peered out the hotel room window and saw a brick wall. Ha. "City View," we called it in our travel brochures. Rain slid down the bricks. I was freezing and had no coat. Fabulous. My suit lay in a crumpled pile on the floor. I reached down and picked it up...still damp. My head pounded. For a moment I stood shivering in my underwear.

"What are you doing?" Naomi asked with eyes closed, barely stirring.

I studied her. Probably just in town for the weekend. She had no idea where I lived, and I liked it that way. Yeah, I could sleep with her, but I didn't want her knowing my personal information. Sex has always made me illogical.

"Breakfast," I told her. "I don't know why, but I'm starving. Howard Johnson's, here I come."

"OK."

And it was that easy. My exit, I mean. Once dressed, I slipped on her black leather deal with the Warner Bros. logo embroidered on the back and slipped out the door. That was that. No muss, no fuss. No awkward exchange of phone numbers. Two minutes later, I was ducking into a cab, begging the driver to please turn up the heat. So long, sucker.

And off we went into the New York morning, zipping down Fifth Avenue at some ridiculous rate of speed. And I was thinking about...jeans.

Her jeans.

How they were stonewashed or acid...washed. Something not yet classic...not ever destined to be classic...but most definitely not current. Not even close to stylish, honey. Not in the least.

I laughed. I laughed until it hurt. No loss, you know. No great catch ever cracked her gum and wore stonewashed jeans.

It was only about two hours later when I woke up in my own bed, hacking so hard I saw flashes of light—Christ, I hadn't even closed my front door—groaning involuntarily from the shocks of pain that racked my body when I tried to get up. In fact, as I lay there silently analyzing the situation, it was rather like a full-body migraine. Oh, goody. The flu.

My apartment had a somewhat slanted, murky look. This wasn't right. A dream, perhaps? The door clicked shut. *Gently.* Afraid, I kept my eyes closed—and heard careful footsteps.

Suddenly I'd had enough. So what if this *was* a psycho killer? So fucking what?

"I don't know who you are," I croaked, "but I'll give you $50 if you bring me a glass of water." *Before you kill me, that is. One last request, you know.* It was only fair.

My head throbbed from the sound of my own voice. Frustrated, disoriented, and just plain scared, I started to cry. Just as I did, a hand lifted my head and a glass was held to my lips. I drank, cool water soothing my throat.

"Mom?" I don't know why I said it.

Someone laughed and said, "No."

I opened my eyes.

Unbelievable.

It was her. The girl who'd been mugged in front of my

apartment. Pretty. Sweet. Girl-next-door-ish. I squinted in disbelief. Yeah, it was her, all right. I closed my eyes and lay my head back against the pillow. It had to be a dream, I rationalized. Some twisted hallucination. Pretty soon she'd have two heads and would start shoving hot dogs into donut holes. No one this attractive could just wander in.

"I'm sorry, the door was open," I heard her say, heard her feet shuffle uneasily. "I just wanted to return your coat. And to thank you. I didn't mean to bother you. It's just that..."

She paused. I opened my stinging eyes and saw that she'd moved closer to my bed, looking at me, into me with those soft eyes. For a moment it seemed she might cry, but she held back her tears and just looked at me like I was Christ himself.

"It's just that most people just turn their backs or walk away, and you didn't." She smiled. "You helped me. I had to let you know how grateful I am."

Nice person, I thought. Manners. Dropping by to return my coat and to thank me personally like that. Dropping by and looking, well, fantastic.

"I've been here," she continued, "in the city, for two years now. Alone. And sometimes it's cool...it's an adventure. But sometimes it just sucks."

And with this, I felt a bit weepy. Not like it took much for that feeling to surface, as I'd been on a self-pity sabbatical from reality all morning. All year, essentially.

She leaned over me, touching my face with caution, touching me with her cool, soft fingertips. I gazed upward to see the smooth, girlish face hovering over me shift into an expression of concern.

"It's my fault." Her gaze moved down with guiltful resignation, as if she was set to confess a homicide or something.

"What?" I had to know what all this tearful melodrama was for.

"You were soaked in the rain when you waited with me

the other day. You gave me your long, beautiful coat." She spoke slowly. "It's my fault you're sick."

"Well, now...it's not as if I have the plague," I began, not entirely sure of that statement at the time, but before I could continue on, I realized the girl had...vanished.

Great, I thought, shaking my head. *A little flu and suddenly I'm Camille, lusting after my young lover on my deathbed. Pathetic. Even my hallucinations let me down.* Embarrassed, I fell into a restless slumber, until several minutes later when I felt her wrapping around me from behind. Cool, silky skin seemed to absorb my fever as her round, naked breasts pressed against my back. Her right arm draped over me as she reached around to caress my ribs. We said nothing to each other, but she knew precisely where to touch me with her tender, delicate hands, pulling the aches out of my body. My skin felt electric under her touch. I had never been so awake, so relaxed, so alive. It was sublime.

For hours, we lay without words or complications. Drifting. Safe. The incident with Naomi seemed distant now, almost like I'd been someone else just one night before. There was no need for games or dances, no roles to play this time. It was a rainy fall Saturday and I lay awake, naked and feverish and held by a beautiful stranger in my own bed. It was the single most perfect moment of my life.

Keepin' It Real

S. Lynn

Maybe it was just the prospect of turning 35 and not having had my "big break" yet, but after eight years as a photojournalist for the nation's leading hip-hop monthly, my dream job was starting to lose its glitter. I had always imagined that by now I would be well on my way to a second Pulitzer and that Caprice Robinson would be a household name; but instead I was well on my way to being bored out of my mind. I was tired of going to concerts and studying one-dimensional people and their one-dimensional worlds. In a very short time, I had seen the music industry change so much that I no longer enjoyed the beat.

Devon had been one of my favorite hip-hop artists since I heard his first single back in college. At that time he was a rising star on the underground scene. His gritty, raw lyrics, delivered with open sensitivity, spoke to me in a way few male artists, especially hip-hop artists, ever had. I'd met him a few times at shows, and he had been my first interview, a project I did for my college newspaper my junior year.

By the time I got my first gig as a reporter, Devon had

really blown up. He was as good as ever, but by then he had the flash and cash to go along with the talent and boyish charm that had made him a household name with so many young ladies. I was thrilled to have the chance to interview him on each of his tours and found him to be friendly and cordial, the perfect gentleman, with no sign of being carried away by his celebrity status. Hell, he even remembered me, which is more than I could say about most of the artists I interviewed. It was no wonder he was so well loved. He was indeed the kind of guy I would date—if, of course, that was my thing. But *that* was not my thing.

Years later, there I was watching him do another concert. Seeing him onstage brought back memories of him working a tiny crowded dance floor in one of those smoky after-hours parties he used to play. Now he was on a huge stage with his own band, DJ, and dancers. I grew tired just from watching him keep step with the young dancers who popped and bounced from one spot to another in perfect sync. But even with all the distractions onstage, there was something about him that made it impossible for me to peel my eyes from his tall, lean frame and smooth good looks. I guess that's why all the teenage girls squealed at his slightest move. And under the hot lights, the heat of which I could feel rolling from the stage, his smooth baby face glistened.

As the set neared its end, I took a few more shots and made my way through the crowd and out of the building. I didn't want to be caught in the mob scene once the show was over. After allowing some time for his entourage to leave the building and get settled at their hotel, I made my way to his hotel suite for my scheduled interview. I was greeted by Devon's manager, who offered me a seat. I waited patiently for a few minutes before Devon emerged wearing a heavy bathrobe emblazoned with the hotel's monogram. This was indeed going to be a very informal interview, and at this very late hour, a very short one.

"Hi, Devon. It's good to see you again," I said extending my hand. "The show was the bomb, as usual."

"Thanks. It's good to see you too, Caprice." Devon shook my hand, then sat across from me on the sofa. His voice was soft and melodic. "Whew! I think I'm getting too old for this." He wiped his face with a thick towel.

"Well, you ready to do this so you can commence to relaxing?" I said.

He nodded.

"You were really working it up there," I began. "How do you keep all the energy going?"

"I don't know. I never really thought about it. I love what I do, so I'm mainly operating on pure adrenaline."

"And testosterone," I laughed. "The girls just love you."

He smiled. "I guess. I never set out to be anything but myself, and I guess that plays well with the young ladies." He blushed slightly.

"And what about offstage?"

"The real me is not the way I am onstage. I try to treat people nice, live right, and just do my thing, you know? It's not just for the image, it's how I really am—well, for the most part."

I nodded. He really was a nice guy. Clean-cut, all-American—so different from other hip-hop artists who've come and gone over the years. He had no facial hair to speak of, except for neatly trimmed sideburns. His hair was closely cropped, and a small diamond stud adorned each ear. Living right must really be paying off, because he looked even younger than when I'd first interviewed him several years ago. He had a gentleness that made me want to hug him and take care of him.

"You haven't been changed by all this fame and glamour? I mean getting to chill in really nice hotel suites, having girls scream your name? Everyone knows and loves you. None of that has changed you at all?"

"Yeah, it's nice," he smiled. "But I never get to be me, the me very few people really know. I don't get much time to myself. And I sure don't feel like I'm really calling the shots. To tell you the truth, I don't even get to eat what I want anymore 'cause my manager doesn't want me to gain too much weight. I miss stuff like home cookin' or just sittin' around trippin' like we used to do back in the day…" His answer was broken up by a noise from the next room. "See, that's what I mean. I can barely fart without someone knowin' about it." The truth in what he said made me feel guilty about my line of work and the role we (the media) played in his sadness.

"So what about your love life?" I blushed. "Your name has been linked with some of the most beautiful women in Hollywood. Anyone special?"

"Most of the women I've been associated with are friends. There's no one special in my life right now. My life is too complicated, and I haven't found anyone who would really be able to understand."

"So can I tell our readers you're available?"

He smiled. "You can tell your readers that I'm not really lookin' right now—for a number of reasons."

"OK." I didn't really get what he was talking about, but I let it slide. After all, what could be more complicated than being on the road all the time? For the first time I watched him, studied him, and for a fleeting moment thought that perhaps he was gay. That would certainly be a complication especially in an industry where a man has to be a "real man" to sell records. His mannerisms, voice, demeanor were all quite feminine, and for a second I felt a glimmer of recognition. "So what's next?" I questioned.

"The tour continues. From here we go to Kansas City and then on to Oklahoma." He tried to hold back a yawn. "I'm sorry. It's been a long day."

"I understand, really," I assured him. But I was a bit disappointed. He'd certainly given me better interviews. This lackluster dialogue would not be the story to give me my big break.

"Hey, maybe we can continue tomorrow. I have the day free. You can come back here and we can do lunch or something."

"I have an idea," I sprang. "It's not the Ritz, and I'm not a gourmet chef, but why don't you come by my place for some home cooking?"

The next day at around noon there was a knock on my apartment door. Collard greens were quietly simmering on the stove alongside ribs smothered in Mama's secret-recipe sauce. The peach cobbler was in the oven and the corn bread was made up and ready to go into the oven just before the meal, so it would be fresh and piping hot when we ate. I gave the apartment a quick once-over glance before opening the door. When I opened it, there stood Devon, looking very nice clad in loose-fitting jeans and a denim shirt, tennis shoes, and a baseball cap that shadowed his face.

"I'm glad you could make it. Come on in," I smiled.

"Well, thanks for inviting me," he said, sliding past me. A whiff of his clean-smelling cologne tickled my nose. "Something smells really good. I could smell it when I got off the elevator. I was hoping it was coming from here. Nice place." He nodded, looking around the room.

"Thanks. It's not exactly a luxury penthouse, but it's comfortable."

"That's the important thing, being comfortable."

"Good, then, just make yourself that way. Would you like something to drink?"

"Iced tea would be nice."

When I returned with two glasses of iced tea, he remarked on how the reading materials on my coffee table revealed my true interests. I suddenly realized that I had an array of feminist material scattered all over my table, including a collection of lesbian erotica. His eyes scanned the titles, stopping on that book, of course. I wanted to snatch it out from under his eyes, but thought it best to be cool. We talked for several minutes about lots of things. The conversation just seemed to flow.

It had been well after 3 A.M. when I finally made it to my apartment the night before, but I had not been able to sleep. I'd found myself wondering why I hadn't noticed certain qualities about Devon before, and why couldn't I find a woman with those same qualities—warm, loving, attentive, sexy as hell?

And now how did I feel? The fan in me was excited about this rare chance to spend time with Devon. The reporter in me was seeing this as the chance of a lifetime. But the woman in me was feeling a rush of something I couldn't quite put my finger on, and the lesbian in me was making damn sure that the woman in me kept whatever it was she thought she was seeing in this man in check.

He was very quiet during lunch, very different from the chatty person who had entered the apartment only minutes earlier. To break the silence I asked about the interview.

"So do you mind if I ask you some questions while we eat?"

"No, not at all. That's what I came here for. Well, that and these slammin' greens," he said, placing a forkful in his mouth. His eyes went to the camera on the counter.

"Can I quote you on that slammin' greens comment?" I joked.

"Hell, you can quote me, take a picture of me with pot liquor drippin' down my chin, whatever you want as long as I can get some more."

"No problem." I moved my chair back to get to the stove.

"Sit down. I'll get it," he said, moving quickly. "I don't get to eat like this very often. The least I can do is get it myself. Would you like some more while I'm at it?"

I shook my head no and reached for my camera in time to get a shot of him piling two large heaps of greens onto his plate. He ignored the flash, piling on some more ribs as well.

"So, Caprice, where'd you learn to cook like this?" Devon asked as he settled back into his chair.

"I guess I picked it up from Mom and Grandma. My Southern roots grow deep."

He grunted in agreement, never missing a bite of food. I chuckled at the sight of him.

"I'm sorry for making a pig of myself, but this is really good. Keep feeding me like this and I won't want to leave."

The thought of it warmed me. I hoped it was because I liked the idea of someone enjoying something I made, instead of who that someone was. My brain was becoming lost. I had not felt like this about a man in many years—ever, actually. I was a lesbian, for goodness' sake. But this man who now sat across my tiny dinette table was making me question lots of things about myself, and I didn't like it one bit.

I tried to keep my focus by concentrating on the interview. I asked my questions and took a few more shots, including one of him with a glob of barbecue sauce on his smooth, dimpled chin. (I had to really fight the urge to lick it off.) The quicker we got through it, the quicker I'd be able to get this man out of here and get my nerves back in check. But did I really want him to leave? I couldn't very well say, "You've had your food, I got my questions answered, so could you leave before I do something I might regret?"

After lunch we sat side by side on the sofa, looking at an old high school yearbook he'd found on a bookshelf. He asked many questions about my high school days, which really were not very exciting, but he seemed to take great interest anyway. He picked me out immediately from each group photo I was in.

"How do you always find me so easily? I looked like a different person back then," I said.

"I'd know those eyes anywhere." He paused. "You have the most expressive eyes I've ever seen."

I don't know if it was the comment or the sincerity of his

stare while making it, but I became even more nervous. My internal battle was creeping to the surface, and my body twitched with an uneasiness he must have sensed. He got up and walked across the room.

"I'm sorry," he mumbled, not looking back at me. "I hope I didn't embarrass you. I didn't mean..."

But he had somehow embarrassed the hell out of me. I tried to coolly recover. "It's OK..." I stammered. He stood very still. As I looked at him the light shone brightly on his soft profile, and I took in the way his neck curved gently up from beneath the collar of his shirt. I had to blink a few times to stop the tricks my eyes were playing on me, but by now it was too late. My body was reacting to him, causing my pulse to race and warmth to grow in my stomach. This was crazy.

"What are you thinking?" he asked, walking away from the window and back to the sofa.

"Nothing." I cleared my throat.

I studied his movements carefully as he moved, the easy stride, the slight roundness in the hips that his baggy jeans until now had concealed. I became embarrassed when he caught me studying him and quickly dropped my eyes to the floor. He gently lifted my chin and looked into my eyes. "Your eyes say so much," he said, placing his other hand atop mine as he sat down beside me. I looked down at his hand, realizing for the first time that it was about the same size as mine, perhaps a bit smaller. Could this really be happening? And what the hell *was* happening, anyway? Devon seemed uneasy. The calm exterior I'd seen walk across the room was replaced by a tremble in the hand that still rested over mine.

He cleared his throat and opened his mouth, but said nothing.

I felt that I had to do something, so I spoke. "Look, Devon, I hope you don't think I'm just being silly, but I don't want you to get the wrong idea about why I invited you here."

"And I don't want you to get the wrong idea either..." His words trailed off into silence as his lips moved closer to and then met mine.

"Oh, God, I'm sorry," I said with a start.

"Don't be," he said.

"But you don't understand. I have to be honest with you. I'm not into..."

"Men," he interrupted. "I understand."

I was glad someone did, because I still wasn't quite sure what the hell was going on. Such a revelation would have made a lot of men leave. The others would have seen it as a challenge to try to change me. He didn't move. I became angry, assuming his motive was the latter, and at my own carelessness at ending up in this situation.

"I think you should..."

"I have a confession to make," he interrupted. He took a deep breath and tightened his grip on my hand. Now I was really confused. He began to explain, "I really don't know how to say this. I am very attracted to you. It's been a long time since I've felt this way, and I'm not really sure how to handle it." Pain welled up in his eyes.

"Devon, I'm gay. I'm a lesbian and..."

"So am I, Caprice. That's why I'm struggling so much with..."

"You're gay?" I couldn't tell if I was angry or hurt.

"No, I'm a lesbian," he said, releasing my hands and sitting up straight.

My heart was pounding so loudly in my ears, I thought maybe I'd heard him wrong.

"*You're a WHAT!?*" Then I saw the tear roll down Devon's cheek. "Talk to me, Devon. Do you know what you're saying?"

Devon nodded, this time staring into my eyes as if ready for a challenge. "When I started rapping about 15 years ago, the industry didn't seem ready for females. Sure, groups like

Salt-N-Pepa did well, but they were groups. The world was-n't ready for a female solo rapper, let alone one who was openly gay. I was too out to masquerade as a straight woman. I couldn't change who I am."

"But you did," I said pointedly. This was getting deep, and I was starting to get angry.

"Eventually, yes. And when I did, people started to notice I had skills. Everything happened so fast that I had no choice but to go with it. At the time it seemed a small price to pay for having my dream come true."

"But millions of people know you as..." I was at a loss for words.

"As Devon. My people, the few who know, and I have been very careful not to say that I'm a man."

"And who the hell is Devon? Is that even your name, or is that a part of this person you've created?" I asked angrily.

"It's my real name," she said. "And I haven't created any-thing. This whole idea got out of hand years ago, and I just felt that I couldn't turn back. I didn't know how to stop hid-ing after a while."

"But your music. You sing about loving women, about having your heart broken by women."

"Because it's true. My music is the only way in my life that I can keep it real, until now. This is all happening so fast, I don't know what I'm doing..."

A steady stream of tears now rolled down Devon's caramel-brown cheeks. I didn't know what to do. I reached over and hugged the broken person who sat before me as she now sobbed quietly onto my shoulder.

"I'm so sorry," I soothed, holding her closer and feeling the outline of tightly restrained breasts for the first time.

She pulled away from me, wiping her eyes on her sleeve. "No, I'm sorry. I should've been real with you from jump, but I didn't know how."

"I'd say you did OK." I tried to smile; my emotions were

still vacillating between hurt and anger—and I didn't want her to see. "But why me, why now?"

" 'Cause I have not been as drawn to anyone as I am to you. I can't explain it. It just wasn't fair for me to go on deceiving you or to let you go on thinking something was wrong with you."

"How did you know I was even thinking that way?"

"Your eyes said it all. And when you kissed me...I knew I had to do something. I had to let you know that you were kissing a woman who wants you just as much." Devon sighed, moving closer to me on the sofa. "Over the years I've wanted to tell you so many times. My manager has always known how I feel about you. Why do you think they never really leave me alone with you? I've been holding on to the hope of this moment for years..."

She leaned in so close that I could smell her breath—familiar, sweet, calming. I softly kissed her lips—and she responded. We continued kiss after kiss for several minutes, each kiss lasting longer than the previous one. I wondered where this was leading. My body was already several steps ahead of my brain, which was still trying to grasp this Twilight Zone I'd found myself thrown into. She took my hand and led me to my bedroom as if she were at her own home.

She kissed me, and my lips parted, allowing her tongue to explore. Then she silently guided me to the bed, sat me down, looked into my eyes, and slowly unbuttoned her shirt—staring deeper and breathing deeper with each button. She let the shirt fall to the floor and stood before me in a black silk tank top. I reached up to pull her close, inhaling the clean fragrance of her cologne as I kissed her neck and strong shoulders. She leaned down to kiss me, and my tongue hungrily tasted her mouth. A soft moan escaped from deep in her throat. She held on to the back of my neck, gently rocking as she cradled my head. As much as I didn't want to let her go, I had to get closer, had to feel her skin.

With the same sense of reluctance, she stepped away from me and pulled her top over her head. As she reached to loosen the fabric that tightly bound her chest, I stopped her. As I unsnapped what looked like a cross between a bra and a girdle, which confined her midsection, I wondered how she lived like this. She let out a deep sigh as her breasts were freed. I nuzzled my face between them, trying to inhale the pain and now relief they must feel. I slowly lifted first one and then the other to my lips and planted soft kisses all over them before gently sucking each to life in my hand.

After a few minutes she was standing before me in only her black lace panties, which were a totally unexpected and very, very (did I mention very?) pleasant surprise.

"Beautiful!" I sighed as my breath caught at the sight of her wide hips, flat stomach, and taut thighs. Her eyes were so deep I thought I might drown. Her body was firm and well defined, but so soft it seemed it would melt to the touch.

"Oh, God! Yes, Caprice! Yes," she sighed loudly before pushing me back onto the bed.

Hearing her say my name like that removed any questions that may have lingered in my mind.

There was an urgency and passion in the way that she undressed me, her lips never losing contact with my body. As she kneeled above me and painted my body with hers, I thought I would surely die.

Her palms were sweating as she gripped my hand.

"You OK, baby?" I asked.

"Yeah, I'm fine," she mumbled, not really hearing what I'd said.

I watched the handsome profile that I'd now had the pleasure of loving for two years glued to the flickering television screen. She jumped slightly as the popular reporter began to speak, and then settled back into the sofa.

"...*the story that has taken the rap music world by storm.*

Rapper Devon, who is at the top of the R&B and rap music charts as a man, revealed last month in this article, 'Life With Devon: Keepin' It Real,' that he is in fact a woman, bringing to light a masquerade that has gone on for almost 15 years. The question in the mind of many Americans is why?"

The first page of my article—which contained a picture of Devon and me smiling from a sofa—appeared on the screen.

The room suddenly fell silent as MUTE popped onto the screen and a cool-looking Devon appeared in the chair across from the reporter.

"Why'd you do that?" I asked.

"We know what I said. I don't need to hear it again. Besides, you know how I hate watching myself on TV. I'd much rather look at you." She smiled, putting the remote on the coffee table. She shrugged. "I'm just keepin' it real, baby."

Dying, But Not Yet Dead, Dream of Love

Cynthia Wilson

Chrys was surprised at herself. After years of knowing Lora, she discovered herself stealing gazes at her whenever Pip, Lora's butch lover, wasn't looking. Seated about the fire, on their camping trip, Chrys felt Lora answer the secret heat by carefully returning the come-hither looks with planned, modulated eye contact.

Chrys was also surprised for other reasons. Lora was a funky country-loving girl who lived in a trailer in the woods, hiked vigorously, made circles around trees in the woods with other nature-loving lesbians, and believed crystals held powers beyond just being pretty. Chrys was surprised to be attracted to a woman like Lora because Chrys prided herself on her intellect, which could not abide heebie-jeebie New Age fatuousness. Chrys would attend a Susan Sontag lecture or read Nietzsche. She didn't even believe in the horoscope, so it was a pleasant surprise to feel drawn to Lora in spite of everything—including that Lora was married.

Chrys was also proud of the fact that messing around with married people was something she herself would never do.

Lora had a tattoo of a phoenix on her forearm 20 years before it became fashionable, but the ink had faded and run a bit under her skin, making it look out of focus. Chrys didn't like tattoos, then or now, but she could ignore it because Lora—illuminated by flickering flames—was looking so...fox-like with her red-auburn hair and slightly slanted upturned eyes, which were a shameless green-turquoise color. Her sunned skin, healthy and weathered, looked dark for a woman of French extraction. Her hair was a happy, fuzzy mass, combed just enough to look sexy-wild. She had a medium build with a sumptuous few extra pounds on her middle-aged hips. Her back was as strong as a 2-by-4 but in spite of her Herculean back, she liked to play the femme. Lora wore "girl shoes" when she dressed up, while Chrys, with her big shock of prematurely white hair and overweight body, wore only men's shoes when she was going formal, partly because she had size 13 feet but also because she liked them better.

So Chrys and Lora found themselves irretrievably attracted to each other against all odds. And against good sense. Their group consisted of two couples, isolated on a camping trip: Lora and Pip, married for seven years, and Chrys and Regina, best friends for three decades. Regina, a known heterosexual, was happy to be on their annual summer camping trip, this time to celebrate her 49th birthday among Northern California's mighty redwoods.

The place was great. There was a good 'n' cold river creek nearby for swimming, and there were trees much taller than buildings and hundreds of years older. Deep-scented forest primeval emanated a spiritual sexiness only a few minutes' walk away, so they exhaled, relaxed, and enjoyed their freedom to lounge, do nothing, sigh. The weather was perfectly hot for cold beer drinking, fat joints, and too many cigarettes because they were "on vacation." They all took turns cooking, and Pip always made the nighttime fire bright orange and snapping. It was at these times that the illicit but heat-making sneak-gazes were most easily accomplished because the darkness shrouded them from the unsuspecting Pip. Hidden from the others but not from themselves, each noticed the fire's blazes reflected in the other's eyes. The two expected nothing from this flirtation—after all, they were "friends"—but each time their eyes met, it was as if they could feel the curvature of the earth.

Chrys and Lora did not touch each other that fateful weekend. Their crotches hurt in silence, and in fact, they spoke to no one, not even to each other, about what was going on. But no matter the silence, the sexy seed had been planted. After Chrys got home, she could not get the movies of Lora out of her mind's eye. She resolved to tell Lora by letter. Chrys attempted to say, "I want you, but I know I can't have you."

I want to tell you about all of the divine (and beyond) thoughts and fantasies that I have had about you. Getting home today from the camping trip, I found myself masturbating, and there I was in your hands. Then I found myself way deep inside you and I was reveling. I came for you like I know I never will because you are married, living elsewhere and all that but it still feels good to tell you the truth because our secret was so painfully silent on the camping trip. After coming with you as sweetly as kissing the pink bottom of heaven, I was resting quietly and you were there, breathing gently beside me. So strong was your presence that for a second I believed it. Even though I have boundaries about being with married people, they do nothing to stop the core of creativity that you agitate in my imagination. And I don't want my imagination to stop where you are concerned.

Lora loved this letter. She read it with pleasure spreading through her like a sunrise in her bloodstream. She caressed the page softly, smelled it, dreamed on it. Her whole body smiled as she read the passionate, carefully chosen words formulated to inflame without calling to action.

Two weeks later Lora was visiting the Bay Area from her mountain home up north to work as a gardener for the wealthier citizens of Oakland. Lora called Chrys to invite her to meet at the local gay watering hole, the Peacock. Chrys was tickled pink and purple by this invitation yet she wondered why because she knew that her feverish sexual creations about Lora would never see the light of day or the perfume of night. She knew damn well that it was not to be. Yet Chrys's crotch had a mind of its own, and Chrys suddenly knew, as she agreed to meet with Lora that she and her pussy were moving onto dangerous ground. As Chrys hung up the phone she was forced to reconcile her hard-on with her integrity. Her hard-on won. If Lora were willing, Chrys thought, Lora who had so much more to lose than she did, Chrys knew that she would hump Lora hard and true, primitive and deep, coming all over her, inside and out. Chrys knew that, if invited, she would be there in a tenth of a flash.

And she was. Chrys greeted Lora in her client's front yard, just as Lora was finishing up for the day. Lora had made, Chrys noticed, the yard look healthy and virulent, nicely designed. Off they went, puffing on a skinny joint, glowing with desire yet resolute not to do anything wrong. Dusk was a soft blue blanket and they walked slowly, noticing more than usual, taking in the dusky night, stopping at a well-endowed rose bush.

"Oh, it's heavenly! Chrys, smell this!" As Chrys positioned her nose above the velveteen orange rose, tinged yellow in the center, she opened her mouth and took in the whole flower, gently crunching down on the perfume, the wetness, and the sour taste of vitamin C.

Lora's eyes widened into poker chips. "I can't believe you did that!"

"Try it," urged Chrys. "This is what I was famous for, growing up in Bakersfield. I ate flowers. All kinds! Roses are the best, though."

Lora followed suit. She chose a smaller one with red burnt petals.

"Delicious!" cooed Lora.

They both swallowed, smiling like Cheshire cats.

The moon beamed down with the heat of the sun in their pants. They walked slowly, arm in arm, both aware that they wanted this walk to the bar to last. They stopped to notice cracks in the sidewalk, eccentric paint jobs on nice houses, the faintly jiggling stars in the night sky.

"I'll tell you what I've been thinking," Lora offered.

"All right, Lora, please do, and then I'll tell you what I've been thinking."

"OK, here it is. I don't know how, but Pip picked up on our attraction over the course of that camping trip, and you know what? She felt secure enough to tell me that we can kiss. She told me that she knew we had the hots for each other and that I should go ahead and kiss you. She thinks she and I are in good enough 'shape'—as she put it—to withstand a kiss! Maybe we should try being together in a limited way, Chrys. I mean, if we don't touch each other below the waist then we haven't done anything wrong that I need to tell Pip, right? I mean, she SAID we could kiss. Besides, what we do together isn't really her concern, is it? I love her the same whether or not you and I get together."

"OK, Lora, you said what you were thinking, now it's my turn. I'm thinking"—Chrys felt frightened of what she was about to say—"the same thing." The thought of being able to kiss Lora "above the waist" sent Chrys's pussy into a paroxysm of sexual celebration because 1) her pussy was starving and Chrys knew that even if below the waist was off-limits;

above the waist wasn't; and 2) she could get extremely happy with hands and mouths on breasts and mouths on mouths. Her pussy was thinking, visualizing the trillion tricks of love that can be committed "above the waist." Chrys immediately obsessed on Lora's mounded, rounded breasts. Her mouth watered. She accidentally drooled. She thrilled to the likelihood that she would get to kiss Lora for days on end.

Lora's heart was beating like a bird's, so quickly she felt she could float away. She was anxious and definitely frightened. But despite her excessive rate of respiration, she was determined to go forward. She turned to look at Chrys, saw her bright-white hair flash in front of her, and then slowly sank to her knees. Lora flopped to the ground.

Chrys was shocked into action, catching Lora on her way down, falling to her own knees, touching Lora's face, calling to her, petting her forehead. Chrys was about to find a phone when Lora opened her eyes and smiled.

"I'm all right, Chrys, just a little shaken. I'll be fine. Here, help me up."

"God, what was that, Lora? Did you faint?"

"Yeah, I do that once in a while when I get truly excited. Don't worry, I'll be fine."

"Lordy! What a scare, girl! I thought for a second you died! Thank God you're OK."

And the wicked part of Chrys was relieved that Lora would still be available for a make-out session. And maybe more.

When they got to the bar, it was beer-smelly and cig-infested but still welcoming. Dark and dreary, it offered an anonymous haven for their illegitimacy. They sat at the most distant table they could find, even though it would be extremely unlikely for them to run into anyone they knew. Chrys ordered a rum with lime and Lora asked for a tequila sunrise. As they drank in small sips to make their visit last longer, they maintained eye contact. Under the table, Lora pushed her knees against Chrys's. This splashed Tabasco sauce in Chrys's pants, and she started fantasizing wildly on the spot. In her imagination, she took Lora's head in her hands, the square of Lora's jaw in her palm, and kissed her with mouth open. Lora's lips were electric wires, burning Chrys just right. Lora, not taking her eyes off Chrys, could sense the overheating concupiscence that caused the floodgates to open as she felt her stomach rush downward. Lora made a small gasp. As the heat rose for both of them, Lora could tell she had made Chrys juicy, and she felt the pull of her own contraction within that made her want to take care of Chrys's hard-on.

"Let's go. Let's sit in your truck. I have to kiss you or I will die."

They held hands very tightly on the way to the truck. The walk back was much swifter than the walk to the bar because their verboten excitement both thrilled and horrified them.

In the cab of the truck they sat, still gripping hands. They both stared straight ahead, too electrified and horny to look at each other.

"I feel like I am about to fly off a cliff, Chrys. My heart is pounding for two reasons: I'm about to betray my lover, and I'm about to kiss someone I've wanted to kiss for years!"

"Now wait a sec, Lora. Pip said we could kiss. No betrayal here." Chrys turned to face Lora, whose lips were open a tiny slit. Chrys knew where her tongue would go.

Slowly, with the windows steaming up even before they kissed, and barely allowing herself to believe it was really happening, Chrys moved her mouth to cover Lora's. Their lips connected, mouths gently opened to let in their love, and metaphorically, out flew Pip, in bits and pieces. Chrys's tongue explored the love cave of Lora's mouth, under her front teeth, in front of her teeth, over the plain of Lora's velvety, responsive tongue. All four of their nostrils were flared and their breaths were *choo-choo*ing for each other like a runaway train. Chrys's hand moved to Lora's breast, mashing softly, then harder. Chrys snaked her way under Lora's thin T-shirt. The suppleness of softness that Chrys found there made her eyes roll back, and suddenly Chrys felt herself expand with the almost unbearable turn-on of having Lora push toward her. The heat in Lora's blood made Chrys press even harder as a burning ring of hot metal encircled her cunt hole with the sudden need to come. Chrys was breathing and humping, talking lust from her throat, navigating the confines of the truck cab, building up, threatening a storm. For Chrys, the tissue underneath, the flesh of this woman, was just too hot. Chrys spasmed into a huge charge of love-energy, rising up on top of Lora by bearing down on her bosom and kissing her hard and wet. Lora answered with a muscular pull on Chrys's larger-than-life ass, forcing Chrys to give over more weight on top. Chrys registered, even in this boiling over, that Lora had touched her below the waist—but it wasn't the love canal, after all. Lora blasted lust inside of Chrys's mouth, scouring her with an electric eel of a tongue, jetting in, jetting out, and almost hurting. As Chrys's passion built pressure, she kept humping and pumping Lora, who was pinned deliciously underneath, and Lora responded with equal undulation, making Chrys rise up and down in demonic waves. Luckily the windows were dripping with condensation by this time, so no one could see in, nor could they see out. Moving against all of her good intentions, Chrys inserted her hand down the now wet jeans of Lora.

Lora dutifully reminded Chrys that she was off limits and pulled Chrys's hand back up and out. "I hope I don't disappoint too much, but I can't. I just can't." Lora was half breathing, half snorting with mounting lust.

"You've given me worlds! Worlds! Don't even think about it. It's totally OK. I'm sorry I got carried away. But you do make me want you. Bad."

Both Lora and Chrys knew damn well that the kind of

kissing they were doing was not what Pip had in mind when she generously offered up permission for her girlfriend to kiss someone else. But the wildfire that seared them both forced them to mutually decide that this affair could not, should not, be stopped. Quickly, Lora justified her explorations outside of her marriage. The burning pair made plans for Chrys to visit Lora within the month.

Two weeks later, in Lora's mountain trailer, Chrys mounted Lora from behind with Delilah, her strap-on dildo. Chrys was standing on her knees and Lora's ass was lifted delicately upward so Chrys could see the dark hairs flattened and wet, smeared into a shiny black line, from around her pinkish-brown asshole all the way down to her exposed, coral-colored cunt. It was into that glistening wetness that Chrys placed the arrow-headed tip of Delilah, just below the stinky rose of Lora's asshole and into the sweet pink canoe. It glided in slowly, carefully, and then a sudden, undeniable push of brutal ardor.

"Ahhrrg!" cried Lora. Chrys was not sure whether it was protest or pleasure, but since she did not know, she withdrew and entered again, this time more slowly, but Chrys forced her way in deeper, all the way. Chrys could feel Lora's soft buttocks halt the trajectory. Lora's gracefully uplifted ass allowed Chrys to withdraw and plunge again, over and over, with musical rhythm and huge carnal pleasure. Chrys loved the slap of her own thighs and hips against the pudding flesh of Lora's pliant ass. Chrys looked down to watch Delilah, slender and forest-green, marbled with dramatic black swirls, disappearing and reappearing with each gratifying thrust 'n' fuck. Chrys watched Delilah sink in deeper and Lora moaned and pushed back and Chrys saw Delilah come sliding out, wet, slick, and ready to dive in again. Chrys felt like the dildo was a root, combining them into one rutting, primitive animal, both of them groaning, squealing, crying out, and laughing.

As Chrys plunged in and pulled out, up on her knees, her ass contracted and relaxed like maniacal billows. Chrys outstretched her arms toward the ceiling, exhilarated beyond anything she had known before. She cried out to God, "How great Thou art to make my life so perfect, so insanely blissful that I can barely withstand it!" Not usually religious, Chrys was sublimely overcome.

"How can you, dear God? How can you make my life so FINE?" Exactly at the moment that Chrys began to come inside Lora like an underwater volcano, shimmering and shuddering above her like a crown of fire, just as she was spewing her mountainous orgasm, on her knees, arms uplifted into a huge prayer of gratitude...Pip walked in.

This Means Nothing

Linda Suzuki

Nicki always walked into a bar like it was her birthday. She would fling open the door and a smile would break across her face as if all the dykes inside were going to yell "Surprise!" and throw confetti.

The fact is, most of the dykes inside would have liked to yell and throw things when they saw Nicki, since she'd fucked most of them—and since most of those she'd fucked, she'd fucked over. Mostly, though, they'd just look away so everyone could see they didn't care anymore, or they'd smile and shake their heads because they knew that was how it was with her, or sometimes, the real pitiful ones—the raw ones—would look at Nicki with big wet eyes and trembling lips. Nicki never saw them. She wasn't attracted to women with problems visible to the eye.

I don't know why I start there, with that image of her, but it is where my memories of Nicki usually begin.

Nicki was Erica Nickerson, star forward and captain of our basketball team. She was at Putnam on a free ride because of the amazing things she could do with a ball—any ball, any shape, any size. If you could punt it, pass it, kick it, hit it, throw it, sink it, slam it, serve it, or dunk it—Nicki could do it better. Not being an athlete myself, it's hard for me to say how good Nicki really was. She was the best athlete at Putnam—a women's college chock-full o' dykes—so maybe she could have been "world class" at any sport she chose. She just never chose a sport. She played whatever sport was in season, played like her life was at stake, then changed uniforms and moved on to the next game. Drove the coaches crazy. If you asked her why, she would say she didn't want to be tied down—and once you understood that women were her favorite sport, it all made sense.

Nicki was my best friend from freshman year on, although I wasn't necessarily hers. It wasn't that she liked anyone else better, she just didn't think that way. People—teammates, friends, and lovers—were incidental and interchangeable. We could be amusing, or useful, or interesting, but if we weren't, Nicki would move on to someone else who was.

At first, Nicki and I lived together courtesy of the Housing Office lottery, and later because it was easier than filling out the paperwork to live anywhere else, and finally because everyone thought of us as roommates—the way two people become a couple and it's hard to say one name without saying the other.

If you're wondering did she ever fuck me, the answer is no, and the reason is that I didn't want to have to find a new roommate and a new best friend.

In the first three months of college, I must have seen 20 women in and out of our room and Nicki's life. She had no self-consciousness about fucking them in front of me (or rather, three feet below me on the lower bunk) or breaking up with them or ignoring them or having all this *lesbo teatro* take place in our Grace Hall 10-by-12 while I sat on the top bunk pretending to study. After a while, I wasn't even pretending to be polite, listening intently to how Nicki made love to women—what she said to make them stay and what she said to make them leave. A finer education could not be had for money.

I don't want you to think less of Nicki for any of this, so let me just say that she always told them first, "This means nothing." Honest to God, she would just come right out and say it, like the airplane chick who tells you to stow your tray table and return your seat to the full upright position. There'd be some crazed-with-lust TA, naked and squirming on the narrow little mattress, and Nicki would just stop and look the poor girl deep in the eyes and say very seriously, "You know, this means nothing. I don't want you moving in tomorrow. It's just sex." Please remain seated until the captain has turned off the FASTEN SEAT BELTS sign.

Granted, the girl was usually wet and moaning and rubbing herself up and down Nicki's thigh by the time the disclaimer rolled and would have said just about anything to keep Nicki's fingers and tongue moving. All the same—and to her credit—Nicki always said it.

Except, maybe, one time she didn't. Which means, of course, that after all those preflight checks, Nicki crashed and burned.

My guess is that Nicki got bored working her way horizontally through the student body. She had started with senior,s and her friends admired her greatly, as this defined upward mobility in our sexually underachieving circle. But by the time we were juniors, she'd had every one of us she wanted, and it was probably then that she set out to have a look at the faculty.

There were a lot of faculty women to choose from, but there was only one first choice.

We were all of us—the English majors—in love with Dr. Flannagan. She taught Feminist Literature and spoke with an Irish accent, wore great bulky fisherman's sweaters over faded jeans and hiking boots, and had long curly red hair and green eyes. All her classes were full all the time.

Her first name was Siobahn, which I pronounced "Siobahn" until I learned it was supposed to be pronounced "She-von" and her friends called her "Vonnie"—as if I weren't already crazy enough about her.

Word was she didn't have a lover, at least not a full-time live-in like most of the faculty dykes. Can't you just guess that this left room for a million stories, like that her lover was in prison for IRA terrorist acts, or that Dr. Flan had been dumped recently and was therefore heartbroken and vulnerable (and available), or that she lived for her writing and didn't have time for a lover unless that lover was prepared to spend the rest of her life serving as muse and wife and working two jobs just so Siobahn could stay home and write, which of course about 200 of us were willing to do.

As an English major, I had an excuse for taking all of Dr. Flan's classes, sitting in the front row, getting there early, and staying late. But not Nicki. Nicki was phys ed, so imagine how surprised I was when she showed up in Dr. Flan's Feminist Poetry class the first day of the winter semester in our junior year. As she slid into the seat next to mine, Nicki flashed me her eat-you-up smile, and, sadistically ignoring my curiosity, turned to face front.

There is something about two strong, virile, desirable women encountering each other for the first time that can make a room vibrate with the fantasy-lust-envy of the rest of us. Straight men, apparently, feel the same way about pro wrestling.

Dr. Flan strode into the room and sat on the edge of her desk, green eyes roaming the rows and brushing across my face like a feather before coming to rest—no, that's not quite it—before coming to dance with Nicki's eyes. Then Dr. Flan—and for this I thought her even more remarkable because I knew how far a talented literary type like her must be able to go fantasizing about somebody with a body like Nicki's—then Dr. Flan just started teaching class. She outlined the course objectives, explained her grading system, distributed handouts, even cracked jokes. And all the while I'm thinking there could not be anything hotter in this world than these two women in bed together. I knew from the way Nicki sat, long legs splayed and the fingers of one hand drumming lightly on her thigh, that she agreed with me.

Dr. Flan taught the whole 45 minutes, and I guess I was a little disappointed that when the class ended the two of them didn't just rush into each other's arms and fall humping to the floor. Instead, everybody stood up and pushed out the door—Nicki and me included—and Dr. Flan sat at her desk reading, waiting for the next class.

I played it very cool, didn't ask Nicki why she was doing a poetry elective. I just waited, and sure enough, over beers that night at the Fifth Quarter (all beers $1.25), Nicki leans back and cocks her head to one side and says all casual-like, "What's the poetry chick's name again?"

"You mean the professor who teaches our poetry class? The one who went to school for 22 years just to attain the qualifications necessary to teach our poetry class?"

Nicki smiled, loving the abuse. "Yeah, the poetry chick. What's her name again?"

"Siobahn Flannagan. Dr. Siobahn Flannagan. We call her Dr. Flan."

"*We* being who?"

"*We* being those of us who can read. *We* being those of us majoring in something other than recess."

Nicki laughed. She loved this part especially. I really believe she became a phys ed major just to be a little more in-your-face about her right to do whatever felt good at the moment. She wouldn't even pretend she wanted to teach. She just said phys ed was her best subject in high school, like English had been mine, so why shouldn't she take the easy A and major in it at college? She also said she liked women's bodies and there wasn't another major that brought you into contact with so many naked ones. I always lost the argument on this point.

For a jock, Nicki did OK in the poetry class at first. I helped her with the homework, and she raised her hand a couple of times to ask questions that were only semi-smart-ass. But mostly she just sat there and turned the beams on Dr. Flan.

And nothing happened.

Nicki ignored the suspense. As far as I could tell, Dr. Flan didn't feel any suspense. But the suspense was killing me.

Nicki gave it as long as she could, but as the last-day-to-drop loomed, my guess is she felt she had to make a move or find another faculty target, so Nicki scheduled some time during Dr. Flan's office hours.

Nicki walks into Siobahn Flannagan's office and perches, leaning forward, on a chair, elbows on knees, hands cupping her chin, beautiful smile that says, "Let me be whatever you want most."

Siobahn pulls up Nicki's records, glances over her home-work, swivels away from the computer screen, and leans forward as well, hands clasped under her chin, eyes unreadable. "If you don't mind the asking, why is a Physical Education major taking a feminist poetry elective?"

Nicki leans back, sprawling casually in her chair, and gestures toward the woman. "Because of you. I've heard good things about you."

Siobahn turns to look out the window, her brow furrowed for a moment. "About me," she says presently, "or about my teaching?"

Nicki, who charges her sexual batteries on being one step ahead of every woman she meets—whether that step be into bed or out the door—is stalled for a moment. Before she can respond, Siobahn continues. "Because there's nothing you could have heard about me personally that would bring you into this class, and I think if you had truly heard anything about my teaching, it would be that I won't give an easy A...even to the captain of our championship basketball team."

Nicki clears her throat. "Actually, we were just finalists." Like this has anything to do with it.

Siobahn nods. "Noted for the record, with commendations for your honesty." She says nothing for a moment and—

*because women just do not do this to Nicki—Nicki does not
know what to do. "Very well, then," Siobahn says, as though
they have agreed on something, "I will prepare a reading list
for you. This will give you some background on feminism,
which you will need if you're to be serious about this class.
Then I'd like to have you submit a list of five possible topics
for your midterm paper. You and I will go over them and
choose the best. Let's say we'll have our two lists together by
this time next week."*

*"Great," Nicki says without much enthusiasm, but then
those turbo hormones kick in and she adds, "but why don't we
meet for coffee or a drink somewhere, instead of back here."*

*Siobahn looks at her quizzically, as though Nicki has just
suggested they get matching tattoos. "No." And then she stands
and walks around to sit on the edge of the desk in front of Nicki
and leans down so that their faces are just a foot apart. "I see
women in this office every day. Sometimes they come in here
talking about literature but end up telling me more than I want
to know about things that are none of my business."*

*Nicki sits frozen, experiencing—maybe for the first time in
her life—that awful sick sensation of control slipping away.*

*"And sometimes when those women talk to me," Siobahn
continues, "I hear names, which I usually manage to forget
the moment after, unless the name strikes me as unusual
somehow."*

*Nicki knows where Siobahn is headed and knows too that
she is powerless to stop the derailment.*

*"And more than once, I've heard your name from some
lovely girl who thought you cared for her and found instead
that you didn't even care enough to pretend. I have you at
something of a disadvantage, I'm afraid. Because no matter
what you may have heard about me, I've heard more about
you. And I haven't liked much of it."*

*Siobahn walks to the door, opens it, and watches Nicki
stand and slip her backpack over her shoulder. "There's still*

time for you to drop this class without penalty to your GPA. If you choose to continue, make an appointment with the departmental secretary and I'll see you back here next week." Siobahn shuts the door firmly but silently behind Nicki, who stands in the hallway staring at the opposite wall.

I didn't hear about this conversation until months later, so I can't say I had the feeling anything was going to come of the whole Nicki-Siobahn thing, but then...

Nicki lies with her cheek resting on Siobahn's smooth, pale thigh, running her fingers slowly through the still-damp hair between her lover's legs, feeling the small jolts that shake Siobahn's body whenever Nicki's fingers sink in too deep and connect with the still-vibrating and tender clit. Siobahn stares out the window at the encroaching spring that marches forward to the incessant drumbeat of melting snow dripping off the roof. They have been in bed most of the weekend.

Of course, Nicki dropped the poetry class—that's how it really started. Nicki walked out of Dr. Flan's office that day and went directly to the registrar's and probably never would have seen the inside of the women's studies building again—except that the next night Dr. Flan handed me a note as I was leaving class. I won't bore you by describing the several thousand erotic fantasies I enjoyed in the split second before she cold-showered them all by saying, "I'd appreciate it if you would give this to your roommate."

I made a beeline for the nearest rest room, locked myself in a stall, and read:

Nicki,
I received word today from the registrar that you have dropped Feminist Poetry. I must admit to mixed feelings. I wasn't sure you had

any true interest in the subject, yet I feel I may
have failed you as a teacher by not encouraging what may be a sincere desire to broaden
your academic experience.

   If, in fact, I have been mistaken, I hope you
will give feminist poetry another chance. I
would like to invite you to attend the reading
on campus Friday night by Henrica Buoni.
Buoni is a new star in our field, and the reading would be well worth your time.

—Siobahn Flannagan

I wanted to scream.

*Siobahn lies burrowed deep in the high feather bed, listen-
ing to a storm batter the shutters. She guesses that it is close
to 3 in the morning, but she feels less like sleep now than
when she crawled into bed near 2 o'clock, chastising herself
because she has a class first thing.*

*Her hand rests lightly between her legs, slowly stroking her-
self in a rhythm that is more comforting than arousing. She has
been thinking of Jolene and then, suddenly, not. She had been
wondering for the thousandth time if either of them could really hold faithful to the other across a distance of miles and
months, neither of them willing to give up promising teaching
posts on opposite coasts. Then she is thinking of Nicki. Her fingers move with more purpose, widening the lips of her cunt,
seeking the heat that rises to meet her. Nicki had entered her
consciousness first as a safe and amusing fantasy—what
teacher doesn't lust after a student or two each year? But when
Nicki had been in the office, Siobahn had seen her as something
a little less safe and therefore a little more arousing.*

*The note inviting Nicki to the poetry reading is an elegant
pretense. She could have just called and suggested they meet*

for that cup of coffee. But Siobahn has an architect's sense of order and appreciates nothing better than the well-crafted come-on structured as its most defensible opposite. She had been the one to invite the guest lecturer to campus. How appropriate that she should spread the word among students who might not otherwise hear of it.

The lecture hall was respectably full. Mandatory attendance for English majors ensured that the department would not be embarrassed by empty seats. Dr. Flan stood in the foyer at the back of the hall, checking off names from the attendance sheets, keeping an eye on the seniors who seemingly had learned more in four years about sneaking out of lecture halls than they had about English.

And then Nicki was standing in front of her. She wore no coat, even though the night was below freezing, her hands stuffed deep in the pockets of her jeans as though that were some great source of warmth. "You wanted to see me?" she asked with a smile bordering on a leer and everything but a wink.

Siobahn is somehow disappointed that Nicki has found her footing so quickly, or rather that she has found it at all. Siobahn has a very small yet well-defined place in her life for which she might consider Nicki a candidate—but only if Nicki can color inside the lines Siobahn will draw for her.

Dr. Flan welcomed Nicki and handed her a program. "If you have any questions after tonight's reading"—she let her words trail off in a pause that was deliciously long—"the library has this writer's work. I'm sure the librarian would be happy to help you."

Dr. Flan then turned her eyes to the next girl in line—who happened to be me. She greeted me by name and with a great smile that almost made me forget she'd ignored me in class only a few hours before, that her smile was simply the period at the end of a sentence in the unspoken dialogue that still floated in the air.

Nicki pushed her way through the line and walked back out the door to the accompaniment of a few raised eyebrows and lips forming the words, "What was that about?" I didn't know what to say. It was the first uncool thing I had ever seen Nicki do.

Nicki wasn't there when I got back to our room that night. Just as well, since I didn't know what I would say to her. My job had always been to voice the conscience I accused her of lacking, to pretend shock at her outrages, to pretend shame at her excesses, to shake my head ruefully—yet indulgently, secretly proud. It was a tough role to play the older we got. But it came as no relief when I finally saw Nicki lose her cool. It came as no relief when I could finally stop propping up a facade that by this time was as much of my own making as hers. It only came as a relief that she wasn't in our room and I didn't have to figure out what to say right then.

"Fuck, fuck, fuck," Siobahn mutters when she turns into her driveway and sees the car. There is no doubt in her mind that it is Nicki's.

There have been other crushes, other students who followed her around, wallowing in unrequited love until some harsh act on Siobahn's part brought them in touch with reality. She has always stayed clean. She has learned to have witnesses, to "cover her ass," as the Americanism goes, to leave no room for charges of misconduct or messy meetings with the dean. She'd thought she had managed it again. She quickly reviews each encounter with Nicki. No mistakes, yet the girl is here. Showing up at a faculty member's home in the dead of night violates many boundaries, and can only mean that the girl is beyond the rules—and trouble.

Siobahn slams the car door and walks up the front steps. No Nicki. A worse sign yet, it means the girl has let herself in. Siobahn feels the first quiver of fear deep in her belly. You let yourself into someone's house—even in a town where no one locks their doors—you expect things are going to get crazy.

But she does not call campus security. To do so would be to admit that there are situations she cannot handle—and Siobahn would never admit that. She is the one who has always relished the confrontations that reduce others to weeping, continuing to take the anguished 3 A.M. recriminations rather than let the answering machine pick up when some just-left lover calls. Every confrontation is a contest, and Siobahn has never said no to the game.

She opens the door. The house is warm. Nicki has turned up the heat. Cheeky, Siobahn thinks, then feels instantly a fool because she knows she means it as a compliment.

Nicki is in the bathtub, up to her neck in bubbles, a bottle of Siobahn's wine and a glass next to her. She smiles when she sees Siobahn standing in the doorway. "How was the reading?"

"Get the fuck out of my bath," Siobahn says evenly, impressing even herself with her calm.

"Sure," Nicki says, and smiles again. She stands, the bubbles rolling away, slowly revealing the long glistening curves of her athletic body. She is leaner than Siobahn had imagined her to be, her breasts smaller, her hips narrower. The lines drawn by the chiseled muscles of her shoulders and arms deepen as she reaches for a towel.

Siobahn turns and walks into the living room. She stands for a moment staring at the phone. She can still call security. It isn't too late. She will be professional and understanding but just a little bit exasperated, and everything will play out fine. And at the same time, she imagines the towel moving across Nicki's body, over her strong legs, feels the smooth hardness of her calves, the muscles of her thighs. She hears Nicki step out into the hall behind her, waiting. Siobahn opens her mouth, the words well chosen. What she means to say is, "You've made a *very serious mistake. However, if you leave immediately, and if it never happens again, I won't feel compelled to bring any sort of disciplinary action."*

What she hears herself say instead is, "The bedroom is at the end of the hall."

"Too far," Nicki whispers in her ear, slipping her arms around Siobahn from behind, drawing their bodies together. Siobahn leans back against her, turning to kiss Nicki's waiting mouth.

I missed Nicki. She hadn't been like this with the others. Even when she was dating the entire tennis team concurrently she still had time for me and our plans. That changed with Dr. Flan. By the second week, Nicki was spending every night over on faculty row, and I was starting to get the idea that this one was different.

What was worse, when I did see Nicki, she wouldn't talk to me about it. With other women, Nicki had given forth with incredible detail on the most intimate particulars—what noise a girl made when she came, how much hair she had "down there." This time, nothing. I would ask how things were going, and Nicki would say "great." She wouldn't change the subject or avoid the question, but that was all she would say. If I asked follow-ups, she would just laugh and shake her head. I started to hate Dr. Flan, but only in a weird, lustful sort of way.

Siobahn knows she must attend the faculty reception, but she leaves at the first moment she can do so without jeopardizing her career. She calls Nicki from the cell phone on her way out of the admin building. Her words are hurried, the skeletal code of their secret mission: "I'm done."

"On my way."

"Can't wait."

"Me too."

They are at a point when they forgive each other even the pretense that there is anything they ought to do sooner upon meeting than begin the all-too-often-interrupted search for pleasure.

Nicki is just pulling into the driveway when Siobahn pulls in behind her, and they step out of their cars and walk toward the door. It is hard for Nicki to look at Siobahn at first, as it always is when they have been out of each other's sight for even a moment. It is hard for Nicki to look at her lover because she is afraid her madness will be visible, her body too small and frail to contain the wave that builds inside her whenever she comes near Siobahn or thinks of her or moans her name.

Siobahn, for her part, thinks nothing of it whenever possible. She does not think of her peers and how they ridicule openly any one of them who fucks students. She does not think of the 15-year age difference. She does not think of what will happen when the school year ends. She thinks only of the burning heat between their bellies when they lie together, the heart-stopping moment when she loses hearing, loses sight, loses herself as she climaxes, shuddering beneath Nicki's driving body. Siobahn thinks only of these moments and how long it will be until she will lose herself in them again.

She especially does not think of what will happen when her other lover—the woman she has been with for five years, the woman she owns this house with—returns for the summer from her teaching job 3,000 miles away.

Of course, Nicki knew about the other lover—Jolene was her name. She slept in Jolene's bed, spent days at a time in Jolene's house, fucked Jolene's girlfriend. But Nicki didn't think much about Jolene. It really wasn't her problem. She would leave campus at the end of the school year, move back home to her parents', and work at the golf course for the summer. Jolene could have her bed and her house and her lover back. That had been the plan from the start.

The phone rings and Siobahn freezes, her lips suspended

just inches above Nicki's. They turn their heads as the answering machine picks up and Siobahn's voice plays back, tinny and impatient. "Sorry, no one's here to take your call, please leave a message."

A very long beep—there are a number of unanswered calls already stored on the machine—and then, "Hey, babe. It's me. Where are you? I wanted to give you my flight info. Ummm, OK, guess you're out. Call me when you get in."

The machine records the disconnecting click, then rewinds.

Ever so slowly, Siobahn turns back and lowers her lips to meet Nicki's. As they draw closer, Siobahn's eyes are open, searching her lover's face, but Nicki's eyes are closed as she returns the kiss.

The weekend before finals began, I saw Nicki for the first time in what seemed like months. She was lying on her bunk when I flung open the door. The lights were out and the blinds drawn, so when I flicked on the overhead she threw an arm across her eyes, and I yelped in surprise. She didn't yell at me or anything, which is how I knew things were bad. I didn't actually see tears, but her eyes were red and she had this look I had seen before on hurt animals who can't understand why they are in pain. I wanted to hug her, but I figured she would punch me if I did, so I pulled up a chair across from her and waited.

"Let's get drunk," Nicki whispered, her voice hoarse and conspiratorial.

"That's original."

"Like I give a fuck."

I looked at the clock; it was 11 A.M. I shrugged and reached toward the otherwise unused drawer of Nicki's desk where we stored the liquor.

"Not here," Nicki stopped me.

I looked up in surprise. Neither of us could afford to drink much commercially, and in our tiny college town not many bars were open at 11 A.M. on a Sunday. "Then where?"

"How about the airport?" Nicki tried for a grin but missed, and I understood.

"The girlfriend comes back today?"

Nicki nodded.

"So what happens now?"

Nicki took a long slow breath. "Nothing happens now."

"You mean you guys broke up?"

Nicki looked at me like I was an idiot. "Broke up? We didn't break up. We weren't together. Siobahn has been with her for years. They're together. If anyone was going to break up, it would have to be them."

"Well, are they?"

"What?"

"Breaking up."

"No," Nicki said. "Why should they?"

"Because one of them has been fucking you six times a day."

Nicki was too far gone to take the compliment. "It's more complicated than that. They have a house."

"Right. A house where one of them has been fucking you six times a day."

"Look, it's over, OK?"

I looked around the room in mock surprise and then back at Nicki. "Oh, I'm sorry, are you talking to me?"

Nicki sighed. "Siobahn knows it's over too."

"You guys talked about it?"

"I don't want to talk about it," Siobahn says, her answer final—even though Nicki has not asked a question.

Neither of them has said a word since they finished making love a few minutes before. They lie in a limp tangle of arms and legs, sweat and the sweet wetness of sex binding them together.

"I just want..." Siobahn stops, and Nicki counts her own heartbeats. It is what she does on the free throw line to focus on

something other than how badly she wants to win the game. "I just want to feel about one of you what I feel about both of you."

After a few minutes, with nothing to say, Nicki gets up and dresses methodically, jeans and a T-shirt, socks and shoes. She picks up a glass of water from the bedside table and drains it. Putting down the glass, she picks up the alarm clock, stares at it for a moment, then walks around the bed to where Siobahn lies facing the window. Wordlessly, Nicki shows her the time.

"Fuck, fuck, fuck," Siobahn shouts, jumping out of bed and running into the bathroom.

Nicki waits until she hears the shower running, then walks out.

Jolene's flight is early, as though hurtled to shore by Siobahn's tsunami of panic.

Siobahn had planned to have a few drinks in the airport bar before the plane arrived, but instead finds herself running down the corridor so as to be standing at the gate when Jolene walks up the ramp. This is only good form when your lover returns from a seven-month absence. Actually, it has not been a full seven months since they have seen each other. They had been together at Christmas and for a few long weekends in between, but they both acknowledge that they will need time to adjust to the day-to-day fact of each other.

But Siobahn isn't prepared for Jolene to be a complete stranger to her. She does not see her lover until Jolene is just a few yards away. Siobahn feels her face color and covers her embarrassment with a long, tight hug. Jolene kisses her exuberantly, slipping her tongue between Siobahn's lips. *And all the while, Siobahn is screaming inside, "I am not ready to give up Nicki. Not yet."* And hears herself saying instead, "Welcome home, lover."

CONTRIBUTORS

K. Bhojwani practiced law for eight years before retiring to write full-time. She lives in Miami, where she has had articles and personal essays published in the magazine *Miamigo*. She is at work on a book about faith, love, and quantum mechanics. This is her first published short story.

Lisa E. Davis has lived in Greenwich Village for many years and loves to write about it. With a Ph.D. in comparative literature, she has taught in the State and City University systems of New York, and often publishes translations from Spanish, most recently in *The Vintage Book of International Lesbian Fiction*. She has also published a novel, *Under the Mink* (Alyson, 2001). Other high points in her life include meeting Fidel Castro and almost drowning in the Colorado River.

Lisa DeSantiago holds a BA in English from the University of Illinois at Chicago. You can find her political commentaries published often in *En La Vida* and her erotica in the anthology *Tough Girls*. Though writing is a passion, Lisa admits that she writes because her brain just won't shut up.

Nena Eskridge is involved in film and video production and is developing a lesbian-themed feature film based on her original screenplay *Careful What You Wish For*. Her short fiction has appeared in the *Harrington Lesbian Fiction Quarterly*. She lives in Philadelphia with her longtime partner.

Amie M. Evans is a white girl, confirmed femme-bottom who lives life like a spontaneously choreographed performance. She is the founder of The Princesses of Porn with The Dukes of Dykedom, PussyWhipped Productions, and *Philogyny: Girls Who Kiss and Tell*. Her works have appeared in *Lip Service, Best Lesbian Erotica, Best S/M Erotica, Set in Stone: Butch on Butch Sex, Harrington's Lesbian Fiction Quarterly, On Our Backs, Bad Attitude,* and *Three Rivers Literary Review*.

Carol Guess is the author of two novels, *Seeing Dell* and *Switch,* and a memoir, *Gaslight*. She teaches at Western Washington University.

Lynn Herr spends her idle hours working up the courage to wear flamboyant shoes. Her stories can be found in various anthologies, including *Faster Pussycats: Live Girls After Hours*.

Lori Horvitz's poetry, short stories, and essays have appeared in many literary journals and anthologies, including *Love Shook My Heart II, Quarter After Eight, 13th Moon,* and *The Jabberwock Review*. She is an Assistant Professor of Literature and Language at University of North Carolina at Asheville.

Yvonne D. Jennings lives in Chicago and makes her living on her bicycle. Writing has always been her passion. She has been published in *Bust* magazine and a few other 'zines and rags. She also has an unpublished manuscript waiting to greet an audience. In the meantime, she has been focusing on short stories and contemplating grad school.

S. Lynn is a native of St. Louis. "Keepin' It Real" is her first published short story. Her nonfiction has appeared in *Common Lives, Lesbian Lives* and in *Our Own Community News* (Norfolk, Va.). Ms. Lynn lives in Denver with her partner and their young son.

Ronna Magy's fiction has appeared in *Love Shook My Heart II, Hers 2, Heatwaves, La Revista Bilingue,* and *The Bilingual Review.* She lives and writes in Los Angeles.

Paula Neves lives and writes in central New Jersey. Although she loves to travel, she finds that the most ordinary circumstances often inspire the most creative wandering. The results of these wanderings have appeared in *Uniform Sex, Early Embraces, All the Ways Home, The Body of Love, The Poetry of Sex,* and other publications.

Dawn Paul lives north of Boston. She has written stories for *Common Lives/Lesbian Lives, Snowy Egret,* and *North Shore Magazine.* Her articles on science, sports, and the outdoors have appeared in *Sojourner, Atlantic Coastal Kayaker, North Shore, Sea Kayaker,* and *Explore.* She writes and teaches poetry and short fiction.

Juliet Sarkessian's first novel, *Trio Sonata* (Southern Tier Editions), was published in fall 2002. She is a frequent contributor to the *Lambda Book Report* and *The Gay and Lesbian Review.* Juliet lives in domestic bliss with her partner of 16 years in Philadelphia, where she is also a practicing attorney.

Michelle Sawyer's "Not Ever Destined to Be Classic" is a condensed excerpt from her novel, *They Say She Tastes Like Honey* (Alyson, 2003). She lives in Michigan with two spontaneously vicious, bipolar rottweilers.

Anne Seale is a creator of lesbian songs, stories, and plays who has performed on gay stages singing tunes from her tape *Sex for Breakfast.* More of Seale's work can be found in *Best Lesbian Love Stories 2003, Pillow Talk, Dykes With Baggage, Lip Service, Set in Stone,* and other lesbian anthologies and periodicals. Her first novel, *Packing Mrs. Phipps*, will be published by Alyson Books in spring 2004.

Elizabeth Sims is the author of the noir novels *Holy Hell* and *Damn Straight*. She gives online writing workshops, and she likes to paint and drive and play the mandolin. Elizabeth can be reached through her Web site, www.elizabethsims.com.

Linda Suzuki lives near Washington, D.C. Her primary purpose on the planet is to amuse two dogs and cat. Sometimes, when Buster, Mitchel, and Whiz are asleep, Linda does a little writing.

Kyle Walker's work has appeared under many names and in many forms: onstage (the 2002 HomoGENIUS Festival) on the page (*Gargoyle, The Catholic Review*), and on the Internet ("Sticks and Balls" on Hottlead.com). "Why They Are Called Bad Girls" is from a novel in progress titled *Innocent Wild*. During the day, Kyle edits nonfiction books on a completely different topic.

Melissa Walker is beginning to spread her wings. Caught in mid flight en route to an MA dissertation, she opened drawers and flew the story "Airport" up north—all the way from Brazil. At 26, learning to leave the nest does not feel like a bad thing. Not a bad thing at all...

Cynthia Wilson, a California native, grew up in spite of living in Bakersfield. She explored her education in the Bay Area, working in the theater. Today, she plays idiophones, birdwatches, teaches theater arts, and writes plays. She finds reality absolutely boggling. Even at 50 years of age, she does not know "the answer."